W9-AUZ-134

Sedro-Woolley Library
802 Ball Ave
Sedro-Woolley WA 98284

Aug 2005

ALSO BY LEA WAIT

In the Maggie Summer Series

Shadows on the Ivy: An Antique Print Mystery
Shadows on the Coast of Maine: An Antique Print Mystery
Shadows at the Fair: An Antique Print Mystery

And Novels for Children and Young Adults

Wintering Well
Seaward Born
Stopping to Home

Shadows
at the
Spring Show

AN ANTIQUE PRINT MYSTERY

Lea Wait

SCRIBNER

NEW YORK LONDON TORONTO SYDNEY

SCRIBNER
1230 Avenue of the Americas
New York, NY 10020

This book is a work of fiction. Names, characters, places,
and incidents either are products of the author's imagination or are used
fictitiously. Any resemblance to actual events or locales or persons,
living or dead, is entirely coincidental.

Copyright © 2005 by Eleanor S. Wait

All rights reserved, including the right of reproduction
in whole or in part in any form.

SCRIBNER and design are trademarks
of Macmillan Library Reference USA, Inc.,
used under license by Simon & Schuster, the publisher of this work.

For information regarding special discounts for bulk purchases,
please contact Simon & Schuster Special Sales at 1-800-456-6798
or business@simonandschuster.com

Text set in Sabon

Manufactured in the United States of America

1   3   5   7   9   10   8   6   4   2

Library of Congress Cataloging-in-Publication Data

Wait, Lea.
Shadows at the spring show: an antique print mystery/Lea Wait.
p. cm.
1. Summer, Maggie (Fictitious character)—Fiction. 2. Prints—Collectors and
collecting—Fiction. 3. Women college teachers—Fiction.
4. Antique dealers—Fiction. I. Title.

PS3623.A42S533 2005
813'.6—dc22
2004065361

ISBN-13: 978-0-7432-4951-5
ISBN-10:   0-7432-4951-8

For everyone who is part of the adoption triangle, with special thanks to Adoptive Single Parents of New Jersey, Concerned Persons for Adoption, Welcome House, World Association for Children and Parents (WACAP), and Spence-Chapin, who provided support and encouragement and helped my children come home. And especially for Diane Veith, Maureen Reichardt, Elizabeth Park, and all the others who traveled the journey with me.

For Sarah Knight, an editor with savvy and understanding.

And for my husband, Bob Thomas, who has always believed in me, with love and thanks that cannot be measured.

Shadows
at the
Spring Show

Chapter 1

⎯⎯᥎⎯⎯

Anatomy: Osteology. Plate I of Cranium. *1808 steel engraving showing skulls of different anthropological groups: Georgian; Turk; Negro; Calmuck* (sic); *Caribs. Engraved by B. Tanner and published by Abraham Rees in* The Cyclopedia, *or* Universal Dictionary of Arts, Science and Literature, *1819–20. 8 x 11 inches. Price: $85.*

The antiques show was dark and hot, jammed with people and oak furniture and tables covered with crystal and china. Maggie forced her way through the throng of customers and dealers. People pressed closer and closer. She could hardly breathe. And then there was light—bright, glaring light—piercing through the roof that was slowly crumbling on top of them.

Maggie emerged from beneath the mound of blankets pulled over her head. The clock radio next to her bed read 6:03 A.M. Her throat was dry. She was sweating.

If she allowed herself more sleep, she'd fall back into the nightmare. She pushed back the hair that had escaped her long braid and focused on her bedroom. Her heart was still pounding. But everything was as it should be: brass bed, yellow, sprigged wallpaper, framed, hand-colored Curtis engravings of flowers, reading chair. A single ray of sunlight was shining through the Victorian, pressed-glass perfume bottles on top of her mahogany bureau, making dancing patterns on the wall. Winslow Homer, her very much stay-at-home cat, was curled in his usual place at the foot of her bed.

She'd been spending too much time organizing the antiques show. That was obvious. The final meeting was at nine this morning.

She swung her legs over the side of the bed. A shower, and then a Diet Pepsi. There was no reason to worry. She'd planned well. Her subconscious must be working overtime.

"Thank you for being here on such a beautiful May Saturday and for volunteering to help with the first Our World Our Children Antiques Show. If it weren't for prospective parent and antique-print dealer Maggie Summer, who suggested this wonderful fund-raiser to support children waiting for families, we wouldn't be here today. Let's all give her a big round of applause."

OWOC Agency director Carole Drummond, trimly dressed in a gray pantsuit, led the clapping. Maggie, who wore a long, flowered challis skirt and soft green V-necked top, stood in the back of the room near the table where refreshments were set out. Hal Hanson, the twenty-year-old currently living with the Drummonds, handed her a cup of coffee, but she shook her head. She'd already caffeinated herself this morning. As he took the coffee back, she noticed his arms were mottled by old scars. Hal had a history of problems, she'd heard. Needle tracks? Self-mutilation? Whatever the marks were, they were healed. The problem was in the past.

Parents and prospective parents filled the room as Maggie wondered for the 453rd time why she'd suggested the agency sponsor an antiques show as a fund-raiser. Of course, then the board had asked her to run the show, and, of course, doing so had taken up most of her past five months. Never again would she complain that an antiques show promoter had not done his or her job well. In the twelve years she'd been an antique-print dealer she'd never appreciated how hard it was for a manager to pull a show together.

"We'll be opening just one week from today." Carole Drummond, a Korean-American in her late thirties, was tall, slim, and an advertisement for the joys of adoption. She'd arrived home to her adoptive parents when she was just four months old. By the time she was six months old she'd probably had those parents organized and scheduled and was changing her own diapers. Carole was the perfect director for a nonprofit organization. Somewhere along the line she'd also found time to include marriage and motherhood on her agenda. She had four children: two biological and two adopted, all between the ages of six and thirteen.

Plus now Hal lived with her. He'd been adopted ten years ago but lost his parents in a tragic fire last winter. How Carole found the time to see whatever hairdresser kept her sleek black hair in place, much less manage her agency and her family and work with social services organizations in Asia, Europe, and Latin America, was a mystery.

Carole was Maggie's new role model. Volunteering to run the antiques show had given her a chance to watch Carole in action.

"Thank you to everyone who's collected ads for the show program. I understand from Holly and Rob Sloane"—Carole gestured toward a plump, smiling woman in her fifties and a taller, slimmer man with graying hair who were seated in the second row—"that seventy-nine local businesses, services, and individuals have bought ads, and The Gentle Reader bookshop, Orchids and Others florist, and Gourmet Goodies have donated wonderful packages we can raffle off at the end of the show."

Holly and Rob had adopted eleven children of assorted heritages, in addition to the three they'd had biologically. Most of the additions to their family had arrived as troubled teenagers. Holly and Rob were poster parents for OWOC, a couple who could supply love, discipline, and a steady home base and support their sons and daughters through the stressful teen and young-adult years. They were the agency experts on troubled older children, the couple who led support groups for other parents. Somehow they'd found time to do a spectacular job for the antiques show, too.

Carole continued, "Thanks to Maggie's help, Somerset College is donating the use of its new Whitcomb Gymnasium."

How did people manage when they had children? Maggie had trouble balancing the demands of her antique-print business and her teaching career at the college. She'd hoped working on this show would help her decide whether adoption—single-parent adoption, unless her personal situation changed—was right for her. And while she was deciding, her efforts would be helping children who needed homes. It was a win/win situation. And she enjoyed working with the adoptive parents and agency personnel. They knew what they wanted to do with their lives and were doing it. Most had full- or part-time jobs, but they managed to put their families first. And put finding families for homeless children a close second.

It had been a good spring. She'd learned a lot about adoption, and a lot about herself.

But right now she was totally exhausted, months behind on matting prints for her business, and after this meeting she'd have to spend the weekend grading final papers and exams. Thank goodness they were *final* papers and exams.

It's a good thing I'm not a mother. Yet, Maggie thought. Tomorrow is Mother's Day, and I'll be reading freshman papers on the causes of the Civil War.

At least school would be over in a few days, and this show would be over next weekend. She'd reluctantly canceled out of exhibiting at two other antiques shows this spring, and her bank balance was missing those contributions. But despite those losses, she'd resisted signing on to teach the summer semester. She needed time for herself, her antique-print business, and for the man in her life.

Will. Wonderful, steady Will. He'd readily agreed to bring his eighteenth- and nineteenth-century fireplace and kitchen equipment from Buffalo to New Jersey for the antiques show. And it hadn't been hard to talk him into arriving two days early to help set up walls and tables for the booths, and stay a day after the show to ensure that everything in the gym was in order before she officially declared the show over.

And a success, Maggie thought to herself. After all this work, it had to be a success. Although if the show *was* a success, then the agency would want it to be an annual event. That was just too much to think about today. But she was keeping notes on everything, just in case. Notes she could hand off to whoever ran a future show. Running an antiques show was a onetime deal so far as she was concerned.

"I'm going to ask Maggie to let us know who is doing what, and when, so we'll all be up-to-date."

Maggie rose and smiled, notebook in hand. This was the easy part. Most parents of OWOC children and prospective parents had volunteered to help, and Carole had divided them into committees months ago. If only coordinating the participation of college officials and dealers had been as easy.

"I'll add my thanks to Carole's for all the work Holly and Rob have done. After I finish going over the names of the committee chairpersons and their responsibilities, the committees can meet and check to make sure all hours are covered. Later this week I'll be meeting with students and administrators from Somerset College who've volunteered to help during the show, so if any group needs more bodies, let me know so we can fill any gaps in coverage." Maggie pushed a strand of wavy brown hair off her face and opened the black binder she'd been carrying for months.

"Publicity is chaired by Skip Hendricks. They've already sent out press releases and arranged for ads, and will be calling local media this week. They'll be the ones putting up signs reminding people of the show and heading dealers and customers to the gym.

They'll also be hosting any visits from members of the press." Skip and his wife, Jennifer, were the brand-new parents of Christina, a beautiful six-month-old from Guatemala. Christina would no doubt be at the show to accept the admiration of her adoring public. And parents.

"Ann Shepard is heading up the café, where customers and dealers can buy light lunches and baked goods. She has a long list of people who've volunteered to make food, but she also needs people to sell and keep the café set up and the tables clean throughout the show. Ann, could you have a couple of people here late Friday afternoon to help while the dealers are setting up? We'll have coffee and soft drinks for them, and Pizza On The Go has donated food."

Ann nodded and wrote herself a note. She was an attractive blonde, forty-two-year-old prospective single parent who was a manager at the Somerset Savings Bank. She'd been baking and freezing desserts for the café since February. Maggie knew that aside from making sure there was enough sugar and cholesterol for everyone at the show, Ann desperately wanted to adopt a healthy white girl under the age of four. For a single parent that was even more of a challenge than for a couple. Ann was making sure everyone at OWOC knew what a wonderful mother she would be. Maybe she hoped the more she did for the agency, the higher she'd be on their waiting list.

"We're looking for a few more porters to help dealers bring their antiques into the gym on Friday, and be here again Sunday afternoon after the show to move furniture and boxes to their vans. If any of your teenagers would like to help, that would be a great way they could contribute. And the dealers will pay them, so they can make a few extra dollars, too. Most dealers will tip ten to twenty dollars for loading or unloading a van.

"Sam and Josie Thomas are in charge of admissions." Maggie gestured toward a middle-aged black couple. Josie was obviously expecting—a classic example of a mother who'd adopted and then been surprised by a pregnancy. Ethan and Michael, the eight-year-old twins the Thomases had adopted last year, were seated between their parents, exchanging light punches. "Sam and Josie will also have someone at the raffle table to encourage people to buy tickets.

"In addition to helping as porters, some of your children have volunteered to help out at the café, and to take messages from the show management booth to the dealers. Be sure to thank them all. We appreciate their help." Maggie had just about finished. "And, of course, Carole and her staff will be at the OWOC booth throughout the show to answer questions, display pictures of children who need homes, and possibly recruit some new prospective parents. Or encourage extra donations!" Maggie smiled at Carole, who raised her hand in acknowledgment.

They'd been able to get enough items donated so the biggest show expenses were padding the floor and providing tables for the dealers—which their booth rent covered—and advertising. If all worked as hoped, the admission fee of $7 per person would go directly to OWOC, as would the money taken in at the café, and a portion of the booth rents.

"If there are any questions during the week, I'll be available, and so will Carole. We're looking forward to a great show—and you're the ones who're going to make it happen!" Along with the thirty-six dealers Maggie had managed to talk into exhibiting in this small, first-time show. And all the customers they hoped would walk through the doors of Whitcomb Gymnasium May 14 and 15.

Carole stood up and announced, "Hal has refreshments in the back of the room. Please enjoy a snack while you're meeting with your committee."

As the volunteers scattered, Carole turned to Maggie. "Is there anything that still needs to be done?"

Maggie glanced at her notebook. "I'm meeting with the school building staff on Monday, and Tuesday I have a meeting with Al Stivali, head of the Somerset College security staff, to confirm he can provide extra coverage for the gym Friday and

Saturday nights, when the antiques will be there. We should have at least one person there all night."

Holly Sloane joined them. "Everything sounds wonderful, Maggie. You've done a great job pulling this together."

"Thanks. And I appreciate everything you and Rob have done to help. I don't know how you find the time, with all those kids to keep track of."

"When you have as many as we do, you have to either be very organized or very lax. We're organized," said Holly. "Teenagers and young adults have constant issues, but at least parenting them is less physically demanding than if we had fourteen kids under the age of ten!"

"Holly, if anyone could manage a family like that, it would be you and Rob."

Holly smiled and shook her head, her brown, slightly askew curls bouncing. "Lots of families manage beautifully with a lot of younger children. Rob and I didn't start out being experts on teenagers. But at this point we can certainly say we've had experience. Although none of that matters when a kid isn't responding."

Maggie had met most of Holly's children at adoptive-parent meetings and parties, but not enough times to keep them straight. Certainly not often enough to know who might be having problems, or why. Carole knew them better.

Carole lowered her voice. "Jackson again?"

Holly nodded. "Do you know another counselor we could call? We've tried everyone we thought might be able to reach him."

"Is he acting out? Violent?"

"Nothing like that, thank goodness. It's just that even after five years—he's twenty-two now—he still hasn't totally bonded with the family, or accepted who he is."

"He's twenty-two?" Maggie blurted. "Then why isn't he out on his own?"

Holly turned to Maggie. "You're still a prospective parent, so don't let this discourage you. But children adopted at older ages have a lot of issues. When they're in their teens, or even older, before they find people to trust, it takes a long time for that trust to become a part of them. Adopted kids will be children longer than other children. Most of them can't take responsibility for themselves before they've had positive role models to show them how to do that. Jackson came to us when legally he could have been out on his own, or in supervised housing. But emotionally he was a lot younger than seventeen, and he wanted a family. We agreed he could stay with us, and we adopted him. He graduated from high school and now he's taking some courses at Somerset College. But he hasn't really figured out where his place is in the world."

"It's wonderful that you and Rob don't pressure him, Holly," said Carole, frowning with concern. "But he does need to pull his life together pretty soon or you'll have him at home for the rest of his life."

"He knows that's not an option," said Holly. "And he is trying. I think a counselor who's an expert in cultural differences might help."

Maggie looked blank. "Is Jackson from another country?"

"No; he's all-American. But his mother was white and his father was black. He's still not comfortable with that, or now, with having white adoptive parents."

"In your family I'd think he'd find plenty of role models!"

"Some of our other kids have had those problems, too, of course. But most of them have accepted who they are. Some issues will last their lifetimes. Being biracial can influence who they marry and where they live and how they bring up their own children. But Jackson is far from ready to do those things. He needs to accept who he is, and what happened to him in the past, before he can make a future for himself."

Carole nodded in agreement. "I'll check with a few of my contacts to see if we can find a counselor."

"Thank you." Holly turned toward where her husband was talking with their committee and then looked back and touched

Maggie's arm. "Maggie, you've chosen a great agency to work with, and Carole is one of the reasons. Postadoption support services are limited at lots of agencies." Holly walked back into the room.

"Don't let it scare you, Maggie. But some of our families need help for years," Carole said with a smile. "And we try to provide it. Adoption is a lifelong journey. Parents and children need to know they're not alone, even years after an adoption is finalized."

"That's one of the reasons I contacted OWOC," said Maggie. "I've read a lot about adoption of older children. I know if I decide to adopt, I'll need all the help I can get." And the more she learned, the more she wondered if she was ready to adopt.

"I think you'd make a great parent, Maggie. Just let me know when you're ready to start your home study and we'll do everything we can to help you." Carole headed Maggie into the hall, out of hearing distance of anyone else. "In the meantime we have an immediate issue. I didn't want to say anything in front of Holly, but that meeting with security you're having Tuesday might be more important than we'd thought. We got an anonymous hate letter yesterday. Someone is threatening to sabotage the show."

Chapter 2

Own Is Best. *1894 chromolithograph by Elizabeth S. Tucker of two elegantly dressed little girls comparing their equally elegantly dressed dolls. Only one doll can be the best. 7.75 x 9.5 inches. Price: $60.*

"Sabotage the show?" said Maggie. "Why?"

Carole shook her head. "Whoever wrote the note didn't say. It could be someone whose application to adopt was turned down." Carole hesitated. "Some people are still opposed to agencies placing children with parents of different races or religions or cultures. It might even be that. At this point I have no idea what the problem is."

Many of the families Maggie had met at OWOC included children who did not "match" their parents. Some families, like Holly and Rob Sloane's, included children of several different races. Some children's biological parents had been of two different races, neither of which was the race of their adoptive parents.

Those children probably wouldn't have parents if they hadn't been adopted transracially. And OWOC had an extensive education program to prepare families who were considering adopting a child of another background, to discuss possible extended-family and community issues, and to emphasize the need for interracial families to live in interracial communities and provide their children with adult role models of various cultures. To raise their children to be proud of both their racial and adoptive heritages.

"It doesn't make sense to me," said Maggie.

"Some people believe that only parents of the same heritage as a child can give that child a sense of history and community. That, for instance, we're destroying the heritage of a Korean child when we place him or her with a Caucasian family."

Maggie remembered the pictures in Carole's office. Carole's parents—her adoptive parents—were white. She had been born in Seoul, Korea.

"How serious is the letter?"

"It's clearly a threat." Carole hesitated. "Not the first contact from this person, either."

"Not the first? How many have there been? Why didn't you tell me?" Maggie felt betrayed. If there was a problem with the show, she should have been told.

"The notes we got in March and April just ranted about the agency. All organizations get strange mail sometimes. This is the first letter that specifically mentions the antiques show."

"What do the police say?"

"To make sure our offices are secure and call again if anyone actually does something. I've contacted them before when we've gotten crank letters. But until someone is actually hurt, our offices are broken into, or our property is defaced, there's not a lot the police can do."

"No one has ever followed up one of these letters with actions?"

"Not so far, thank goodness."

"So it's likely that the author of today's letter will just fade away. There's no reason to think it's a real threat." Maggie breathed more easily. If this wasn't a unique situation, then it was a concern, of course, but not a major concern.

"That's possible. But this note specifically mentions the dates May fourteenth and fifteenth. To be safe, we have to make sure security for the antiques show is more than cursory."

Maggie thought of the thirty-six dealers who'd be bringing their inventories to the show. Of the customers and the college and agency personnel and volunteers who would be at the college that weekend. Not to mention all the adoptive parents and their children. "Have you talked to the police specifically about this letter?"

"I'm meeting with them later today," Carole said. "But based on their reactions in the past, I'm not anticipating they'll be able to do anything."

"I'll talk to the college's 'rent-a-cops.' But they're not law enforcement people. If there were a serious problem, the best they could do would be to call 911." Maggie hoped the campus security force wouldn't panic at the possibility of real trouble. They were more geared up to cope with students who'd had too much to drink, or who'd fallen asleep in the library and been locked in, than with any serious crime or violence.

"People who can keep an eye on things and call 911 would be a plus. I'm going to ask the police to patrol the gym area from the time the dealers start arriving until everyone has gone home."

Maggie nodded. "They should be willing to do that. Have you any idea what kind of trouble is being threatened?"

"The note said 'close down' the show. I have no idea how." Carole seemed calm, but her fists were clenched. "I've already arranged to get extra security for the agency offices themselves that weekend. Just in case. Most of the OWOC staff will be at the college, and there are papers at our offices that can't be duplicated. Especially documentation from abroad. Any files destroyed might mean children who couldn't come home. Or whose adoptions couldn't be finalized."

Maggie quickly reviewed all the possibilities. None of them made sense. This was a New Jersey suburb. A quiet community college hosting an antiques show to benefit an adoption agency.

Who would want to disrupt it? "I'd guess some crazy person is just hoping to make us nervous."

"Believe me, I hope that's all it is."

But why? The question hung in the air, and Maggie couldn't make it go away.

Chapter 3

—⟋∾⟍—

Oliver's First Meeting with the Artful Dodger. *Illustration by Jessie Willcox Smith (1863–1935), originally done for* Scribner's Magazine, *December 1911. From* Oliver Twist, *chapter VIII: "'Hello, my covey! What's the row?' said this strange young gentleman to Oliver." Smith studied with Thomas Eakins and Howard Pyle and was the best-known American woman illustrator in the early twentieth century. Although she never married or was a mother, she is remembered for her paintings and prints of children. 7.25 x 5.25 inches including printed border. Price: $40.*

Maggie was glad Carole had told her about the threat. But that didn't mean she was happy to know someone intended to disrupt the show in any way. Getting it organized had been enough of a problem.

She'd started by calling every promoter she knew for advice; then she'd contacted all the dealers she knew to ask them to add a show to their spring schedule. It hadn't been easy. Most dealers knew six months to a year or more in advance which shows they would be doing. Many wouldn't risk the time and money to do a new show. They'd rather take a chance on a show that had

15

been around for a while; that had an established base of customers. A new show could have a great location, wonderful dealers with exciting stock and strong advertising and still not pull in customers. Reputation and word of mouth sometimes took years to develop.

Maggie had tapped a lot of friendships and heartstrings. ("The show is to help children waiting for families!") If the show wasn't a success, facing those dealers wouldn't be easy. And if the show was disrupted in any way . . . She didn't even want to think about it.

There were exams and papers to grade at home. But how could she give students' work the attention it deserved when her mind was on the show?

What would happen if someone was thinking of property damage? Some dealers would have their entire inventories in that show. Never mind the college's reaction if its new Whitcomb Gymnasium was damaged in any way. Any kind of destructive act could not only mean antiques dealers losing their stock; it could mean Maggie losing her teaching job.

Maggie paused at the wheel of her faded blue van, unable to head home. She'd have to grade papers late into the night, but right now she needed to take her mind off whatever might or might not happen at the antiques show next week. There was nothing she could do about it now.

She wanted—no, she needed—to do something positive for herself.

A movie? A museum? A manicure? A long walk? A massage would be nice . . . but getting a last-minute appointment on a Saturday afternoon wouldn't be easy. She tried to remember what she'd seen in the entertainment section of the paper the night before.

Yes! She turned the car southwest, toward Lambertville, a small New Jersey town across the Delaware River from New Hope, Pennsylvania. Lambertville was a center for antiques shops and malls, but Maggie headed for an elementary school that was hosting a small paper show. Last night she'd ruled out going; it would take too much time, and she'd seen most of the paper dealers in the Northeast at the two days of shows in Allentown in April. But now she needed to take her mind off the antiques show she was running. Even if she didn't find anything at the paper show, the distraction of checking out the booths there would help keep her calm.

Red and purple azaleas were blooming, and the last of the daffodils and the beginnings of iris and tulip blossoms brightened yards along the way. She passed farms where colts capered near their mothers and calves followed cows across meadows.

Perhaps three dozen vans or station wagons (no doubt dealers' vehicles) were parked in a lot to the left of the school, and about twenty other cars were in the parking lot next to the entrance. Maggie paid her $3.50 to enter the cafeteria, now filled with rows of tables covered with all sorts of old paper and ephemera.

Paper shows were a world of their own. Antiquarian-book shows tended to be very serious, with high-priced merchandise. Antiques shows, although they might attract a few print or book dealers, featured furniture, glass, crystal, and all manner of household goods, often including vintage fashions and jewelry. Most print dealers did antiques shows; only a few did paper shows. Paper shows were buying grounds for print dealers.

Maggie walked slowly up the first aisle. The majority of paper dealers were men, and they made few attempts to dress up their booths in any way. Magazines, postcards, advertisements, books, instruction brochures, fruit-crate labels were all displayed (or piled) on cafeteria tables. Some dealers had brought wire "walls" on which to hang their merchandise, or folding bookcases to display books, but few had bothered with the niceties required at antiques shows—such as covering the tables with floor-length drapes. A paper show looked to the uninitiated like a flea market. To the collectors and dealers who shopped there, it was an adventure. You never knew what you might find on those cluttered tables.

Maggie passed five postcard dealers displaying their wares in long, low, marked boxes ("New Jersey Towns A–M," "Halloween," "Santa Claus," "Automobiles"). Postcards weren't of interest to her, but several people seated in front of the tables of postcards were intensely going through those boxes. They might be looking for cards picturing specific places, or printed by specific manufacturers, or on specific subjects. Postcards were collectibles many people could afford, and they offered an almost unending selection of variables to specialize in.

The next booth belonged to antiquarian-book dealer Joe Cousins. "Joe! How are you?" Maggie said. "What are you doing here? I hadn't seen you in a year, and then I saw you at Allentown, and here you are again! I'm looking forward to seeing you at the OWOC show next week."

"Hi, Maggie." Joe grinned as he pushed a shock of thick brown hair back from his forehead. A year ago he'd inherited a more diverse art and antiques business, but after a few forays into the world of Art Deco and furniture he'd sold off the new business and was back to concentrating on the books he loved. Although now he could choose between staying at his home in Connecticut or his loft in New York City, his increased financial assets hadn't changed his appearance. Today he was wearing his usual slightly baggy corduroy pants and a shirt that could have used ironing. "Don't think I have anything you'd be interested in. You cleaned me out in Allentown."

"It's good to see you anyway."

"This is a new show, so I thought I'd give it a try. Two new shows in New Jersey in two weeks is a little difficult. But"—Joe's voice lowered—"I have a new friend, who lives out here. And he gets tired of driving to Connecticut or New York to see me."

"Congratulations," said Maggie. "And I'm really glad you're doing the OWOC show. You'll be the only antiquarian-book dealer there. Although I can't promise dealers won't bring books to decorate their booths." Joe was one of the few book dealers who occasionally did antiques shows. He had a great inventory of both nineteenth-century leather-bound sets and twentieth-century first editions.

"That's never a problem," said Joe as he stepped aside to let a young man in jeans enter his booth. "By the way, I'm cleaning out an estate library Monday and Tuesday. If I see anything you might be interested in, I'll bring it to the OWOC show."

"Wonderful," said Maggie. "See you on Friday for setup!"

Joe knew exactly what sort of eighteenth- or early-nineteenth-century natural history books Maggie was looking for: breakers, whose bindings were broken, which decreased or eliminated their value to a book dealer or collector, but which contained hand-colored natural history prints. Since the books were already imperfect, removing the plates could be done without guilt.

Maggie browsed through two other booths of books, but both collections were too modern for her business. She was looking for seventeenth-, eighteenth-, or nineteenth-century engravings or lithographs. Definitely not the photographs or pictures in mid-twentieth-century books.

"Have you any automobile repair guides from the 1930s?" she heard a young woman ask. Someone else was looking for Pennsylvania road maps from the early twentieth century. There were people who collected high school yearbooks or *Playboy* magazines or the cards that were packaged with single packs of cigarettes in the early twentieth century. Maggie paused at a booth piled high with comic books. She remembered reading *Archie* at a friend's house the summer after sixth grade.

She was halfway through the small show. It had been fun to see Joe, but so far she hadn't found anything for Shadows, her antique-print business. *Shadows* because old prints were shadows of the past that let us see the shape of the world as it once was.

Another postcard dealer. A poster dealer. Maggie paused again. She liked some posters, especially World War I recruitment posters, and the travel posters used by transatlantic steamship lines in the 1930s. But posters were very different from prints, and she didn't know enough to invest in them. Just enough to know their prices were high, and they took up so much space in her booth that they crowded out the prints she did know well, and that her customers looked for.

If she didn't find anything today to add to her inventory, that was all right. It happened. But if you didn't look, you wouldn't know.

The next booth was full of children's books, from early-nineteenth-century primers with woodblock engravings to Golden Books and twentieth-century first editions of children's classics like *Charlotte's Web* and *The Dark Is Rising*. There were even copies of the UK editions of the Harry Potter books, with the different covers for adult and child readers. Paper shows specialized in "old paper," but the definition of *old* was increasingly flexible, and first-edition Harry Potter books were certainly collectible.

There was only one more booth, in the corner, filled with twentieth-century magazines. Cartons of *Life* and *Saturday Evening Post* issues and stacks of *National Geographic, Time, Good Housekeeping, Redbook,* and *Sports Illustrated.*

There were a few magazines she looked for. December *National Geographic*s in the 1940s had ads for Coca-Cola on the back covers that featured the classic Santa Claus that the Coca-Cola Company now reproduced as cards, toys, and prints. Maggie included a few in her portfolio of Christmas prints.

Twentieth-century ads weren't exactly in the same category as eighteenth-century engravings. But they were collectibles for some people. Ads featuring dogs and cats, from White-Cat cigar labels (1890–1910) to the dog on a Ken-L Ration lithographed tin door push (1932), were hot sellers.

She sorted through the *Good Housekeeping*s from the 1920s and found two that interested her. Both had covers of children by illustrator Jessie Willcox Smith. The address label on one cover had torn the picture slightly, but the other was in excellent condition. "How much to a dealer?" Maggie asked.

"Twelve . . . oh, you can have it for ten dollars," said the dealer, an elderly man whose clothes were immaculate despite the dust on some of his inventory.

"Okay," said Maggie, handing him a $10 bill. Not exactly a treasure, but she could mat the cover, complete with the *Good Housekeeping* logo, and price it at $40. Although she preferred earlier prints, people loved Jessie Willcox Smith illustrations, and some collected her *Good Housekeeping* covers. They weren't seventeenth-century astronomy engravings, but they might sell faster.

She wouldn't make a fortune on this afternoon's buying trip, Maggie thought. But the search was part of the game, and the paper show had taken her mind off the antiques show. And whoever was wishing it harm.

Why? And who? The questions haunted her as she headed for home.

Chapter 4

⎯⎯∽⎯⎯

Godey's Fashions for February 1873. The Ladies Book, founded in New York in 1830 and renamed for publisher Louis Antoine Godey when he became the sole owner, was the first successful magazine for women. It featured fiction, recipes, patterns, and hand-colored fashion plates, some the size of one magazine page, and some foldouts. This engraving is a foldout, with the two fold lines visible. It pictures five elegant women in a salon, wearing pleated and ruffled and bowed dresses. There is very little color in the plate: a blue ribbon on one dress, a pink on another, and a lavender on a third. In front of the women stands a young boy, perhaps six years old, dressed in a bright blue suit with orange tights and a hat with an orange feather. He is holding a child's bow and arrow and is pointing the arrow at one of the women. 9.6 x 11 inches. Unmatted. Price: $65.

It was late Sunday morning. Maggie moved Winslow off her lap, stood up, and stretched. The world outside her window was glorious, but she was stuck inside with piles of paperwork to do, and she was restless. She'd eaten one "everything" bagel, toasted, with cream cheese and lox and onions and capers. She'd skimmed the Sunday *Times*. She'd corrected a dozen exams, finished a glass of Diet Pepsi, and answered all of her e-mails. Maybe she should check her computer again.

Yes! A message from Will.

Dear Maggie,
And Happy Mother's Day to someone who is not (yet!) a mother, but who's helping families and children find each other by organizing a great antiques show! Buffalo is still chilly. I spent yesterday morning at an auction, and then went to the antiques mall to reorganize my exhibit for spring. Too bad you're not closer. You could add some feminine touches. Although I did get carried away and put a leafy plant in one of my hand-forged copper saucepans. (A plastic plant, of course. Wouldn't want dripping water to damage the copper.) Somehow my new shelf of sadirons doesn't brighten the place up much, however I rearrange it. Hope exams are almost over, grades are in, and you can get some downtime before showtime. Have you decided what you're taking to the Rensselaer County show over Memorial Day? Hard to believe that show will be our one-year anniversary. But what better place to have met than at an antiques show! Looking forward to helping set up those rented tables with you (am I a manipulated male?) in four days. And wishing you a happy Sunday, Mother's or otherwise.

Will

Maggie teared up a bit and blew her nose. Mother's Day. It was sweet of Will to mention it. She looked down at the regard ring he had given her last fall, and that she'd worn on her right hand ever since. R-e-g-a-r-d. A small Ruby, Emerald, Garnet, Amethyst, Ruby, and Diamond set in a line in classic Victorian fashion.

The ring meant a lot to her. But every time she looked at it she remembered Will didn't want to be a father. That part of her life would be so simple if he just wanted children, too. At thirty-eight—almost thirty-nine, she reminded herself—she was flexible. No matter how hard she tried to stop herself, she felt a few pangs of envy every time she saw Josie Thomas. Two adopted sons and a baby on the way. And a caring husband to help out with all three.

Will was caring, but he'd decided years ago he wasn't cut out to be a father, and he hadn't changed his mind. Maggie paced the room. Winslow wove his way between her feet and meowed his sympathies.

It just wasn't fair; a widow at thirty-eight, she had finally found a wonderful and even antiques-loving man. But if she didn't have children, she'd always regret it. Why couldn't she have both the man she loved and the children she longed for? Why did life seem so simple for some women, and so complicated for her?

She was tired, she was confused, she was bored with grading exams. Last night she'd finished the pile of term papers, but the exams never seemed to end. And they deserved her full attention.

She stopped and looked around the room that was both her office and the headquarters for her antique-print business. Her prints and even Will's sadirons were bits and pieces of life as it had been 150 years ago. Or more. Had life always been so complicated?

Right now her life was filled with portfolios of prints ready to take to antiques shows. The labels were clear: "Fashion," "Anatomy," "Insects," "New York/Hudson River," and dozens more. She'd need them all for the show in New York State over Memorial Day. Will was right to remind her. Getting ready for that show was a major project.

And there were three piles of prints waiting on her matting table. Just yesterday she'd carefully removed the cover of the *Good Housekeeping* she'd bought and placed it on the top of one of those piles. Everything there had been purchased this pring and had to be sorted, matted, and inventoried before it could be put in a portfolio.

She didn't want to set up a major show with the same prints she'd had the last time she'd been there. At minimum, she needed to update her Winslow Homer inventory. And she'd bought some beautiful Cassell ferns that would be just right for that show, if only they were matted; preferably in dark green. But when would she find the time? Maybe she should call Brad and Steve, her local framers, to see if they'd be able to do some work for her in the next two weeks.

She looked back at her desk.

Exams had to be finished. Today. The spring session at Somerset College was over Wednesday. Will and her friend Gussie would arrive Wednesday. Thursday they'd start setting up the gyms. There'd be ten days between the OWOC show and the one at Rensselaer County: enough time to at least check the signs and prices on her framed prints, clean the glass and frames, and pack her van.

The ringing telephone interrupted her planning.

"Carole? . . . What? . . . No. I haven't had the radio or TV on today." Maggie sat down.

She hadn't expected to hear from the director of OWOC today. Carole was strict in designating Sundays as family days.

Carole's voice was uncharacteristically shaky. "I almost didn't call you, because, after all, you're not officially an OWOC parent yet, but you are in charge of the antiques fair, and all the publicity is not going to be good. Someone is bound to ask you questions."

"Questions about what? Carole, what's happened?"

"Someone shot Holly Sloane as she was bringing in her newspaper this morning. And her son Jackson is missing."

Holly Sloane. The woman with fourteen children; the woman who counseled others on how to deal with traumatized children. "Is she all right?"

"I think so."

Maggie took a deep breath.

"Rob got back from the grocery and found her almost immediately. She was shot in the hip, and she bled badly. She's at Somerset County Hospital."

"And Jackson? That's one of her sons who goes to Somerset College, right? Was he shot, too?" Maggie had a vague picture of a slender young man with a shy smile.

"No one knows anything about Jackson. He's just gone. Rob called me from the hospital to let me know. Jackson went out with friends last night, and Rob and Holly thought they'd heard him come in late. But maybe he never got home. The police are looking for him, since he's missing, and he's got a history of problems." Carole took a deep breath. "Rob kept a gun locked in his desk. The gun is gone, too. The police think Jackson might have shot Holly."

Chapter 5

———✦———

Accidents and Emergencies: How to Stop Bleeding. *Illustration from a medical textbook published by I. W. Wagner, New York, 1912, showing arteries, veins, and pressure points. Includes such notes as "For snake or mad dog bite put pressure above the wound on the veins." 7 x 9.75 inches. Price: $45.*

Maggie put the telephone down. There must be more to Holly's being shot. She'd said Jackson was having problems, but she'd also said he wasn't violent. Was he more seriously troubled than she'd known? Some of Holly's children had major emotional problems. They'd survived abuse and neglect for years before finally coming home to Holly and Rob. But that didn't mean one of them would shoot their mother! Had anyone else threatened the family? Had anyone nearby seen anything?

All questions the police must be asking.

She could already see the headlines Carole Drummond was imagining: "Mother Shot by Adopted Son on Mother's Day!" It was horrible that Holly had been shot, no matter who'd fired the gun. But somehow the shooting was worse because it was on Mother's Day. It was just the sort of publicity adoption agencies and adoptive parents dreaded. When biological children acted out,

they were just called "children." When an adopted child g
media attention, the word *adopted* was almost always a part of th
headline, emphasizing that adopted kids were different. And, the
media often assumed, more troubled than other children.

Which, of course, might be true if they'd lived in five or six
neglectful or abusive households before they'd come home.

Maybe Rob's missing gun had nothing to do with the shooting. But why did he have a gun in a house with so many children
in the first place? Even if it had been locked up. Probably the
police would find Jackson at a friend's house and establish he
had nothing to do with the shooting. Maybe someone nearby
discharged a gun by accident and it just happened to hit Holly.
Maybe . . . but no matter how optimistic she was, Maggie
couldn't think of a lot of positive scenarios. She just hoped
Holly would be all right. And Jackson would be found.

She rinsed out Winslow's water dish, emptied his litter box,
opened a new bottle of Diet Pepsi, and poured herself a glass,
with lemon, on the rocks. How could she concentrate on grading exams or papers now?

Winslow jumped up into Maggie's chair and meowed at her,
then rolled over. That meant she was supposed to sit down and
rub his tummy.

"It's good to know someone needs me." Maggie sighed as she
moved Winslow over so they could share her chair.

But she couldn't concentrate, not even on the task of rubbing
Winslow's tummy.

She'd call Gussie. After talking herself out, she'd be ready to
settle in to more grading.

She and Gussie had been close friends since they'd met at an
antiques show ten years ago. Gussie had a shop on Cape Cod
and also did shows with her antique dolls and toys. Since they
both knew Maggie would be too busy to have her own booth at
the OWOC show, Gussie had suggested they share a large booth
this time.

"You'd just better make sure every print on display is well

abeled," Gussie had said when she volunteered to act as cashier for their joint booth. "I'll keep some of your cash books. The only challenge will be if someone wants two Henry Alken hunting prints, and one Shirley Temple doll."

"I guess that will just have to mean two cash books," Maggie had agreed. "And some true-up accounting between the two of us after the show. Are you sure you want to do this, Gussie?"

"What are friends for? It would be a shame if you'd organized this great show and didn't have any of your prints in it. If we have everything in one booth, I can handle it without any major difficulties. Plus, Ben will be with me to lift toys or framed prints down from the walls and help pack things up."

Ben was Gussie's nephew. He often helped Gussie in her shop and traveled with her when she did shows. Gussie's postpolio syndrome now kept her in a motorized wheelchair. Ben's Down syndrome meant he had trouble making out sales slips. Together, they were a team.

Maggie dialed her number by heart. "Gussie! I'm so glad you're home."

"I'm not celebrating Mother's Day either. Where did you expect me to be? The Boston Marathon is over for the year!"

Maggie relaxed and chuckled. "I just needed to talk. I'm feeling overwhelmed."

"So what else is new? You're the one who has two jobs, a house, and keeps saying you want to add motherhood to your résumé. Maggie, if you're serious about that, you'd better get used to being overwhelmed."

"Guess you're right. Will sent me an e-mail today. It was sweet. But he's in Buffalo, and I'm here. I'm exhausted from grading papers and planning the show. And every time I think life is organized, something else happens."

"No, Maggie. In your life? I can't believe that." The sound of Gussie's laugh reassured Maggie. Maybe she wasn't crazy. "Your problem is you think you *can* organize life. Once you accept that most life events refuse to fit on a list, you'll feel much better."

"You're right. And school is out for the summer on Wednesday."

"And you've still resisted signing on to teach this summer?"

"I have. I could use the money, but I keep thinking that when I'm not teaching, I can do more shows, and travel a little, and maybe make as much money as I could sitting here in New Jersey and grading papers. Have more fun, too." And, if she should adopt a child, it might be the last summer she could do whatever she wanted. Much as she yearned to be a parent, the reality of what it would mean to be a mother twenty-four hours a day for the rest of her life sometimes felt overwhelming.

"Good! I'm glad having fun is on your list. Because I hope you're planning to come to the Cape for at least a week."

"You've got it. For the Provincetown Show, and then for a good visit, if you'll have me. And I'm going to do some traveling in New York State, and other parts of New England."

"Would Will have anything to do with those travel plans?"

"I hope so! He even mentioned possibly visiting Quebec. I haven't done that in years and would love to go. French food, wine, small antiques shops in the country . . ." Maggie was momentarily distracted from her daydream. How would she manage seeing Will when she was a parent? Especially since he didn't want to be involved? She changed the subject to Gussie's love life. "How's Jim?"

Jim and Gussie had been a couple for over a year now. "He's fine. Busy, as usual. Lawyers always are, even in small towns. He's catching up with paperwork and then coming over for dinner later."

"Give him my best."

"I will. Now, what's gotten to you this afternoon? Sounds as though Somerset College issues are under control. Any problems with the show?"

Maggie paused. But there wasn't much she didn't tell Gussie. "The logistics are all in order, although I'm sure little things will pop up in the next few days. And maybe I'm crazy for being concerned about anything else. But some strange stuff is happening at the agency. It may have nothing to do with the show. I hope it doesn't. But it's upsetting Carole Drummond, the director of OWOC."

"And that upsets you. Of course, Maggie. So what's the problem?"

"Two problems, actually. The first is that the agency's gotten a couple of threatening letters, and the one received Friday mentions the dates of the antiques show."

"That sounds serious."

"And this morning one of the most well-known parents from the agency, Holly Sloane—she and her husband have adopted eleven hard-to-place children, Gussie, most of them teenagers!—was shot."

"Shot!" Even unflappable Gussie sounded shocked.

"No one seems to know if it was an accident, or if it was intentional. She was shot right in her own driveway, when she went out to get the morning paper."

"How is she?"

"Carole said she's injured, but not critically. She's in the hospital. But one of her sons is missing, and the police are looking for him." Maggie paused. "The cops are implying he's a suspect."

They were both silent. Then Gussie said, "Maggie, do you think there's any connection? Between the threatening letters and the shooting?"

"I don't know! I don't think so." She hesitated. "We don't know why the person sending the letters is upset about the agency, so I guess anything is possible. Carole said it might be someone who's disgruntled because their home study wasn't approved. But how would that connect to the shooting? I don't think the letters mentioned any individuals. And Holly is an adoptive parent. She's an active member of their adoptive parent organization, but she's not an agency employee."

"But she did adopt her children through OWOC."

"Yes. She and her husband." Maggie gave Winslow an extra scratch behind his neck. "No. I can't imagine the letters and the shooting are connected. But the timing is awful for everyone."

"Is Carole talking about canceling the show?"

"She never mentioned that." Maggie sat back in her chair, scrunching Winslow a bit. "And I hadn't thought of it. Now you've really given me something to worry about. Can you imagine what I'd have to do to call things off at this point?"

"Unfortunately, yes. But it does seem strange to have two violent, or potentially violent, events connected to the adoption agency you're supporting. I don't normally turn on the TV to check on terrorism at adoption agencies."

"That's why it's all a bit unreal. And the shooting is close to home. I wish we knew for certain that it was an accident."

"No wonder you're on edge. But you said your grading will be done today. Then you can concentrate on the show, and on slowing down a bit."

"And on doing everything I can to ensure there aren't any more problems at OWOC. Although I really don't know how anyone can do that."

Maggie took her Pepsi to the study and switched on the local news. Would they cover Holly's shooting? Or maybe something else was going on in the world. Something positive.

Temperatures in the high seventies tomorrow and sunny. That was nice. A car bombing in the Middle East. Not so nice. A meeting of the relatives of 9/11 World Trade Center victims from New Jersey to discuss a memorial to those who'd been killed. Maggie sat up and stared closely for a minute. She knew the young man sitting in the second row. It was Abdullah Jaleel, the bright star of her Myths in American Culture course this semester. Someone in his family must have died in the World Trade Center disaster. Unfortunately, he wasn't unique. Twenty-five percent of those killed— murdered—in the World Trade Center had been from New Jersey. It didn't matter what your background was or where you were from if you happened to be working in one of the Towers that day.

A commercial for SUVs was blaring as Maggie sat back. What did she have to worry about? So many people in the world had lost so much. She was one of the lucky ones. She had a home, food, two jobs, and people who cared about her.

The newscaster went on to a story about a fire in a Paterson warehouse. Maggie clicked off the television and refilled her glass of Diet Pepsi. Winslow had just settled himself on the floor next to the French doors to watch robins in the backyard when the doorbell rang.

Chapter 6

Farmer and Farmer's Wife. *Pair of prints by Grant Wood (1892–1942), American artist whose work featured stern Midwesterners and stylized landscapes; best known for his painting* American Gothic. *Only occasionally did Wood illustrate books. These stark, two-dimensional portraits are from* Farm on the Hill, *1939. The farmer is sitting on a tree stump, eating a sandwich from his lunch bucket. His wife is peeling apples into a wide wooden bowl. Both portraits are on orange backgrounds. 6.75 x 9.5 inches each. Price: $110 for the pair.*

She wasn't expecting anyone to stop in. Feeling ridiculous for being paranoid, Maggie peeked out a front window. A woman was standing on her front steps. It wasn't a woman she knew, but, probably irrationally, she felt safer with an unknown woman than an unknown man. She opened the door.

The woman was bent, her hair graying, and Maggie noted that her hands, clasping a large leather-bound volume in front of her, were heavily veined, and their joints were swollen and deformed by arthritis. She wasn't wearing makeup, and her green, patterned dress hung loosely on her slight body.

"You're Maggie Summer. The print dealer?"

"Yes."

"I'm Agatha Thurston, from over in Somerville. I'm sorry to bother you without calling, but I was visiting my grandchildren here in Park Glen. One of them, Storm Hayden, took a class with you last semester. He told me how you teach at the college and have a business, too."

"Yes?" Storm Hayden. A tall, skinny boy with thin, blond hair. "That's right. I teach and I have an antique-print business."

"So I thought maybe you'd be interested in buying this," continued Mrs. Thurston, thrusting the large volume she was holding toward Maggie.

Maggie's heart sank. She hated unexpected visits like this. "Won't you come in, Mrs. Thurston?" She directed the elderly woman to her small living room just to the right of the front hall. It wasn't a room she used often, so it was kept neat and "readied up for company," as her mother would have said. Maggie had hung five dramatic Seguy lithographs of butterflies on one wall, and the upholstery on two modern couches and a comfortable armchair reflected the blues and pinks of the prints. Other people bought prints to match their furniture. Maggie upholstered to match her prints.

Both Mrs. Thurston and Maggie sat on the couch nearest to the front windows, and Maggie turned on a cut-glass lamp so they could see better. She piled up the copies of *Time, Antiques, Smithsonian, Folk Art,* and *New York* on the glass-topped coffee table. Then she took the book out of Mrs. Thurston's hands and put it on the table so they could both see it.

Her first guess had been right. It was a Bible.

People often brought books and prints to show to Maggie. Sometimes they just wanted to know the value of what they owned or had inherited or bought at a yard sale. Sometimes they were interested in selling. Sometimes Maggie bought. But all too often the cherished possessions they brought her were treasures only to their owners. Just because something was old didn't mean it was valuable.

"This was my great-grandmother's Bible," said Mrs. Thurston. "Her family was from up in New York State. She left it to me."

Maggie nodded.

"But I haven't looked at it in years. I have a small Bible I keep next to my bed to read in the morning. This one is just too big. And my children and grandchildren aren't interested in it. I'm trying to decide whether I'll sell it or keep it. Could you give me some advice? My grandson said you were a very nice, honest lady."

"I'd be happy to look at it." Maggie opened the heavy black book. In the front was a traditional family listing of births, deaths, and marriages framed by an elaborately chromolithographed scrolled decoration.

Mrs. Thurston pointed at one of the listings. "That's my mother, Emma, and the date she was born," she said proudly. "The minister read from this Bible when my mother was married, and then when I was married."

"It has a very special history," agreed Maggie. She turned the pages carefully. The Bible had been printed in 1878 and contained a dozen lithographs illustrating famous biblical stories such as the Garden of Eden, Noah and the animals, and the birth of Jesus. "And this is a lovely edition." Maggie noted that some pages were more worn than others; some passages had been underlined. "It's meant a lot to your family."

"Yes. It has," agreed Mrs. Thurston. "But I'm the only one who seems to care now, and I'm getting older. Is it worth any money?"

Maggie hated to disappoint the woman. "I'm afraid not very much. There are so many family Bibles, even lovely ones like yours, and very few people are interested in collecting them. They really should be kept in the original families for as long as possible. It's sad to see Bibles selling at auctions for thirty-five or fifty dollars when they contain the history of a family."

"But this one has such pretty pictures in it!" Mrs. Thurston paged through the book and pointed at one of Moses. "That's why I thought maybe a print dealer like you would be interested in it."

Maggie shook her head. "I'm sorry. The lithographs are lovely. But there isn't a big market for biblical engravings or lithographs." Of all the prints, Maggie thought, the one of Noah and the animals might be salable. But not quickly. She didn't even have a category of "religious prints" in her business. They just weren't what people were looking for at antiques shows today. "I'd hate to see this Bible leaving your family. Are you sure none of your grandchildren would be interested in it? Perhaps in a few years, if not now."

Mrs. Thurston smiled at her. "They aren't yet, but you're right, maybe as they get a little older they will be. I'll keep the Bible. At least now I know it doesn't have a large dollar value." She stood and picked up the book.

"It's a lovely family treasure," agreed Maggie, also standing. "I hope someone in your family appreciates it someday."

"And in the meantime it will stay right with me, as it has for the past fifty years. Thank you for taking the time to tell me about it."

"I'm sorry I couldn't give you better news," said Maggie, as they walked back to the front door.

"But you have, you know. You've reminded me that this book means something to me and to my family, even if they don't realize it just now. Young people today are just so busy with their computers and TVs and such they don't pay much attention to the past. But one of the jobs of us older folks is to keep the stories of our family alive. I've been thinking about writing down the stories of our family. Leaving the stories with the Bible might mean more to some of my grandchildren when they get a little older and have children of their own."

"That's a beautiful idea," said Maggie. "I wish my grandmother had written down the stories of her world, so I'd have them now."

The ringing telephone interrupted her.

"You go and answer your phone, Ms. Summer. And thank you, again. You've given me a new reason to keep going a few more years: to keep the stories alive."

Mrs. Thurston walked down the front steps decisively.

Maggie watched her for a moment, and then went to answer her telephone.

Chapter 7

⸻

Colored illustration by Jessie Willcox Smith for A Child's Garden of Verses *by Robert Louis Stevenson, 1905. Smiling young woman in long pink robe holds three toddlers in her lap while five more surround her. One is putting a rose in her hair; one holds a cat. Smith, who lived in and just outside Philadelphia, is known as an illustrator of children's books. She and several of her fellow women artists were called The Red Rose Group. 7 x 9.25 inches. Price: $65.*

"Maggie? This is Ann Shepard."

Ann was the other single prospective parent involved in the OWOC show, the one in charge of food for the café and bake sale. Of all the show committees that was the one Maggie worried least about. She knew Ann had been baking muffins and cookies for months.

"I'm going slightly crazy and wondered if you'd like to have dinner tonight? I need to get away from my house and my office, and I thought of you. After all, we're both prospective single parents."

"You picked a good night to call. I'd love to get out of my house."

"Nothing formal," said Ann. "What about Thompson's, down on Bridge Street?"

Thompson's was a family place where you could order a glass of wine but you could also have a cheeseburger and fries.

"Thompson's sounds fine," agreed Maggie. She would like to know Ann better, too. She should get to know other people interested in single-parent adoption. It could be the beginning of a support system for them, and then, for their children, after they all had families. *If* I adopt, added Maggie to herself. "About half an hour?"

"See you there."

Ann was already sitting in a booth when Maggie walked in. "You got here quickly! I thought I'd be early." Maggie slid onto the other red plastic seat.

"I cheated a bit," Ann said. "I was calling from my office at the bank. I went in to clean up a pile of papers and just couldn't face going home to an empty house."

Maggie nodded. "I have times like that, too." Usually she went home anyway. I've been acting like an old married woman, she thought. Why not be like Ann and call a single woman friend to have dinner? It was better than having frozen pizza and watching the news alone with a cat. "But you won't have too many more quiet evenings, will you? I heard a rumor your home study was finished."

"Yes. I'm approved." Ann did not seem enthusiastic. She turned to the waitress who had materialized next to their table. "Dewar's on the rocks, please."

"A glass of the house chardonnay," said Maggie.

"I'm having second thoughts. Maybe thirty-second thoughts," continued Ann.

"Adoption's a big step. I'm so uncertain I haven't even applied to have my home study done yet."

"I really do want a child. And I'm definitely tired of trying to get pregnant."

Maggie tried not to react. She hadn't realized Ann had been trying to conceive.

"I've been inseminated four times. It hasn't taken. I don't want to waste all my savings on sperm and then have nothing left to cover adoption costs."

Maggie didn't feel comfortable hearing the details. She knew one couple who were going through fertility treatments while they were trying to adopt. She also knew agencies frowned on the practice. They wanted to work with people who had put any fertility problems in the past and were ready to adopt with a whole heart. An adopted child shouldn't be expected to replace a child someone had dreamed of giving birth to. That wouldn't be fair to the child.

Of course, there was always the classic stereotype of the adoptive mother who, like Josie Thomas, adopted and then got pregnant. But applying to adopt was definitely not a way to increase your chances of conceiving. "I didn't know you wanted a baby. I thought you wanted to adopt a toddler."

"If I can't get pregnant," Ann agreed. "My first choice would be to adopt an infant, but that's hard to do if you're not married. And now the agency is hassling me about wanting to adopt a child as young as a toddler."

"But they must be ready to work with you. Your home study's been approved."

"To get it approved I had to agree I'd adopt a child up to the age of six. And I couldn't specify a white child. Or a girl." Ann took a good drink of her Scotch. "I'm not sure I'm ready to adopt a child of another race. And I really want a little girl. A little blonde girl with pigtails and big blue eyes."

"That's pretty specific."

"Oh, I know enough not to tell that to my social worker! I might be able to cope with adopting a boy; and at first I thought I might be able to adopt a child of another race. I know lots of people do, and some of the kids are really cute. But the more I think about the future, and about what it would mean to bring up a child of another race or color, the more I'm not sure it's something I'm ready for."

"OWOC only makes placements across racial lines when a family is sure," said Maggie. But they expect you to be honest about your feelings, she added to herself.

"I told them I didn't think my parents would accept a grandchild who wasn't white. But they said there were very few Caucasian children available for adoption, except older children who'd have emotional problems of some sort, or children who were physically disabled. And that when young, healthy white children were available, couples were preferred over single parents. Carole told me, gently but firmly, that I'd have a much better chance of getting a placement if I'd accept a child from Latin America or Asia."

Maggie nodded. "They can place infants and toddlers from China with single women."

"Well, I don't think it's fair. I don't think I should be emotionally coerced into adopting a child from abroad because it's my only option. Adoption applications from single parents should be treated the same as applications from couples. I could give a child as good—or better!—a home than a couple. I wouldn't have to divide my attention between my husband and my child. I could devote myself totally to my child." Ann took another drink. "It isn't fair that the Hansons would get a healthy baby before I would, even though they already had a son."

The Hansons? The couple who'd died when their home had burned down last winter. Their son, Hal, escaped because his bedroom was on the first floor. She hadn't remembered until now, but, yes, she'd heard they'd been applying to adopt another child. She focused back on Ann. "A single parent can absolutely be the right parent for a child," Maggie agreed. "But if there's a qualified couple waiting, too, it's not as simple. I think if I were the agency, I'd place the child with a couple. After all, two great parents would be better than one."

"But they're discriminating against us, just because we're not married!" said Ann.

Maggie hesitated. "I don't think it's discrimination. I think the agency really wants to find the best family for each child. If there were a three-parent family, I suspect they would be considered the best."

Ann gave her a dark look. "What's so good about having more than one parent? Lots of couples get divorced. Mine did. At least a single parent will always be there."

Unless there's a death, Maggie thought. A child with only one parent could be orphaned again more easily than a child with two parents. That's why single prospective parents had to name someone else to back them up in case of illness or death. That requirement was an issue for Maggie. Her parents were dead, and she hadn't been in touch with her older brother in years. She had no obvious family or extended family backup. She sipped her wine. Ann was still talking.

"Even supposedly perfect parents, like Holly and Rob Sloane, aren't perfect couples."

"They're pretty impressive. Adopting eleven hard-to-place kids, in addition to the three biological ones they started with." Maggie was much less comfortable now than when she'd walked into the restaurant.

"But I've heard their marriage is rocky. That they spend so much time with their kids they have no time for each other. And if they're such great parents, then why did one of their kids shoot Holly?" Ann sputtered.

"We don't know that's what happened," Maggie said quietly.

"But it seems obvious. Otherwise Jackson would be at home, or at least in touch with the rest of his family. At last year's agency Christmas party I overheard one of Holly's kids say her mom spent more time talking about adoption with other parents than she spent with her own children. I don't want my daughter ever to say that about me."

"No," Maggie agreed. "But children always complain about their parents. Most of Holly's and Rob's children seem to be doing well. And they all started with the odds against them. Let's just hope Holly heals quickly and can get home."

Maggie picked up her menu. "Have you decided what you want?"

Ann chose poached chicken breast in white wine sauce with rice; Maggie ordered a rare hamburger with sautéed mushrooms and onions. They were both quiet for a few minutes before Ann began again.

"Have you thought about what adoption will mean to your social life? About what kind of a man would be interested in dating a woman who adopted a child of a different race?" Ann said. "I'd like to get married someday and I think I'd have more of a chance of finding the right guy if my child were white."

Maggie swallowed deeply. "I'd like to think any man who loved me would love my children, whatever they looked like. After all, some men like children, and some don't. So, yes, some men will be turned off by our adopting. But they won't be the men we're looking for." Will didn't want children. Of any color. Other than that, he might be the man Maggie had been waiting for. She took a breath. This conversation was moving uncomfortably close to some of her own private concerns. "We can't plan our lives around what some man someday might expect of us."

That was the "right" answer. But what if Will was the one for her? Did she have to choose between having a man in her life and being a mother? Was that the reason she hadn't agreed to begin her own home study? Was she really hoping Will would change his mind? She wanted to be a parent. But adopting was an enormous gamble.

"You can say that. You've been married, and you have another man in your life already." Ann's face was flushed, from the Scotch or from emotion. Maybe both. "I don't want to wake up and be fifty or sixty and alone, without a husband or a child. You don't know what it's like to be forty-two and know you probably can't give birth, and then be told you can only adopt a second-class child. I make more money than a lot of couples, and I would be a wonderful mother. It's not fair that I can't be one!"

A second-class child? No child was second-class! What if Carole knew Ann was thinking that way? Or did she know already? Agency personnel were experts in analyzing and questioning motives for adopting. "But OWOC has said they'd place a child with you."

"Not the child I want to parent. Even though I've spent months working on this damn antiques show, smiling and making enough blueberry muffins to feed Calcutta. I had to buy a freezer just to hold all the pies and cookies I've baked!"

Maggie took a bite of her hamburger and another sip of wine. She tried to keep her voice calm. "The way I understand it, OWOC is looking for families for children; not children for families. There are very few healthy white babies in need of homes."

Ann looked at her with disappointment in her eyes. "You're on their side. I thought since you were single, you'd feel the way I do."

"I want to be a parent, Ann. But if I adopt, then I'll apply for a child who needs a parent. Probably a school-age child. I want to adopt a child who needs a family." Maggie hesitated. "I guess I need a family, too. That's why this decision means so much to me."

Ann shook her head. "It means a lot to me, too. And I'm getting older. I don't have time to put my name on long waiting lists." She waited a moment. "An older child would have more emotional baggage and issues than an infant or toddler. Those are the children who need the most help. If there is a preference, I'd think an agency would want to place them with a two-parent family that had more time and energy to help them."

Maggie nodded slightly. That had occurred to her, too.

"But there are so many children on waiting lists. They're getting older every day, too, and less adoptable. Have you told Carole and your social worker how you really feel?"

"I've told them I want a young white girl without handicaps." Ann put down her glass of Scotch. "I've even talked with my lawyer about it."

"Your lawyer? You mean the one who'll handle the adoption?"

"I haven't taken formal action yet. But OWOC is treating me, a single woman, differently than they treat couples who apply to adopt. That's one reason I thought we should talk, Maggie. You might like to talk with my lawyer, too. She thinks we'd have a good chance of proving discrimination against prospective single parents. If we got enough people involved, it might even be a class-action suit."

"You're thinking of suing OWOC?" Maggie put her glass down, too. The remaining wine sloshed from one side to another.

"This may be my last chance! I want to do something to make OWOC and other agencies wake up and help people like me adopt the children we're looking for."

"Ann, I don't agree. I don't agree about the discrimination, and I don't want to talk with a lawyer. This isn't like going to the Bridgewater Mall and picking out the best pair of shoes for the money. This is wanting to share your life with a child who has no one. A child who needs love, and attention, and someone to help them grow up and find out what their life could be like. It's not about lawyers, or about getting what we want. It's about giving what we can."

Ann's face reddened, and then a tear slid down her cheek. "But I can't give up my dream."

Maggie reached out and put her hand over Ann's. "Then maybe adoption isn't the right choice for you. Or maybe you're just not quite ready."

"Maggie, will our lives always be this complicated?"

"At least," Maggie answered. "That's the one thing I'm sure of."

Chapter 8

―⁓―

"Hark! hark! The dogs bark, The beggars are coming to town; Some in rags and some in tags, And some in a silken gown. Some gave them white bread, And some gave them brown, And some gave them a good horse-whip, And sent them out of the town." From Kate Greenaway's Mother Goose, *1881. Lithograph of two little girls holding on to each other and looking through their gate at several beggars standing on the outskirts of town. 3 x 4.5 inches. Price: $40.*

It was after nine when Maggie got back from dinner with Ann. It hadn't been the relaxing evening she'd hoped for. Ann's concerns had increased Maggie's own fears.

Was she ready for adoption?

What *would* a man's reaction be to a woman who'd adopted alone? She hoped Ann was overemphasizing the issue, but it wasn't an imaginary one. And while Maggie was sincere in wanting to adopt an older child, she couldn't help thinking of what experienced adoptive parents like Holly and Rob Sloane were dealing with. If they couldn't cope with some of the problems of their adopted children, how could she, who had never had children, possibly believe she could handle them?

She wanted to help a child. But what if the child she adopted didn't want her help? Could she deal with that kind of rejection? Could she hang in and be a loving and caring parent for the years it might take to win a child's trust and love?

Her mind was too full of questions for her to forget them. She finished grading exams, then decided that, late as it was, she'd clean the house. After all, she was expecting company Wednesday.

Winslow thought cleaning was a game. He pounced on her dusting cloths until Maggie wouldn't play any longer and shut him in the bathroom so she could clean in peace. She relented and let him out in less than half an hour, but when he heard the vacuum, he dove under her bed.

It was almost midnight when she finished, but she still couldn't settle down. She pulled out her Arthur Rackham (1867–1939) prints. Because Rackham was one of her favorite illustrators, she could rarely resist purchasing his prints. That meant she almost always had new prints to replace those she'd sold. But those new prints needed to be matted. She hadn't done that for months. She could check the prints she had now and choose the ones she'd mat as soon as she had time.

Spending time with Rackham was a delight. Just looking at his work took her into another, magical, world. Although others of his period, such as Kay Nielsen and Edmund Dulac, had done similar work in the early twentieth century, no one else was like Rackham. Maggie'd heard there were organizations in England formed just to celebrate and share his work. She wasn't surprised. It was getting more difficult to find his early prints, and prices were going up. Some had been carefully reproduced in the past twenty years, too, so she never bought Rackham prints whose origins she didn't know.

Rackham was an illustrator of stories for adults and children; often traditional stories, but his vision of the world was anything but traditional. The worlds he pictured were fantastic and mysterious. His line drawings contained incredibly fine details. Trees were formed of faces and arms, and elves lived in attics. Flowers, roots, and ferns had human features.

Maggie smiled at an illustration from *Peter Pan in Kensington Garden* of a tiny, gnarled gnomelike creature hiding behind a tulip. He had long, pointed toes and ears, striped socks, and a feather half his size jauntily stuck in his hair.

But despite the imagination showed in his prints, Arthur Rackham himself had lived a rather ordinary life.

For eight years he'd clerked in an insurance office during the day and attended art school at night. In 1900 he married Edyth Starkie, a portrait painter, and got his first major commission: to illustrate *The Fairy Tales of the Brothers Grimm*. About this time color reproduction techniques improved, thanks to photographic separation using filters. Only heavy and highly glazed art paper would retain the colored inks well, so publishers using this new technique printed the color illustrations separately and "tipped in" the prints after the book was printed. This operation had to be done by hand, so it cost more, but the resulting prints were so lovely that people were willing to pay more for the books.

Every time Maggie looked at Rackham's illustrations, she saw more. The details were extraordinary. Her longtime personal favorites were the ones Rackham had done for *The Wind in the Willows* and *Ondine,* but there were none she disliked. She had about forty in her current inventory, and in the late-night peace she chose another twenty to be matted.

She refused to think about threats or shootings. Or adoptions. There had been three calls while she'd been at dinner with Ann: Carole asked whether they could get two extra tables for the admissions area, and if there would be coatracks customers could use. A dealer from Ohio wanted to know if there was a reach number at the show; another dealer, from New York State, needed directions. None of those were problems. She could return the calls tomorrow.

Maggie had almost forgotten how good it felt to have her print files updated and the house clean and in order. She added the Rackham portfolio to the pile she had already started next to the French doors in her study. Most of the portfolios featured children, but she'd added her Winslow Homers, and Thomas Nast Christmas prints (they included children, after all). The pile also included tools, display racks, and table covers.

Tomorrow she would add several portfolios of flowers, one of birds and nests, anatomy, and astronomy and astrology. Might as well have the stars on her side.

As long as she finished before Gussie and Will arrived on Wednesday, she'd be fine.

Even if Holly had been shot, her son Jackson was missing, and someone was threatening to sabotage the antiques show.

Chapter 9

—⟡—

Illumination of Manuscripts—Arabian. *Chromolithograph from* Dekarative Varbilder, *printed by E. Hochdanz, Stuttgart, 1891. Beautiful example of Middle Eastern design patterns in gold, blue, and red. 9.75 x 13.5 inches. Price: $90.*

"Professor Summer!"

It was Monday morning. Exams and papers were graded, and Maggie was in her office at Somerset County College filing grade reports and copies of exams.

"Yes, Abdullah?" The tall, muscular, dark-haired young man in her doorway had become a fixture in the American Studies offices during the past few months. In his late twenties, he'd registered at the college for the first time this semester and was one of the most enthusiastic and bright students Maggie had taught. She wondered sometimes what he'd been doing between high school and college. Saving money? Supporting his family? Whatever it was, it had prepared him well for college.

"Have you graded the Myths in American Culture papers we handed in last week?"

"I'm not finished, and you'll have to wait for your grade report, in any case." Maggie smiled. She remembered Abdullah's paper, an incisive analysis of the myth of America as a melting pot. Amazing work for a first-semester student.

"I understand. I just wondered. And I wanted you to know I've volunteered to work on the antiques show you're running. The one that's going to benefit the adoption agency."

"I saw your name on the list; thank you. We can use your help. Make sure you come to the meeting Wednesday morning in the lobby outside the basketball courts at the gym. We'll go over assignments and make sure everyone knows what they're going to help with."

He turned to leave.

"Abdullah," said Maggie. "Did I see you on television last night? I thought I saw you at a meeting about creating a memorial for the victims of 9/11."

His body stiffened, but he turned back toward her. "I was there."

"Did you lose someone at the World Trade Center?"

"My brother was on the ninety-seventh floor of the South Tower."

"I'm sorry. That must have been very hard."

"Life is not easy for many people." He turned again to leave.

"Good luck with getting support for the memorial."

He nodded and left.

What a relief it would be to lock this office for the summer, even though she'd done her best to brighten the small room. She'd hung several hand-colored prints near the window overlooking the front of the campus: an Alexander Wilson engraving of eider ducks, a lithograph of a clump of naturalized daffodils, and a self-portrait of George Catlin painting a Native American family. She'd reframed her Currier & Ives print of *Maggie* and hung it between a high bookcase piled with books on American history and literature and a four-drawer file cabinet full of lecture notes, papers, exams, records of past students, and clippings and notes for articles she might write or lectures she might give. Someday. May 11, the last day of the semester, was circled on the calendar next to the window. Even heavier lines were around May 14 and 15.

When the college and the agency had finally agreed those would be the dates for the antiques show, Maggie had considered it a good omen. May 23 was her birthday. She wasn't particularly excited about tearing another leaf off her life. Thirty-nine. It seemed impossible. But it did seem auspicious that the antiques show would be over before her thirty-eighth year ended. What would the next year bring?

Not that she'd be able to relax and contemplate the future even after May 23. Memorial Day weekend was the Rensselaer County show in New York. But the stock market had been up recently. Maybe that was an omen of better shows ahead.

She'd read somewhere that time passed more quickly when you were older. No wonder she sometimes felt she couldn't keep up with it. Seventeen months ago her husband, Michael, had died of a stroke, leaving her with regrets, bills, and the knowledge that Michael had been unfaithful. It had taken months to get through the grief and anger his death had left behind.

So much had happened since then that sometimes she had trouble absorbing it all. This spring the antiques show had taken up so much of her time she hadn't had time to step back and think. She hoped the show made lots of money for the agency. And if she did apply to be an adoptive parent (when she did, Maggie mentally corrected herself), she'd know a lot more about adoption than she had a year ago.

Last night's conversation with Ann kept coming back to her. She didn't agree with Ann's limitations on what child she might adopt, but Ann was correct in thinking that adopting an older child, one who came with emotional baggage and might be another race, or from another culture, would change her life completely. Was she ready to cope with all the issues Holly and Rob dealt with every day? How was Holly this morning? Had Jackson come home?

"Professor Summer?" Claudia Hall, the American Studies

department secretary, was standing in the door of Maggie's office, a cup of coffee in one hand and a bag of chocolate kisses in the other. Her blouse strained a bit at the buttons, she wore a bright yellow-flowered skirt, and her tangled brown hair was under more control than usual.

"Yes, Claudia?" Maggie took a sip of her Diet Pepsi. It was never too early for Diet Pepsi.

"Have you seen Uncle Sam?"

"I haven't," Maggie answered. Since she'd removed the large potted snake plant from her office, she didn't see the American Studies cat as often as she used to. "Have you checked Paul Turk's office? Sam's taken a liking to the schefflera in there."

"I'll check," said Claudia. "I'm not worried. He'll probably appear as soon as I open a can of cat food. Maybe he's avoiding me because he knows that today's the day he goes home with me for the summer. He hates the cat cage. Anyway, I meant to tell you that Oliver Whitcomb called Friday afternoon, after you'd left. He wants to be at the meeting with the facilities management staff you're having this morning. I told him it would be in the conference room over at the gym. I hope that was okay."

Maggie sighed. "That was fine, Claudia." The gymnasium was technically WHITCOMB gymnasium, and Oliver was the benefactor who'd made it possible. He was no longer a member of the board of trustees, but he still kept involved with events on campus. Especially events involving *his* gymnasium. He'd been the one to convince the board to donate the space as a gesture of community support for the antiques show, so he was welcome at the meeting. As long as he didn't get in the way. Sometimes Oliver forgot he was no longer running a corporation.

"Two more students called to volunteer to help with the antiques show—Kendall Park and Kayla Martin, from Whitcomb House. I told them about the meeting on Wednesday." Claudia bent down and stage-whispered, "I've seen Kendall and Kayla together a lot recently. Wouldn't it be great if they got married? Two single parents. They'd have an instant family."

Claudia looked closely at Maggie. "You look tired this morning. Late night grading exams? You need some fast energy." She poured a dozen chocolate kisses onto Maggie's desk.

"Thank you. I guess I am tired." Maggie glanced at her watch. "You're right; I was up late. I'd better get moving if I'm going to be at the gym on time." She picked up her black binder and one of the chocolate kisses and headed for the door. "You know my schedule; just try to keep the place from falling apart while I'm gone." She hesitated. "And lock my office, Claudia; there are exams in here."

Once last fall, Maggie's office had been trashed. Now she locked it even when she was going to the ladies' room.

"Don't worry, Professor Summer. I'll take care of it." Claudia popped a chocolate kiss into her own mouth. "You don't have to worry about anything here. In fact, I wondered if I could go to the meeting with you. I've been thinking about all you've been doing for Our World Our Children, and I'd like to help with the show. Would you mind? I could take notes. Or run any errands you needed help with."

"Claudia, I'd love to have your help. But we're so close to the end of the semester, I think you'd better stay here this morning." Maggie hesitated. "If you'd really like to help, maybe you could come to the meeting Wednesday, with the volunteers for the show, and help me keep that organized."

"I'd love to! And if it's all right with you, I've cleared my schedule for Thursday through Sunday so I can help with the show." Claudia shrugged and brushed back her hair. "I guess all the advertising for Mother's Day got to me this weekend. I'm not ready to be a mother, but I figured maybe I could do something for kids who needed one."

Maggie almost hugged her. "Claudia, that's the nicest thing I've heard all morning. You know a lot of the players, and you'd be a great help."

"Thank you!" Claudia's smile was broad.

Claudia was Maggie's right-hand person on campus, and she

could use all the help she could get before and during the show. Especially if there were any unanticipated problems.

Maggie was the last to arrive at the conference room in Whitcomb Gymnasium. The room had originally been designed as a small library on sports and athletics, conveniently located between a large conference room and the offices of the gymnasium director and coaches. But it turned out the college needed more space for weight machines and treadmills than for sports reference materials, so the college library had absorbed the books, the conference room was now a weight room, and the space designed for a library contained two small oblong tables, one of which was now topped by a coffeemaker and remnants of what must have been doughnuts for an even earlier meeting.

Maggie's stomach growled. She'd skipped breakfast, and there would be no time for food until midmorning. She should have brought some pastries for the meeting.

Oliver Whitcomb was there, dressed in shorts and a T-shirt and dripping a bit. He used the gym as his personal exercise site. Still, he was elegant despite the sweat. Oliver had retired from Wall Street, and last fall he and his wife, Dorothy, had rediscovered Sarah, the daughter she'd relinquished for adoption many years before, and Sarah's five-year-old daughter, Aura. Oliver had accepted their entry into his life with remarkable grace.

Sarah had taken this semester off to manage some medical issues and get to know her mother. Maggie hoped she'd be back in class next fall. She'd volunteered to help out at the antiques show, so she would be at the Wednesday meeting.

Maggie put down her notebook. George Healy, the facilities manager who had responsibility for the gymnasium, was there, plus two men she didn't recognize. One of them looked familiar. He was in his early twenties; a tall, light-skinned African-American. She'd seen him somewhere. Had he been in one of her classes? She tried to get to know all her students, but some years her classes were larger than she would have liked.

He looked at her, smiled, and raised his hand in greeting.

He'd been leaning back in his chair, but now he put his hands squarely on the table and looked at her intently.

She must know him. Drat. She hoped she wouldn't have to introduce him to anyone. The other man was perhaps ten years older; receding brown hair, an athletic body, and a frown on his tanned face.

"Good morning, everyone! Thank you for freeing up your schedules so we could get together one last time. And a special thank-you to Oliver Whitcomb, who donated this wonderful facility, and helped me convince the Somerset County College Board of Trustees that this benefit antiques show would be a good use for it. Our World Our Children is thrilled that we'll be setting up the show in the two gymnasiums usually used for basketball and indoor tennis. I hope everything is set for this weekend; today we're just going to review the final details."

The older of the two men she didn't recognize spoke first. He was attractive. And not happy. "I'm Mike Colletto, Professor Summer. I haven't met you, but I teach tennis here, and no one asked me what I thought about a bunch of people moving in tables and chairs and then asking hundreds of people wearing hard shoes to walk on my courts. As I told Mr. Whitcomb, those floors could be ruined. And he knows how much they cost to maintain."

"Maggie, what about that? I told Mike here you'd have an answer, but I didn't know what it was, so he should just come this morning and ask you himself." Oliver looked at Maggie with confidence.

Maggie nodded, hoping her answer was acceptable. "When the president of OWOC and I first approached the board of the college, we promised not to damage anything in this wonderful new facility. The floors of both the tennis courts and the basketball courts will be covered with plastic liners, and then with padding and thick indoor-outdoor carpeting on Thursday, the day before the dealers arrive. Even if it rains, no dampness will get onto the floors, and the padding will protect them. We've told our dealers nothing can be attached to the walls of the gyms or the hallways. Not even masking tape."

Mike hesitated. "I'd like to be here to make sure no damage is done, even by the people putting down the carpeting."

Maggie pulled out a pad of paper. "That's one of the reasons I wanted us to meet today. Mike, if you'll take responsibility for making sure there are no problems with the floors, I'd really appreciate your help. The company putting down the plastic and padding will be here Thursday morning at eight thirty."

Mike nodded slightly. "I can't take total responsibility, but I'll be here. I still don't understand why an adoption agency has to use a college fitness facility for something like an antiques show. One mark on that floor and thousands of dollars could be needed to restore it."

Oliver just smiled at him.

The young black man leaned back in his chair again and started drumming on the table with the fingers of his left hand.

Maggie went on, "And, George, I'd appreciate some members of your staff being available when we set up and then during the show itself. I need someone who can take care of possible maintenance problems. We hope there'll be hundreds of people here over the weekend. We need to make sure the doors are locked or unlocked when needed, the lights are on, and the bathrooms are clean and working and we don't run out of soap or toilet paper."

Maggie grimaced to herself. Never had she thought of antiques shows in terms of logistical issues involving toilet paper. As a dealer, she never had to. As an organizer of a show, whatever went wrong was her fault. "George, when we talked before, we estimated how much power we can use. We may need air-conditioning this weekend; there's no predicting what kind of weather we'll have in May in New Jersey. Have you arranged for your electricians to lay down wires with outlets? The dealers who've paid extra for their booths to have power will want it there when they check in Friday afternoon."

"When can we start working on the electric?" asked George. "The floors would have to be covered by then, and we'd have to know exactly where you want the wires and outlets."

"The electric will have to be finished by Friday afternoon, before four. It might help if someone could work Thursday night," said Maggie. "The carpeting company estimates it will take most of Thursday to cover the two gyms and tape the carpet so it won't separate. Thursday night I'll be here with several other people to measure out booths and lay tape on top of the carpet to show the dealers what spaces they have to set up in."

"Okay. We'll work together on that. I'll see if I can get someone to at least start working Thursday night, to follow you as you outline the booths." Healy took some more notes. "And I brought Eric Sloane with me today so you could meet him."

Eric Sloane. Of course. That's who the young man was; one of Holly and Rob's children. She'd met him at an adoptive parent picnic at their house. She wanted to ask him how his mother was, and whether his brother had come home. But this wasn't the place. If anything disastrous had happened, he wouldn't be here. Maybe there would be a moment after the meeting.

"Hi, Eric," she said, hoping he would think she'd recognized him all along. "Good to see you again." No wonder his T-shirt looked crumpled and his hair was askew. He and his family were living through a nightmare.

"Eric's been in charge of basic daily cleanup in the gyms for the past couple of months. He's volunteered to be available from the beginning of your setup until the show closes to help with small emergencies like spilled coffee and missing toilet paper. I'll be in and out and so will the electricians, but Eric will also have reach numbers for everyone you might possibly need during the show."

"That's wonderful, Eric. Thank you for volunteering, and I'll look forward to working with you," said Maggie, nodding at him. "Sounds as though you'll be an important point man during the setup and show, although I hope to have enough volunteers to take care of minor emergencies like spilled coffee!"

Eric smiled and nodded, but he was still drumming his finger. nervously on the table.

She looked down at her notes. "So, we were talking about taping the outlines of the booths Thursday afternoon and evening." She already dreaded that part of the exercise. Spending long hours with duct tape and tape measures was not her idea of an exciting evening, but some of the dealers would bring their own measuring tapes and check to make sure they got exactly the size booth they had paid for. They would also be arriving with portable walls and heavy furniture, and no one would be in a mood to adjust boundaries at that point. Thank goodness Will would be here to help.

Maggie touched her regard ring for luck.

"We'll leave a note in the middle of each space with instructions for the electricians as to which booths get power and which don't." Maggie hesitated. "I think I'll have the carpet rental people do the basketball courts first, since they're farthest away from the main entrance. As soon as they're finished I'll start measuring the booths. That way, by afternoon, maybe even by one o'clock or so, your electricians could start working in that gym, George. If they don't finish by the time they have to leave that afternoon, they can work Friday morning while the tables and chairs are being put down."

George looked relieved. "That would be a lot easier. My guys weren't enthused about working late hours, especially between semesters." He looked at his list again. "You were going to check on the furniture. Are the tables and chairs ours?"

"The chairs, yes, but not all the tables. The college has enough folding chairs to allow two for each booth and extras for the café area, for admissions, and for some seating at the ends of the gyms. We've had to rent"—Maggie glanced down at her notebook—"ninety-six extra folding tables."

"Will you need help with them?" Healy was taking notes again.

"The company we're renting from will bring them into the gym, but, yes, they'll still need to be put in the right booths Friday morning or early afternoon. If you have some people to help, that would be wonderful. Again, I'll have a map. Some booths get six-foot tables, some get eight-foots. Others don't want any, because dealers are bringing their own furniture and display areas.

"The dealer contracts say they can start unloading their vans and cars at four, but some will be here early, and anxious to set up. I'd like everything to be absolutely ready by three thirty."

"I can help with tables," said Eric.

"Great," said Maggie. "Maybe I can get a couple of the student volunteers, too."

"And then everything will pretty much stay as is until the show is over?" said George Healy.

"Yes and no. Everything will be as it should be, but I'll still want some backup help. Toilet paper, remember. And once the dealers all turn their booth lights on, and the air-conditioning is operating, we don't want any surprise blackouts."

"There's an emergency generator. If there should be a power problem, there will still be small lights in the corners of the gyms by the exits. But the room would be pretty dark."

"Then let's hope we don't have to rely on the generator," Maggie said, mentally crossing her fingers. "Will you have any problem getting people to work that weekend? I know Eric is going to be here, but just in case we need anyone else." Maggie hoped she wasn't being too obvious. Eric might be great for cleanups, but he probably couldn't handle a major electrical or plumbing emergency. And with his brother missing, how could he concentrate on housekeeping details?

"It'll be double time for some of them." Healy hesitated. "But I'll do what I can."

Oliver, quiet until now, spoke up. "If you have trouble finding people to work, or getting the money to pay them, let me know. I'm in back of Maggie and the OWOC antiques show one hundred percent, and if there's anything I can do to help, I will."

Ever since Oliver had found out his wife had given a child up for adoption long before she'd known him, he'd been interested in adoption, and Maggie hoped he'd write a nice contribution check to OWOC as well as using his influence with the board of the college to let them use the gym.

"And, Maggie, if you need help setting up tables or measuring out booth spaces, let me know. I can be here, too."

"Thank you, Oliver," said Maggie. She didn't really need another boss to help set up the show. But, then again, if there were any problems, Oliver had the influence to take care of things. "I'll let you know once I talk to each of the committee heads one more time." She hesitated. Should she mention anything about the potential security issue?

No. That would just be between her and the people responsible for securing the building. Why bother the electricians and plumbers and tennis coach? They had enough problems to worry about in their own areas.

"I think we're all set, then," said Maggie. "If you have any questions about the schedule, please get back to me as soon as you can." She handed them each a card with her home and college telephone numbers. "I'll be at the college off and on through noon Wednesday, but after that I can be reached most easily at my home. Leave a message if I don't answer. I really appreciate all the work you've put into getting this show ready to go. And the earlier we know about a possible problem, the better chance we have of solving it." Maggie thought about the problems she couldn't solve, such as someone who sent hate letters. Or someone who shot Holly.

She stopped Eric as they were leaving the room and asked quietly, "How's your mother doing?"

Eric looked at her, then past her, into the empty hallway. "She had surgery yesterday. Mr. Healy asked me to come in for this meeting, so I did. But we don't know how she is yet."

"I've been thinking of her."

"So have we." Eric looked at her. "I'm just here for the meeting. We decided to stay home this week. All of the family. Sort of moral support, you know." Eric shifted his weight from one foot to another. He seemed full of nervous energy.

"And have you heard where . . . ?"

"No one knows anything," he said, and turned and walked away quickly.

No one knew where Jackson was? No one knew who had shot Holly? Or maybe Eric meant exactly what he said. "No one knows anything."

Chapter 10

Foreign Children. *Illustration for Robert Louis Stevenson's* A Child's Garden of Verses *by Ruth Mary Hallock. Caucasian child eating porridge at small tea table with Japanese doll seated opposite, with rice bowl and chopsticks. Pictures of Native American, Inuit, and Japanese children on wall. 1923. 8.75 x 7 inches. Price: $40.*

Winslow Homer was waiting as Maggie turned the key in the back door of her 1920s-era suburban colonial. She might be weary, but Winslow's winding his way around her legs reminded her he was glad to see her. And that it was lunchtime. He had priorities. When Maggie came home, he expected at least a tidbit.

Maggie dropped her armload of books on the nineteenth-century pine kitchen table, bent down, and scratched his head. He'd been part of her life since last September, when he'd arrived and refused to leave. Since then she'd looked at prints of cats with a new eye. But no cat in a print looked enough like Winslow to convince her to take a print out of her inventory and hang it on the wall. After all, she had the original. Winslow was just a basic gray and white cat. Perhaps like the cat she had named him after in Winslow Homer's engraving *The Dinner Horn,* but a more domesticated creature. His idea of a wild adventure was peeking out the door to the ramp leading from her workroom/study to her driveway. Winslow was definitely an inside cat. An inside cat who wanted a taste of mackerel. Now.

Maggie complied and rinsed and filled his water dish.

It was a beautiful spring day, she noticed belatedly, realizing she should have left some windows open. She walked through the downstairs and opened several to let in fresh air. Despite her work last night, in the daylight her study looked more disorganized than usual. She sighed. At least she'd finished grading exams and filing the grades. And she'd made a start at sorting her prints for Friday's show.

She kicked off her shoes. Winslow was speedily working his way through the mackerel. He looked up and meowed a loud "Thank you" and then returned to his dish.

Even Diet Pepsi was elegant in Edinburgh crystal, Maggie thought, as she selected one of the tall glasses she'd purchased with abandon at a show last winter when she'd realized they matched the brandy snifters she'd bought the year before. She took a long drink and looked around.

The house had become more hers since Michael's death. Little changes, such as the crystal glasses, and the forest green recliner she'd bought last month, had made a difference. The recliner helped her muscles feel less as though she were reaching the "vintage" stage herself. It was so comfortable, in fact, that she'd rearranged her study to accommodate it.

The small table next to it was now covered with her telephone and answering machine, paper, pens, and a coaster with a picture of Pemaquid lighthouse on it. Literally, all the comforts of home.

She'd picked up the Pemaquid coaster in Maine last summer as a souvenir. That seemed a long time ago. She was definitely ready for another summer. And for a vacation, if she could afford one.

This was the closest to a vacation she could get right now. Caffeine. A comfortable chair. No immediate panics.

Knowing this week would be crazy, she'd stocked up on her favorite brand of frozen pizza and the fresh mushrooms, onions, and black olives she liked to add to it. Easy, filling, and if not totally virtuous, well, that was too bad. There were a few advantages to being widowed. Not being expected to put a full three-course dinner on the table every night was definitely one of them. Now the small refrigerated wine cooler was almost empty, and her freezer held more cherry vanilla ice cream and Lean Cuisine dinners than she'd care to admit.

Maggie put her glass down on the coaster. She reached for her blinking answering machine. Twelve messages on a Monday afternoon? People who managed antiques shows for a living were masochists. She had no clue how some of them managed to organize a show every three or four weeks in different states.

She hit the speaker button and readied her paper and pen.

Two dealers who were coming to the show wanted to change the number of tables they'd ordered. Luckily, their change-of-table needs canceled each other out. She made a note to adjust her floor plan.

One dealer wanted more posters advertising the show. She'd call Skip Hendricks about that. It shouldn't be a problem, but it needed to be done today.

A student wanted to know if he could get his grades early; his father had promised him a new car if he got all As. Maggie sighed. That was certainly not a critical issue. He could wait for his grades like everyone else. She wondered for a moment what grade she had given him. Whatever it was, he'd earned it. Whether he'd earned a car or not was up to his father.

Gussie had called to check up on her and find out whether Jackson was home with his family by now and Holly was feeling better.

The next message was from Carole Drummond. "It's important, Maggie. Sorry to bother you, but call me as soon as you get this. At home or at the agency."

Maggie hit the stop button on the answering machine and dialed Carole's number.

Chapter 11

———〜———

Baa, Baa, Black Sheep. Hand-colored steel engraving, 1860, of classic nursery rhyme, showing brother with crossbow and sister with a bouquet of flowers talking to a black sheep on a hill overlooking the ocean. 4 x 6 inches. Price: $40.

"Carole? It's Maggie. What's happening?"

"Thank goodness you called. How was your meeting with the facilities people today?"

"No problems. We'll have the building maintenance coverage we need for the whole weekend. Holly's son Eric knows the basic setup and will be our contact for the weekend. What he doesn't know, I'm assured, he has telephone numbers to find out."

"Eric Sloane. That's interesting. But you feel there's no problem there." Carole's voice implied there might be an issue of some sort.

"Should there be a problem? Eric seemed fine today, and I guess he's been working in the gym area for a couple of months." Maggie paused. "How's Holly? Eric said she'd had surgery."

"She's much better, but still in the hospital. They removed the bullet. The police still haven't figured out who shot her, or why. It's pretty scary. Her family is taking it hard."

"I was surprised Eric was at work today, but he said he'd come in especially for the meeting; that the family was staying home for the week."

"Of all the kids, I think Eric is probably the closest to Jackson. They came to the Sloanes about the same time, and they share a room. He must be upset, even if he didn't show it. Some of the younger children are having strong reactions, too. After all, they've all lost mothers before. This one promised to be there for them. There's some real fear and anger there."

"But they can't think Holly wanted to be shot! It wasn't her fault!"

"No, of course not. But, emotionally, they feel she left them. After all, she's not with them right now."

"Carole, are you serious?"

Carole paused. "Absolutely. Separation and desertion are major issues for adopted children. Especially for older children who've repeatedly been moved from one family to another. It's not an issue of understanding, Maggie. They know something happened to Holly that she didn't plan. It's an emotional response."

"I still have a lot to learn about adoption."

"Don't worry. You're learning every day!" Carole's voice dropped. "Even Hal, who didn't know the Sloanes that well, has spent the past couple of days in his room, just playing with his computer. Losing a mother is an issue much too close for his comfort. And I haven't been free to spend as much time with him as I should."

Maggie grimaced a little. Last night she'd heard some negative thoughts about adoption from Ann, and now this cheerful information from Carole.

"Maybe this is none of my business. But at the meeting Saturday I noticed scars on Hal's arms. Are they from the fire?"

Carole's answer was blunt. "Those are scars from where his bio parents burned him with cigarettes when he was little."

"I didn't know; I'm sorry."

"He's had a rough life. No doubt."

Maggie felt uncomfortable knowing too much about Hal. But no wonder he had needed an adoptive family. Not all children who needed homes were orphans. "What about Jackson? Has he come home yet?"

"No one knows where he is. He's probably with a friend, but it's strange he hasn't called. The news about his mother has been on the radio and in the newspapers. Maybe he feels guilty; maybe he feels if he'd been home, nothing would have happened. According to Rob, he's never disappeared like this before. I just wish he was with the rest of the family. They don't need to worry about him as well as worrying about Holly."

Maggie hesitated. "Is he still a suspect?"

"There is that missing gun. But since it *is* missing they don't know for sure it was the one Holly was shot with." Carole hesitated. "It was the right caliber. But Rob doesn't know how long the gun's been missing. He says he hadn't unlocked the box it was in for months." She paused. "Rob also says Jackson and Holly had a big argument before he went out Saturday night. Nothing major; she didn't like one of his friends and she wanted him to stay home. But under the circumstances . . ."

"The police are considering every possibility." If only Jackson would go home. Then maybe the police would investigate other suspects. Maggie didn't know Jackson, but she knew she didn't like the idea of an adopted son shooting his mother. On Mother's Day! No matter how big their argument had been. The media coverage implying he'd shot her was awful. And no matter how it turned out, people remembered dramatic headlines, not the articles that corrected them.

"Is there anything Holly or Rob were doing for the antiques show that now needs to be done by someone else?" Carole asked, ever the efficient manager.

"I can't think of anything. Most of their work was on the program and in getting the raffle items, and that's been done.

The program is at the printer. It just has to be picked up. I don't think there'll be a problem with coverage. I'm more worried about their family, actually. Is there anything I can do to help them?"

"Several of the kids are in counseling, and all the counselors have been notified. Rob's taken time off from his job, and Holly should be able to come home in a couple of days." Carole hesitated. "If you'd really like to do something, maybe you could drop off a meal for the family. With about a dozen people at home—the oldest two kids went back to their apartment in Philadelphia—they can always use more food. A couple of the kids are cooking, and Rob is trying, but they have other priorities just now, and even spaghetti for twelve or thirteen is a major job."

"I'd be glad to." What could she make in quantity? Maggie's specialties were quiet dinners for two, or maybe four. Not the sort of repast she suspected the Sloane family was used to. "I'll stop at their house tomorrow with something, after my morning meeting."

"Actually, that's what I called about. Your security meeting."

"Have the police find out anything about the person who sent those letters?" Maggie asked.

"No. They took the last one and said they'd check it for fingerprints, but they didn't seem confident they'd be able to identify anything."

"And there haven't been any more letters since Friday?" Maggie asked, not sure she wanted to know the answer. Maybe if she didn't know, she could forget she'd heard about them in the first place.

"No more letters."

"That's good news!"

"But the police do have some new information. It seems whoever is sending us letters may have other targets, too."

"Other adoption agencies?"

"An agency in Trenton. There was an article about some of their families in a Philadelphia newspaper around Valentine's

Day. One of those 'loving families make the world go around' stories. It featured several large transracial families like the Sloanes. Right after the article appeared, that agency received the first of several letters like ours, although none connected threats with specific dates."

Maggie suddenly thought of an article she'd read in *The Star-Ledger.* "Weren't Holly and Rob featured in a similar story earlier this year?"

"Yes. It's scary."

"How did the police here know the other agency had received threats?"

"Pure chance. Someone on the force here has a cousin who adopted through the agency in Trenton, and the cousin mentioned the notes at a Mother's Day family picnic. Click. They realized it sounded like the same person sending the letters. Or group of people, with one person writing the letters."

"What about fingerprints?"

"None they can identify. But the letters are all postmarked in Somerville, so it sounds as though the problem is in our court." Maggie could almost see Carole wincing. "Literally."

"What are the police going to do about it?"

"They're digging through old files to see if they can come up with any similar cases from the past. They'll also patrol the school and the agency during the antiques show. There's not much else they can do."

Maggie hesitated. "What about Holly? Is there any chance her shooting has anything to do with the letters?"

"None of the adoptive families from the Trenton agency have been bothered. The police still think Jackson had something to do with the shooting here; that it had nothing to do with the agency. That's why I wish he'd come home and tell everyone where he's been."

"How much should I tell the security people at Somerset College tomorrow?" asked Maggie. "I want them to be extra vigilant, but I don't want to panic anyone."

"No one should go overboard. Just tell them there's a crazy out there who's been sending hate letters. The police know about it and will be patrolling, but we need to be extra careful and aware during the days of the show." Carole stopped. "There's no reason to connect this to Holly's shooting, Maggie."

"Got it. I'll talk to them, of course." Maggie paused. "Anything else I should know about?"

"I think that covers it. And don't worry, Maggie. You're doing a great job. I'm sure we'll be laughing at all this a week from now."

Chapter 12

"He presently reappeared, somewhat dusty, with a bottle of beer in each paw and another under each arm." Arthur Rackham (1867–1939) illustration for The Wind in the Willows, _1940. Badger presenting Mole with their evening's supply of liquid refreshment. Rackham was one of the foremost Edwardian illustrators, known for his work with magical, mystical, and legendary themes. 9 x 6 inches. Price: $65._

Winslow jumped up onto Maggie's lap and settled himself in. He'd finished his snack and was ready for his nap. She idly scratched his neck as she contemplated the answering machine and its still-blinking light. Six more messages to go. She might as well listen to them all at once. Then she'd call Gussie back.

She moved Winslow a bit so she could take notes if necessary.

"Maggie? This is Vince. Vince Thompson. Just thought I'd check in and see how my newest competitor in the antiques show promotion game was doing. Sorry I won't be able to come to your show, but will see you Memorial Day weekend at the Rensselaer County show. Unless you have time before that to meet me in the city for a glass of wine, and whatever? Give me a call." Maggie shook her head. Vince was one of the best promoters in the business, and she had called him several times earlier this spring to get advice about setting up this show. She hadn't wanted to forget anything, and Vince knew the game well. He knew other games, too.

She'd call him sometime next week, after the show, and hope she'd miss him and just be able to leave a message. Too much was on her plate to even consider "a glass of wine in the city." Especially with Vince. She'd see him over Memorial Day. For work; not wine.

"Maggie, this is Elsie, from Old Things and New. I'm signed up for your show, but my mother just had a heart attack and I'm going out to the coast to be with her, so I'll have to drop out. Can you send my refund for the booth deposit to me in California, please? Thank you!"

Elsie was the third person who'd dropped out in the past two weeks. Maggie made a note to send Elsie her $50. Most shows had nonrefundable booth-rent deposits. But with a new show . . . She had just hoped no one would cancel out. At this late date she'd never be able to get someone to fill Elsie's booth. Would one of the current dealers be interested in expanding their space? Drat. This was not the fun part of managing a show. She wondered when—or if—that part would start.

"Maggie, it's Carole again. I'm really worried about—oh, never mind. We just have to go on. I've already left you a message. Talk with you later."

That was strange. Carole sounded much more upset than she had on the telephone a few minutes ago. What had made her call twice? Maggie hesitated. Was there something happening Carole hadn't told her? Or maybe Carole was just tired. Managing an adoption agency all day and then coming home to her own family must certainly be stressful. Not to mention little problems like hate mail and an adoptive mother being shot.

Would Maggie be able to handle the conflicting demands of jobs and children? If she did adopt, then she'd have to. All day, every day. And she wouldn't have a husband, as Carole did, to share responsibilities.

She sipped her Diet Pepsi. Some days she had trouble just managing the stress she was dealing with now. If she were a parent, she'd have to put all that aside to meet a child's needs. Could she do that? Do it well? If she was going to be a parent, she wanted to be a good parent.

Three more messages. One from the mother of a student who'd missed his exam: he'd been in the hospital having his appendix out. Pretty decent excuse. She'd give him an incomplete and have Claudia call his mother and set a date for a re-exam when he'd recuperated.

One from a local Chinese restaurant, alerting Maggie to their new delivery service. Chinese sounded good. A little moo shu pork, and some hot and sour soup.

She hit the play button once more for the final message. The voice was high and effeminate and obviously disguised. "Hey, lady, America is heating up, and prints and papers and people can burn. Adoption is a cause, not a solution. Kill the antiques show. Now. Before someone else does."

Maggie shivered. The words were angry, but the tone was frighteningly calm. This was not a random call. She played it again, hoping to recognize the voice. The tone was familiar, but she couldn't place it.

She stood up, brushing Winslow off her lap. Something dangerous was going on. That was for sure. And she was in the middle of it.

Chapter 13

~~~~~~

October. *1888 print of small Victorian girl dressed in white, holding a spray of red maple leaves above her head, by Maud Humphrey (1865–1940). Today she is best known as the mother of actor Humphrey Bogart. Her drawings have been reproduced in ceramics, as dolls, and as posters. Printed by Frederick Stokes & Brother. Stokes also edited several books Humphrey illustrated. 6.5 x 8.5 inches. Price: $85.*

Maggie paced the length of her study. Winslow watched, but didn't join her.

Should she call the police? Probably. But not this minute. The voice sounded so familiar. Maybe if she listened to the message often enough and thought hard enough, she'd remember where she'd heard it. The more information she could give the police the better. She'd call them as soon as she could identify the voice. Tomorrow, at the latest. From what Carole had said, the police couldn't do much anyway. And, Maggie admitted to herself, she just didn't feel up to coping with the police.

There was no doubt the threat was to the OWOC antiques show. She shivered. The reference to "burning" was frightening.

All of a sudden Maggie felt very alone. She checked the lock on the outside door to her study and then walked through the house, closing the windows she'd opened. The house might be stuffy, but at least she'd be certain she was the only one in it.

She sat down at her computer. Right now she didn't want to talk to anyone. Not the police, and not even Gussie. She needed to think. E-mail seemed the solution. Communication without involvement.

Hi, Gussie,
Got your message. I'm fine—not to worry! Holly is healing and won't be in the hospital long. Her son still hasn't come home. But there are no major problems with the antiques show. I'm going to make some food to drop off tomorrow for the Sloanes. Hope weather at the Cape is warming up. Will see you and Ben in two days. Can hardly wait!
                                                                    Maggie

That should let Gussie know she was all right. And she was, wasn't she?

Nothing had actually happened. Carole had said the police couldn't do anything unless more than threats were involved. The old rhyme "Sticks and stones can break your bones, but words can never hurt you" came to Maggie's mind. But Holly had been hurt by more than a stick or stone. She shook her head and started writing another message.

Dear Will,
All looks OK for the show so far, although it will look a lot better after you get to Jersey. Only two days! Drive carefully. The agency has been getting nasty letters from someone angry about something, but it's all a little unclear. We'll up the security a bit for the show, just in case there's a problem. Probably just someone who wants to picket or send a nasty letter to the editor. They say any publicity is good publicity, right? We need droves of customers! I

haven't started on inventory items for the Rensselaer County show. Just turned my grades in, so maybe tomorrow I can do a few things. Looks as though I'll be recycling my inventory, not displaying a lot of new items. Hope this summer is going to be one long buying spree. Still looking for some early (pre-1840s) astronomy prints, should you happen to see any. Looking forward to seeing you Wednesday. I miss you. And I could use a hug. Would be willing to share!

Yours, Maggie

Maggie pressed "send and receive." The two messages she'd sent disappeared. The only new message that appeared asked, "Would you like to make your date as hot as the Equator?" Delete.

Maggie stared at the computer screen and realized sitting and thinking were just driving her crazy. What could she do that would make a difference?

What had women done for centuries when there was a problem, or when nerves needed to be soothed?

Well, a couple of things, actually. But, above all, they cooked. She, who had planned to eat frozen pizza until her guests arrived and then distribute menus for Chinese restaurants and pizza parlors, had promised to supply food for a small army called the Sloane family.

The occasion called for large amounts of food that were soothing. Pasta was an obvious solution. Maggie assessed the contents of her kitchen cabinets and decided: macaroni salad with tuna fish. She'd add some of the vegetables she'd bought for her frozen pizza. Mushrooms, peppers, red onions. Plus mayo. A touch of mustard. Maybe she'd sneak some capers in, too. She could make it tonight and it could be eaten hot or cold. Perfect.

She heated a large pan of water to cook the packages of whole-wheat macaroni she found in her cabinet and got out her largest mixing bowl for the salad. But what if someone didn't like tuna or salad? What did teenagers eat?

Maggie looked in her freezer for inspiration. Two lamb chops. A sirloin steak. Hamburger. And the solution: three packages of hot dogs she'd bought to take to a neighborhood barbecue a couple of weeks ago. The barbecue had been rained out, so she'd stuck the hot dogs in the freezer. She knew Will's aunt Nettie in Maine would have palpitations that she wasn't cooking them from scratch, but she'd combine canned baked beans with the sliced hot dogs, add some tomatoes and onion and . . . voilà! Baked bean and frank casserole.

An hour later, the casserole ready to heat and the salad made, Maggie sat down. She'd nibbled a hot dog and a little pasta herself along the way. Not exactly gourmet, but she was full, and she had two containers of food ready for delivery tomorrow. How were the Sloanes doing? How was Rob coping with fourteen children—no, make that eleven, assuming Jackson was still missing and the oldest two were still in Philadelphia—who wanted their mother safe and available? She hoped Jackson had returned by now. She hoped Holly was healing quickly and would go home soon. She hoped the police found whoever had shot her.

And she hoped whoever had shot Holly Sloane had nothing to do with the letters sent to Our World Our Children. Or with the message left on her own answering machine.

Tomorrow morning she'd meet with the head of security at Somerset County College. She'd tell him security might be a bigger issue than any of them dreamed.

Then she'd go to visit a family missing a mother. And a brother.

Before she went to the police.

Chapter 14

Council with White Man's Horse. *Plate XVII, lithograph (1855), engraved by Stanley and published by Sarony, Major & Knapp*, NYC, *for the* General Report of the United States Surveys, 47th & 49th Parallels. *Blackfoot Indians meeting with a group of white men on the prairie, outside what appears to be a Native American village. All in shades of black, white, and orange/tan. 8.24 x 11.5 inches. Price: $50.*

It haunted Maggie that she couldn't identify the voice making the telephoned threat. She was sure she'd heard it before. At five in the morning she went downstairs and listened to the message over and over. Why couldn't she recognize the voice? It made her angry, and it scared her. If the person making the threat was someone she knew, the possibility of real danger was a lot greater than if the caller was a stranger.

But how would a stranger know her connection to the show, and her unlisted home telephone number? She kept hoping that at any moment the caller's name would somehow emerge from her subconscious. Then she could call the police with real information.

In the meantime, she went ahead with Tuesday's schedule. Her meeting with the security staff was in their basement office at the far end of Somerset College's administration building. If office location meant anything in terms of prestige, then security was not a priority at Somerset College. Thank goodness it had never needed to be. The college was just over a highway hour west of New York City in an area of suburban sprawl that was threatening the existence of small dairy farms and stables. An area where most crimes involved automobiles or burglaries.

Where did her caller fit into the picture? What kind of person tried to scare people working on behalf of abandoned children?

Maggie walked with a determined stride. She wasn't going to let anyone scare her. Whether or not she herself ever had the courage to adopt, Our World Our Children was one of the most deserving organizations she knew. No crazy person who didn't understand the needs of children could discourage her from helping them.

Al Stivali, a retired policeman in his midfifties, was Somerset College's head of security. He'd walked the beat in Newark for twenty years and deserved every hour of peace he'd found after that. His profile was no doubt a bit more paunchy than when he'd been chasing drug dealers and angry kids in city streets, and his hairline had receded, but his senses and brain were still alert. Maggie noted a copy of *The House of Seven Gables* on the corner of his desk next to a pile of well-worn notebooks. Stivali had been auditing some courses recently, including one of Maggie's. She'd enjoyed having him in her front row.

One wall of his office was covered by a white board listing schedules for the college guards who reported to him. Some of the guards were also retired cops; some had been MPs; some had little experience but were looking for a quiet second or even third job.

Al put down his coffee cup as Maggie walked in. "Professor Summer! Glad you stopped by. Can I offer you some coffee? It's strong."

"No, thanks, Al. And call me Maggie. *Professor* sounds so formal."

"Then, Maggie." Al smiled as Maggie sat down. "I think we've exchanged enough notes to have a good idea of what you're looking for." He got up and pointed at the dates May 12 through May 15 on his white board.

"You've got suppliers coming in Thursday and Friday morning, and then the antiques people are arriving around four o'clock Friday afternoon. They'll do their thing and be out by ten. You'll have people in the gym Saturday morning starting around eight and going until six in the evening, and then again Sunday, from nine until six. That cover it?"

"Pretty much. There will be some people working later Sunday night, after the dealers have packed up, to pile up tables and chairs. Monday morning the rental people will pick up their tables, and the company that put the pads on the floors will be back to take them up. If all goes smoothly, everything should be back to normal by noon on Monday."

Al had returned to his desk and was making a couple of notes. "There shouldn't be any problems. I've got a couple of guys who can work overtime that weekend. The new semester doesn't begin until June, so we usually operate with a skeleton crew at this time of year. But we can pull people in."

"Two things I'd like your help on. The first is parking. I'm going to ask the dealers to move their vans and trucks into the dorm parking lot during the show so there'll be lots of space for customers to park by the gym. I'd really appreciate your guys keeping an eye out for any dealers who don't move. You tell me license plate numbers and I'll find the owner of the vehicle. All dealer vehicles should have placards stuck on their windshields. And I know you always check for unauthorized cars in the handicapped areas, but I'd like special attention paid there during the show. I don't want any potential customers to leave because there aren't enough handicapped parking spaces. Antiques shows tend to have older visitors than most events here on campus."

"No problem, Maggie," Al said, making another note. "We

have temporary handicapped designation signs. Shall we increase the number of handicapped spaces by the gym?"

"That would be great! Three or four more spaces should be plenty. And make sure at least two are wide enough for vans with wheelchair lifts. There's one space there already, but I'm going to reserve it for one of the dealers. There should be at least one other for customers." Gussie wouldn't ask for any special privileges, but there was no reason someone using an electric wheelchair should have to maneuver her chair all the way from the dorm parking lot. So far as she knew, none of the other dealers doing this show were disabled. If someone was, she'd make adjustments.

"Okay, parking. What else do you need our help with?"

"Friday and Saturday nights the dealers are going to be leaving their antiques in the gym. I know the college has insurance, and most of the dealers do, and Our World Our Children took out a separate policy to cover this show. But none of us want to test those policies. There will be valuable inventory items in the gyms. They're even priced, so someone who doesn't know antiques could figure pretty quickly what was worth stealing. The estate jewelry dealer will take his top-end merchandise home every night, but most people will leave everything here. I'd feel better if there were someone in the gyms overnight—we could even put in a cot, if they were a light sleeper—to make sure no one tried to break in."

"You want one of my guys to sleep in the gym?" Al raised an eyebrow. "Those antiques must really be big-ticket items."

"Perception is reality. Tell people there's a building full of antiques and they'll imagine hundreds of thousands of dollars worth of items. And when you multiply the retail value of even a relatively small inventory by thirty-six dealers . . ."

Al nodded. "Got it."

"I'd planned to ask one of the adoptive fathers connected with the agency to stay overnight. But now the situation is more complicated. The agency has asked the local police to keep an eye on the gym, but that just means they'll drive by once an hour or so. I'd like someone there who knows what to do in case of an emergency."

Al put his pen down. "Professor, I mean, Maggie, what's the real deal? There's something you're not telling me. What's this 'complicated situation'?"

Al seemed incredibly sane and easy to talk with. And trustworthy. "This has to be just between you and me. But Our World Our Children has been receiving threatening letters from someone who is angry about something the agency does. Or did. We don't know what."

"My niece and her husband out in Ohio adopted a real sweet little girl from China. I don't see how anybody could be upset about people bringing kids and families together." Al leaned back in his chair.

"Exactly. I have no idea what the problem is either."

"They must be nuts!"

"Maybe. A lot of nuts are out there."

"You don't have to tell me." Al sat up straighter and paid close attention. "Talk to me about these threats."

"Carole Drummond, the head of Our World Our Children, has gotten several hate letters in the past couple of months. They were nasty, but they weren't threatening. The local cops said there was nothing they could do."

"Right. Can't arrest anyone for words. Just actions."

"Then last week the agency got another letter. This one said they should stop the antiques show. It specifically mentioned the dates. Carole talked to the police yesterday and they connected it to letters sent to an adoption agency in Trenton."

"Same sort of language?"

"Apparently. But all the letters are postmarked near here, in Somerville. I haven't told anyone yet, Al, but yesterday someone left a threatening message on my home answering machine. It sounded like the same sort of rhetoric. And mentioned the show."

Al looked sternly at her. "You haven't told the police?"

"Not yet."

"You need to do that, Maggie. Today. Did you erase the message?"

"No. I listened to it several times. And that's what stopped me from calling anyone. Al, I think I've heard the voice before. I'm pretty sure it was a man, but he was speaking in a high voice."

"You need to get to the police, Maggie. Whether you recognize the voice or not."

"I will. Today. Right after I drop some food off at the Sloanes' home. Did you see in the paper? Holly Sloane is the adoptive mother who was shot Sunday morning."

"I did see that. And she's connected to the same agency that you're doing the antiques show for?"

"She runs a support group at OWOC. She and her husband have adopted eleven hard-to-place kids. And one of her sons is missing. They're trying to find him, too."

"This could all be connected, Maggie."

"I don't understand how, or why. But that's why I really need your help on security for this show."

"Any chance you or the agency will cancel the show?"

"No! We're not going to give in to this . . . adoption terrorist!" Maggie slammed her fist on the arm of the chair she was sitting in.

Al smiled slightly, but his eyes were steady. "*Terrorist* is probably a strong word. But I think you should take him or her, or even them, seriously. I'll stay at the show myself Friday and Saturday nights. Pretty quiet at my place, since my wife died. Give me something different to think about. So don't you worry."

"I'd really appreciate that. I don't think we should panic anyone about this, either, right?"

"Absolutely. Although most of my guys are pretty calm about stuff like this. I'll tell them some crazy has been writing letters and we hope he doesn't show up. If he does, we call the police. That's all. They'll be more alert, and no one will start carrying as a result."

"Good. That sounds just right."

"But keep me tuned in, Maggie. If you get any more messages from this guy or find out anything about whoever shot Mrs. Sloane, let me know. Or even if you just need someone to talk with. I haven't been a detective for a while, but I'm not totally out of the loop. This is a lot to have on your shoulders. I'd like to help."

"Thanks, Al. I promise. I'll tell the police. And I'll let you know what I find out."

"And, Maggie? If you remember the voice? The one that called and threatened you? Tell someone. Right away. I don't want to scare you, but that could be critical. If that man doesn't want anyone to know who he is, and you do know, you could be in danger."

Chapter 15

———∽———

Who Is Coming? Charming Victorian lithograph of three small children, one holding a doll, peeking out a doorway with their dog into a snow-covered yard. C. 1885. 6.5 x 9.5 inches. Price: $70.

Maggie knew she had to report the threatening telephone message to the police. But priorities were priorities. She'd packed the tuna salad and baked-bean casserole in large coolers filled with ice, and the warm May sun had already turned some of the ice to water.

Her next stop would have to be the Sloanes' house, before the food went bad.

Their large Victorian-era home had once been the center of a farm. The barn now housed cars instead of cows, and more cars, in various stages of repair, were parked in the yard. Usually broken-down cars on property indicated a broken-down house. But here the house was intact and newly painted. Maggie pulled into the wide driveway and parked her faded blue van between a small navy sedan and a large brown station wagon.

The girl who answered the door looked about thirteen and might have been part African-American and part Asian. She wore faded jeans and a cropped T-shirt. "Yes?"

"I'm Maggie Summer, a prospective parent from OWOC. I know your parents, and I was here for the picnic in April."

The girl opened the door a little farther. "You're not a newspaper person?"

"No! I just brought by some food. Carole Drummond said maybe you could use it."

"Hey, Dad! Some lady's at the door who says she knows you!" The girl kept the door half-closed.

Maggie suspected a number of unknown, and unwelcome, people had knocked on this door in the past couple of days. In the background several radios or CD players were loudly emitting contrasting sounds. A couple of figures walked through a room at the end of the entrance hallway.

"Dad!" The girl's voice was piercing.

Then Eric appeared at her side. "Hey, Kim, what's the deal?" He looked at Maggie. "Hi, Professor Summer. What're you doing here?"

At least this was someone who recognized her, who didn't think she was a reporter or some other unwanted voyeur. "Carole Drummond suggested you and your family could use a little sustenance, so I brought a couple of things you could have for lunch or dinner." She thrust the large bowl into his hands. "This is a tuna-pasta salad. I have a casserole in my van."

By the time she returned to the door, Eric had deposited the salad in the kitchen and Kim had disappeared. "Why don't you come in, Professor Summer?"

"Just for a moment," said Maggie, curious about both the house and its residents. The picnic had been held outside, and so many parents and adopted children had been attending she hadn't been able to connect most of them with their families. She held the casserole and followed Eric through a hall lined with racks of jackets and baseball caps, softball bats and umbrellas, into a large kitchen.

Eric put the casserole in one of the two large refrigerators. "Would you like something to drink, Professor Summer?"

"Water would be fine, Eric," Maggie said. "How's your mother doing?"

"She's healing." Eric handed Maggie a glass of ice water. "She's going to need physical therapy, but she should be home in a couple of days. Thanks for the meals, though. We seem to go through a lot of food."

Maggie noted a dozen empty pizza boxes piled in the corner.

"Dad's back and forth to the hospital. Astrid and I try to keep everybody together, but it's not easy. Right now she's at the grocery store with some of the kids. Dad just left for the hospital, to see Mom."

"Kim was calling him." Maggie took a drink of the water.

"She usually has her headphones on and doesn't keep in touch with the real world." Eric smiled. "It's a little crazy here, but we're fine. We'll be better when Mom's home. Somehow she keeps it all together." He hesitated a minute, and despite his bravado, Maggie suspected she saw tears in his eyes. She looked away, so he wouldn't be embarrassed. "We miss her. A lot."

"Of course you do. Are you and Astrid the oldest two at home, then?"

"Right now. Tom and Beth live in Philadelphia. Tom has a job, and Beth's in college there. They were home for the weekend. For Mother's Day." Eric swallowed hard. "Dad sent them back when we knew Mom would be okay. Dad's word is the rule. And"—he paused—"you know about Jackson."

"You haven't heard from him."

Eric shook his head, and his voice was quiet. "We've called everyone we could think of, and the police have been looking."

"Has he ever disappeared before?"

Eric hesitated. "Well, you're involved with the agency, so I guess you know, our family isn't exactly a calm place. Just about everyone's taken off at some point or another. But Jacks hasn't done it in a while. And never for this long. He wouldn't leave if he knew Mom was hurt, for sure. He talks up a storm in public about how horrible his life is, but he's really close to Mom. That's why it's weird he hasn't come home."

"It's been on the news, and in the papers."

"I know. And the cops've been saying maybe he shot her." Eric's voice rose in controlled anger. "He wouldn't have done it. I mean, they had some arguments. Everybody has arguments. Saturday night, sure, he and Mom were yelling pretty loud. But not as loud as Mom and Dad did after Jacks left! Yelling is just part of being a family, sometimes. If no one cared, no one would yell. But to take a gun . . ."

"I heard the gun was your father's."

Eric was clearly frustrated. He paced across the kitchen. "They don't know that for sure. They just know Dad's gun is missing and the bullet that hit Mom came from the same kind of gun he had. Hell. I've lived here for six years and I didn't know he had a gun. How would Jacks know? Mom and Dad never even allowed water pistols in the house. And Jacks may have weird friends, but I don't think they carry. I told the cops. But they don't listen. I'm black, and so is Jacks, so they probably figure we're guilty of something."

"Is that what they said?"

Eric stopped and looked straight at her. "See, you're white. You don't know. They never *say*. They just *imply*. And they sure *implied* that since Jackson wasn't right here, then he was the one responsible. Easier saying that than trying to find the person who's really guilty."

"I'm sorry, Eric. This must be awful for you."

"It's sure not fun."

"You know I'm a prospective parent, Eric. If it isn't too awkward for you to answer, it would help me to know. Do you think your parents understand what it's like for you to be black?"

Eric frowned, but the question didn't seem to bother him. "They try really hard. They've read all the books and they know what happens. But they're not black, so they don't feel race the same way Jacks and I and the other kids do. Sometimes Jackson's really angry about being in this family. He thinks it would have been easier for him if Mom and Dad had been black. I'm not so sure. No parents are perfect. I'm a whole lot better off here than I was anywhere else. After seven foster homes you'd have to be pretty dumb not to figure that out. And about half of us in the family are at least part black, so it isn't as if we're isolated or anything." Eric paused. "I guess there isn't an easy answer. I think the kids who are Asian or white or Hispanic have it easier, but they might not agree. And I know kids who live with one or both of their biological parents, and the parents don't match, if you know what I mean?"

Maggie nodded.

"Some of those kids are a lot angrier than anyone I know who's been adopted. At least if you're adopted, the issue of race, or culture, is right out there. The agency talks about it, and your parents talk about it, and they're always trying to look for role models and cultural stereotypes to talk about and books about heritage. Most kids I know who live with their bio parents don't have a lot of that. I guess their parents just figure they're living the experience; they don't need to talk about it. Maybe more of them should. Especially when the parents are two different races. Or even two different religions."

Maggie took a sip of her water. "Thank you for sharing that. I know it's pretty personal."

"Yeah. But that's another thing about being adopted, especially when you have parents like ours. We're always talking to other parents, and prospective parents. You hear this stuff all the time. So it isn't as big a deal as it might be. Sometimes I think I could deliver the message as well as Mom and Dad do—or better."

"The message?"

Eric grinned and struck a pose, listing his points on his fingers. "'Don't adopt a child of another race unless you have friends of that race. Study the culture. If language is involved, at least learn some key words. Learn to cook the food. Celebrate the holidays. Value your child by valuing his heritage!'" He relaxed. "You've been around the agency long enough to know the drill."

Maggie laughed. "I guess I do. But it can be intimidating to someone who's considering adoption."

"That's good, though. Because adoption isn't simple. That's part of the message—'love isn't enough.' And it isn't. But it's still a damn good place to start."

"I've kept you too long, Eric," said Maggie, getting up. "But thank you for talking with me. I've left heating instructions on the casserole. The salad can be eaten cold or hot."

"Thank you. We all thank you."

"Well, I appreciate all your parents have done for the antiques show. And you, too, Eric. I look forward to working with you this weekend."

Eric nodded. He seemed much more relaxed than he had only a few minutes before.

"I'll see you at the gym, right? Thursday morning, if you can be there. The floor coverings will be put down then."

"Right, Professor. At the gym."

"And I hope Jackson is home soon. Your mom, too."

Eric hesitated. "Professor Summer, if someone knew something that might help find Jackson, but that they didn't want the police to know, what should they do?"

Maggie looked at him. His gaze was steady.

She pulled one of her cards out of her pocketbook. "I'd be willing to talk." She thought of Al Stivali. "And I know someone else who might be able to help."

Eric took her card and slipped it into his pocket without looking at it. "If my friend wants to talk, then I'll tell him. Thank you."

Maggie backed her van carefully around two bicycles in the driveway and waved toward a blonde girl, maybe sixteen, who was working under the hood of one of the cars. As she pulled out of the driveway, an old tan station wagon full of teenagers pulled in. Maybe Astrid, returning from grocery shopping.

What had Eric meant about knowing something but not

wanting to tell the police? Was the "friend" really him? Or was there someone else who could help but who was keeping quiet?

Either seemed possible. Some of the Sloane kids had been in trouble with the law at different times, she knew, and might not want to talk to the authorities.

No matter what, Jackson needed to get back to his family. And so did Holly. Healing was more than physical.

And Maggie needed to get to the police station. How could she expect Eric—or his friend—to share something with the police when she hadn't even told them about her threatening phone call?

Chapter 16

—∽—

Mistress Mary, Quite Contrary. *Print of the classic nursery rhyme, drawn by children's illustrator Clara M. Burd for* The Brimful Book, *1927. 9.5 x 12 inches. Price: $60.*

Detective Dawn Newton, a serious, young black woman with a no-nonsense, cropped hairstyle, followed Maggie home, complete with her own tape recorder, to make an official copy of the threat left on Maggie's answering machine.

They listened to it together. Newton shook her head. "Not sure how much help this'll be. How many people have heard about the hate letters OWOC's been getting?"

"Carole told me. I assume her whole staff knows. She told the police. The only person I've told is Al Stivali, the head of security at Somerset College. And I told him after I got this message. Oh, and I told a friend of mine in Massachusetts."

"Your message could be a copycat. You said you recognized something in the tone of the voice, which means the message was probably left by someone you know. The other contacts were by mail. Usually someone sending anonymous letters doesn't switch to anonymous phone calls." Detective Newton took a few notes.

"You think someone heard about the letters and then *that person* called me?"

Detective Newton shrugged. "It's possible. I'll take this recording and see if we can find out anything. May we check your telephone records to see if we can identify where the call came from?"

"Sure. I haven't got any secrets. And I'll admit the call's made me nervous. At this point I'll be very glad when this antiques show is over."

"Truthfully, so will I," agreed the detective. "Chances are, nothing will happen. But you never know. In the meantime, if you get any more messages, from any source, call us immediately."

"The show opens in four days; we start setting up Thursday," Maggie reminded her. "We're not talking about a lot of time."

Detective Newton nodded. "I know. Just keep in touch, and remember he's probably not going to hurt anyone. He's trying to scare you."

Maggie grimaced. "He succeeded."

"Don't let him know that. If he should call again, and you answer the phone, let him talk and take down as much as you can of what he says. His exact words. I doubt he wants to have a conversation with you. He'll probably hang up if you answer the phone. But once in a while someone surprises us. If he does talk to you, you may recognize the voice or get some valuable information."

"Will you tap my telephone? To hear if he calls again?"

"I don't think that's necessary. You've only had one call, and it basically left the same message that was in the letters. If you start getting more calls, or calls that escalate to anger or threats, then we'll consider getting permission to put a tap on." She turned toward the door. "Take a lot of deep breaths and make sure your car and home are well secured. You'll feel better, and probably nothing more will happen. I think this whole thing will blow over and disappear after the antiques show."

"But what about Holly Sloane being shot?"

The detective hesitated. "At this point we don't see that connected to the letters or to your phone call. It's probably a domestic matter. But we're looking at every angle, of course. We can't rule any possibilities out."

A domestic matter? They must still think Jackson was responsible.

Maggie's head was throbbing by the time Detective Newton left. She'd done the right thing. She'd told the police. And she'd felt like a fool when Detective Newton had pretty much told her the call meant nothing.

She got out her black binder and checked over her to-do lists for the show. Everything seemed in order. Tomorrow she'd meet with the volunteers from the college and finalize planning. Tomorrow Will would arrive, and Gussie and Ben. Doing the show was so much more complicated than she'd imagined in January, when it seemed a great way to earn some money for the agency. And to make some money for dealers in the area, too.

Maggie crossed her fingers and knocked on her wooden desk. People would come. People would buy.

Chapter 17

Untitled angel. Young girl in white fur coat and shawl, standing in snow, cradling a nest full of birds. The girl has large pink wings. German lithographed die cut from about 1885. Figure, 4.5 x 11.5 inches. Mounted on a lavender background, matted in mauve, in a modern gold frame. Price: $125.

Maggie sorted her piles of prints in waiting and separated out the Cassell chromolithographed ferns. She had some left from an earlier purchase, already matted and in her "Ferns" portfolio. She'd file the ferns that were duplicates. She had enough forest green, acid-free mat board to mat six additional prints to take to the New York show. There wasn't time to order more; she should have done that a couple of weeks ago. After the OWOC show she'd order all she'd need for the summer. Or at least enough to catch up with her recent purchases. "Investments," Maggie mentally corrected herself. Her prints were investments.

She was debating whether to mat six vertical ferns, or three horizontal and three vertical, when the telephone rang.

"Maggie? It's Al Stivali, in security."

"Yes, Al! No problems, I hope?"

"Everything's fine. I just wanted to make sure you'd told the police about that telephone call you got."

"I stopped and told them earlier this afternoon, and Detective Newton came and recorded it."

"Good. Things were easier with the old answering machines when you could just take the tape out and hand it over. Glad you got that taken care of."

Maggie didn't admit that the police had first asked her for the remote-access code for her answering machine so they could listen to the message at the station. She'd never paid attention to the remote-access feature and didn't remember how to make it work.

Winslow slumbered happily on a sunny windowsill. He didn't have to worry about log-ins and access codes.

"They didn't seem very concerned. They said I should call immediately if I got any more messages like that, though."

"They're right. I'm sorry to have called you, Maggie, but this whole situation is nagging at me. Maybe I'm itching to get back to my detective days. But I keep thinking about your friend who adopted all those kids. It's hard to understand why one of her kids would have shot her. But if he didn't, then why hasn't he gone home? There are some really troubled kids out there, I know. But it seems logical that if the boy isn't involved he'd at least call the police and tell them whatever alibi he has. It doesn't make sense for him to disappear. Unless he's guilty. Or unless he's hiding something else. Or someone else."

"I visited the Sloanes' home after I saw you. I brought them some food and talked with Eric. He's one of their older sons and works for George Healy over at the gym. Sort of a general helper, custodian, and so forth."

"Healy's a good guy. If he hired the boy, I'm sure the kid is doing a good job."

"Anyway, he's black. And Jackson, the boy who's missing, is biracial, black/white. I got the feeling Eric wasn't comfortable talking to the police. So maybe Jackson isn't either. Although Detective Newton, who came to my house today, is black."

"She may be the only black detective on the Somerset County force. Some of the other detectives around here can be a little rough on certain potential suspects."

"But Eric isn't a potential suspect! He's the brother of the boy who's missing, and the son of the mother who's been shot!"

"Doesn't mean he's not a suspect. I know what the Constitution says, Maggie, but when you're in police work, everyone's a suspect until you know they're not. What's your young fellow's alibi?"

"I assume he was in the house with everyone else. Except Jackson, of course."

"So everyone was at home except the one boy when the mother was shot."

"Rob, her husband, was out, I think. Carole told me he'd gone out to do an errand and drove in and found her right after she was hit. He's the one who called 911."

"What is their relationship like, do you know? The husband and wife's?"

"Fine, I'm sure! Al, you don't think . . ."

"Maggie, I was a policeman for too many years. When the wife's shot, the husband's the first one you check out. In this case, with the boy missing, they've got two potential suspects. I'm sure right now they're keeping a tight eye on everyone who lives in that house."

"I hadn't even considered that Rob might be a suspect."

"Remember what I said: everyone's a suspect. Until you know who did it, or you know for sure someone didn't." Al paused. "Anyway, I just wanted to check that you'd told the police, and that you were okay. You're a good lady, Maggie, and I don't want you to have any problems."

"I appreciate the concern. I'll let you know if anything else develops."

"My card has my pager number on it. Call me anytime."

Maggie put down the telephone and walked into her kitchen. Frozen pizza. Diet Pepsi. The good things in life. Winslow fol-

Sedro-Woolley Public Library

lowed her and meowed meaningfully toward the cupboard holding cans of delicacies such as tuna fish. Maggie opened a small can of tuna, changed Winslow's water, and preheated the oven. While Winslow devoured his meal without even a word of thanks, Maggie sliced a portobello mushroom, some black olives, and part of a red onion and added the results to the top of a frozen pizza.

Dinner, plus Diet Pepsi on the rocks.

If Al was right, then the police were looking at Rob Sloane and his son Jackson as suspects in Holly's shooting. No one had mentioned a gun being found, so there couldn't be direct evidence linking Rob's gun to Holly's wound. But it didn't look good that her husband owned the same caliber gun she'd been shot with.

If they were still investigating suspects, the police must have ruled out other possibilities, like someone cleaning their gun across the street and shooting Holly accidentally.

It was Tuesday evening. The pizza was heating. She switched on the television; maybe somewhere there was good news.

"This just in." The commentator interrupted Maggie's thoughts. "The body of a man has been found in a wooded area of Somerset County, New Jersey. No identification has been made, and no cause of death has been announced. The Somerset County Police Department asks that anyone who believes they have information about this situation should contact them as soon as possible." An 800 number flashed on the screen.

Somerset County, New Jersey. Maggie shivered. The newscast hadn't mentioned any identifying information. No age, race, or even the town where the body was found.

If only she knew Jackson Sloane was safe at home.

Chapter 18

The Last Load. *Winslow Homer wood engraving, from* Apple-ton's Journal of Popular Culture, *August 7, 1869. Homer frequently drew haying scenes. This one shows two women and a man wearily looking over a recently mowed hayfield, an oxen-drawn, hay wagon in the background. 4.5 x 6.5 inches. Price: $150.*

Maggie paced her study, her mind racing. She kept hearing the broadcaster's voice: "The body of a man has been found." How long had the body been there? Could it be Jackson's? Or if Jackson was responsible for shooting Holly . . . could he have killed someone else? Maybe there were other missing men in Somerset County. Or maybe the body was of someone from another place. Someone who had just happened to die in a deserted wooded area in Somerset County, New Jersey.

It was already Tuesday night. Will and Gussie and Ben were arriving in less than twenty-four hours. Thursday night they'd be setting up in the gym. Friday morning she'd be arranging booth locations and tables, and she'd hoped to set up her own section of the booth she and Gussie would share before the other dealers arrived. That way she could concentrate on their needs on Friday.

Right now her inventory was only partially organized, and it wasn't in her van. And she couldn't focus on any of the mundane chores she had to get through.

What a joy it would be if someone were there to talk to.

She took a deep breath. Prints. She could manage prints. They wouldn't talk back, and she had to get them ready. Thank goodness she only had to fill half a booth at this show.

Because of the adoption theme of the show, she'd decided to feature prints of children. They would also fit well with Gussie's dolls and toys.

She needed to keep from thinking about a dead man lying in the woods. How was Holly coping? How would it feel, wondering whether the body found was that of your son? Maggie refused to allow the thought to fill her mind.

The first portfolio on her list held prints by Maud Humphrey (1865–1940). Humphrey was a major illustrator who worked out of New York City in the late-nineteenth and early-twentieth centuries. She'd specialized in drawing babies and children. Maggie looked through the prints she had. The children were sweet and pretty and immaculately dressed. Maggie's thoughts flashed to the bulletin board of "waiting children" at the agency. Those were not the sorts of children Maud Humphrey had painted. Not the sorts of children artists in the late-nineteenth century were paid to draw, especially for popular magazines, newspapers, and books. People liked to think of Victorian America as a gentle place, full of sweet and loving children.

Although there certainly were many American children in the late nineteenth century living in squalid city streets and in need of love.

Maggie forced that thought from her mind. Today Humphrey's work was more popular than ever. People collected it not only because of the charm of her drawings, but also because she was the mother of actor Humphrey Bogart. Supposedly mother and son hadn't gotten along well, but any family issues hadn't diminished the value of Humphrey prints.

Maggie put the portfolio near the French doors that opened onto a ramp leading down to her waiting van. Tomorrow Gussie would be using that ramp.

Gussie and Will! They were arriving tomorrow and she hadn't even turned on her computer to make sure they hadn't had a last-minute change of plans. Or had any questions. Or . . .

What had the world been like without computers and answering machines? More peaceful, no doubt. Sometimes being informed was overrated.

She skimmed three spam messages (she did not need a new mortgage, an internationally based supply of Viagra, or a business contact in Liberia) before finding the note from Gussie.

Dear Maggie,

Thinking of you! I know you're zooming around with last minute details, so I don't expect you to answer this. I just wanted to assure you we'll be seeing you tomorrow! Ben finished packing his suitcase three days ago. Can you tell I haven't taken him to an out-of-town antiques show for several months? He's very excited about visiting you again. Here it is the last minute—we'll leave tomorrow morning—and I'm still dithering about how much of my inventory to take with me and what to leave in the shop. My sister will be watching Aunt Augusta's Attic, as usual when I do shows. After this month I'll owe her several dinners and some babysitting since between your show (I can't help thinking of it as your show, even if I know it is the Our World Our Children show) and the Rensselaer County show at the end of the month, she'll be shop-sitting a lot. Thank goodness I can settle in for a couple of months at home after that.

Has the agency heard from their anonymous correspondent again? And how is your friend Holly? I know you're busy, but let me know!

See you tomorrow, probably between 2 and 4.

Love, Gussie

Maggie read the note over again. She hoped Gussie was all right. Gussie became exhausted more easily now than she had a couple of years ago. Two out-of-town shows in one month was pushing it. In the last year Gussie had cut the number of shows she did in half and was concentrating on her shop. Maggie felt a wave of guilt for asking her to do the OWOC show, but Gussie would have been hurt if she hadn't been asked. Friendships were complicated.

Dear Gussie,
I'm a bit panicked about everything that has to be done by
tomorrow, but I'm fine, the weather is okay, and there have
been no more anonymous letters.

Was it wrong to keep the anonymous telephone call to herself? Not when Gussie and Ben were going to be staying with her. Why worry Gussie any more than she already was?

Holly is better, but I haven't heard whether they've found
whoever shot her. The planning for the show is going
pretty smoothly, but I've just started pulling my own
inventory together. I'm going to feature prints of and for
children. Okay with you? I figured it would go with your
booth, and you know Kate Greenaways as well as I do, so
it would be easier for you if anyone asked questions when I
wasn't around. Give Ben a hug for me and tell him I'm
looking forward to seeing him. See you tomorrow!

Maggie

P.S. If I'm not home when you get here, have Ben check
with Jerome and Ian next door. I'll leave a key with them.
My schedule is a bit unpredictable just now!

No message from Will. She hadn't written to him yesterday, either, Maggie thought guiltily.

Dear Will,
Can hardly wait to see you tomorrow. It's a long drive
from Buffalo. Be sure to get lots of rest and coffee and
drive carefully! I want you intact and in my arms. Soon. I
won't expect you until tomorrow night. Gussie and Ben
should be here in the afternoon. In the meantime I'm stay-
ing busy with last-minute planning details and figuring out
what I'm going to display at the show. At least the semester
is over. I can concentrate on only one job for a change.
Although managing this show is taking more time than I
ever thought it would. I have nightmares about truckloads
of tables arriving and being the wrong lengths, or sizing the
booth spaces and finding I measured the gyms wrong to
begin with, or, worst of all, having no one come. No deal-
ers, no customers. Never again will I volunteer to run an
antiques show!

                                        Maggie

(If you have time—pick up some wine from that vineyard
we liked upstate!)

No more excuses. Maggie looked at her portfolios, poured
herself a small Edinburgh crystal glass of Dry Sack, and added a
twist. She'd savor her sherry and then sort through more children's prints. She needed to check her Jessie Willcox Smith
prints to make sure their labels were straight and prices correct.

About four years ago she'd "retired" some of her Smiths,
after taking them to several years of shows. It was time to bring
them out again. If an antique dealer's inventory was large
enough, he or she took different merchandise at different times
and let some "rest." But you couldn't just pick up an old portfolio or carton, put it in your van, and then unpack it at a show.
Retail values varied over the years, both up and down; labels
and the tape holding the mat to the backboard dried; and
despite caution, dampness might have damaged a print. She'd

have to check every one of the Jessie Willcox Smiths before she could make sure all were ready to load.

All of her portfolios of artists who specialized in drawing children, or in illustrating books for children, were waiting. She pulled out a thick brown envelope of illustrations done by Randolph Caldecott (1847–86). Not many people today remembered who he really was, an illustrator born in the English countryside who decided as an adult that sketching was more interesting than his career at the Manchester and Salford Bank. Antiquarian book dealers knew his hand-colored wood engravings of traditional eighteenth-century scenes and his sixteen "toy books": tiny books that illustrated old rhymes or nursery rhymes. Caldecott was only thirty-nine when he died while on a sketching trip to America.

Today people might not recognize his drawings, but many knew his name. In 1936 the American Library Association introduced an annual award for an illustrator of children's books and named it after Randolph Caldecott. The name *Caldecott* was now on a gold seal affixed to some of the best illustrated children's books in America. Maggie tried to keep a small portfolio of Caldecott illustrations in her inventory at all times.

Now she only had five left. She wrote herself a reminder in a small green notebook she always carried in her pocketbook: "Look for more Caldecotts!!!" In the meantime, the five she had would have to do for the OWOC show.

Her Beatrix Potter (1866–1943) portfolio was much thicker. Two years ago an elderly woman had brought a small Altman's shopping bag to a show Maggie had done on Long Island. "These were my mother's," she'd confided in a wavering tone. "I'm afraid when I was a girl, I loved them as much as she did. I hate to part with them, but with the price of medications these days . . ." She handed Maggie the worn bag containing twelve of the small original Beatrix Potter books published between 1901 and 1913. Unfortunately, they were, as their owner explained, "well-loved." The covers were off, and many of the pages were separated. Some pages had been colored with crayons, and a good number were torn. Several books had been put together with tape, and the tape had left marks on the pages. "I took them to a book dealer, but he said they weren't worth anything. But you like pictures. Maybe you can find a use for them."

A book dealer wouldn't be interested in them: they were "breakers," books with broken bindings, in the worst of condition. But although Beatrix Potter books were still in print and had become a brand now encompassing stuffed animals, lamps, wall hangings, and furniture, these pages from the original books held a charm missing from even the best reproductions today.

Maggie'd paid the woman as much as she thought they were worth (and a bit more), and then faced the challenge of deciding which pictures were worth matting and showing to customers, and which weren't.

Condition, of course, was a primary consideration. Crayon marks might be marks of love, but they ruined any monetary value in the page. As did tape marks. And mothers and grandmothers who might buy these prints wanted Potter scenes they recognized. *The Tale of Peter Rabbit,* of course, and *The Tale of Benjamin Bunny.* But some of the scenes in *The Roly-Poly Pudding* or *The Tale of Two Bad Mice* were obscure, or the images so small they couldn't be seen and admired on a wall.

Not for the first time, Maggie wondered why none of the major illustrators for children were parents themselves. Beatrix Potter had been a solitary woman brought up by servants in London and in England's Lake District. Her brother Bertram was sent to boarding school, but Beatrix stayed home with a governess. The solitary child began keeping journals and notebooks of sketches when she was in her early teens.

She admired Randolph Caldecott's drawings and tried to imitate them, but then developed her own style. She was especially inspired by nature, and by her own pets, whose ranks included hedgehogs, rabbits, snails, frogs, a tortoise, and several mice. In her twenties, while caring for her parents, she wrote illustrated letters to her friends' children. In 1900 she copied some of those letters and sent them to Frederick Warne & Co.

They rejected *The Tale of Peter Rabbit*. Instead of giving up, Potter had 250 copies privately printed, in black and white. Warne himself saw the finished version and changed his mind. They would publish Peter in color. Beatrix Potter's career had begun.

And Frederick Warne asked her to marry him. Unfortunately, he died during their engagement.

Maggie tucked the pile of small matted prints back into the Potter portfolio. Peter Rabbit had always been a special favorite of hers; after all, he was a spunky maverick rabbit and had escaped (if barely) capture by Mr. MacGregor. Maggie remembered a Steiff Peter Rabbit among the stuffed animals in Gussie's inventory. Like many Steiff animals, it was hard. Steiff animals were made to collect, not to cuddle. Luckily, other manufacturers made cozier versions of Peter. Maggie wondered if someday she'd have a chance to choose one of those for her own child. *If* she were a parent. And *if* her child were young enough to need an animal to hug at night. Although everyone needed something, or someone, to hug at night.

Since Michael's death Maggie'd slept next to a pillow turned lengthwise that she could snuggle against. Children weren't the only ones who felt alone in the dark.

Thinking of the dark brought back her fears about the antiques show.

In two days she'd be at the Whitcomb Gymnasium supervising the company putting down the floor coverings.

On the surface, all seemed in order. But she couldn't forget that the show had been targeted by someone. She was the show manager. Somehow she had to prepare for the unexpected.

Dealers' issues she could manage. Too little food or too few parking spaces could be worked around. She'd alerted the police, and campus security. What more could she do? Maggie imagined the worst-case scenarios.

Someone could pull a fire alarm. They could call in a bomb scare. Or—she swallowed deeply—there could be a real fire. Or a real bomb.

More likely, thank heavens, the show could be disrupted by people. Protesters, maybe. But protesting what? The motive for all of this was murky. Or what about vandals? In any case, there would probably be more than one person involved.

Maggie shuddered. If a person or persons were determined to be violent, there were also guns. And Rob Sloane's gun was still missing.

Chapter 19

~

Pomfret Russett. *Lithograph of three views of a green apple done "on stone by F. J. Swinion," and published by* R. H. Pease, Albany, for Natural History of New York, *1851. 8.5 x 11.75 inches. Price: $60.*

Classes had been over for a week, but Wednesday was the official last day of the semester. Claudia had piles of papers for each American Studies professor to verify or fill out or sign. Maggie spent the morning at her desk on campus. Claudia was a treasure at times like this. Never once had Maggie been late with a required document, and it was all to Claudia's credit. At this stage in the teaching year, students, unfortunately, were the lowest priority. Feeding the great paperwork mill in the administration offices was the all-consuming goal.

"Maggie, I've been reading, and I just wanted to make sure you knew." Claudia stood on the other side of Maggie's desk, a grim expression on her face.

"Yes, Claudia? You've been reading. What?" Maggie pulled her thoughts away from the two makeup exams she still had to schedule.

"I've been reading about—that." Claudia pointed to the second of the Diet Pepsi cans Maggie had finished in the past two hours.

"You've been reading about Diet Pepsi?"

"Not just Diet Pepsi. All diet sodas. They're not good for you, Maggie."

"No?" Maggie asked in mock disbelief.

"Have you read the ingredients on this can?" Claudia delicately picked up the offending can with two fingers. "This is serious. This stuff has no vitamins in it. No minerals. Not one thing that is good for you. It has zero nutritional value."

"But it has caffeine, which must be a nutrient," Maggie replied, trying to find some humor behind Claudia's serious expression. It was the last day of the semester. She didn't really need a lecture on nutrition.

"I knew you wouldn't pay attention. But I'm concerned about your health. That's why I wanted to talk to you before vacation, since I'll bet you drink a lot of that stuff during the summer."

Maggie nodded. "True."

"I read on the Internet that the chemicals they put in to sweeten soft drinks can kill you. They might cause brain cancer. Or bladder cancer. Or stomach ulcers! You should be drinking milk. Or water. Or juice."

"Juices are full of carbohydrates and sugars. They'd make me fat," said Maggie, reaching into her bottom drawer, where she stored a backup supply of Diet Pepsi.

"Then drink water. Maggie, this is your health we're talking about. After all, you're not getting any younger!"

And my birthday isn't for another ten days, thought Maggie. Do I need a reminder? "And I suppose I should be eating more chocolate?" It was hard to think of Claudia without thinking about chocolate. There was always a dish of chocolate kisses on her desk, and she left them like a trail of bread crumbs when she visited people's offices.

"Actually, yes," said Claudia, her curls bouncing and her glasses a bit askew. "Eating dark chocolate can lower your blood pressure. And it makes you happier, not more jittery, the way cola does. And it has the caffeine you want. And antioxidants! Red wine is good for you, too."

"That's what I need to do. It will really secure my job to keep a bottle of red wine in my bottom drawer."

Claudia shook her head.

"I'll think about the cola connection," said Maggie. "But in the meantime I'll definitely eat more chocolate. Maybe the good ingredients in chocolate will counteract all the evils I'm drinking. Speaking of chocolate, did you happen to bring any in today?"

Claudia smiled. "It's on my desk. I'll get you some. But you should really think more about the cola. I almost didn't tell you. After all, you're the professor and I'm just the administrative assistant."

Maggie wondered when Claudia had stopped being a secretary.

"But it wouldn't be right to hold back information. Eating or drinking the wrong things could ruin your life. Or end it prematurely."

"Claudia, I promise to drink more water and red wine. Within limits. Will that make you feel better?"

"A little." Claudia looked doubtful; red wine was clearly not the substitute she'd prefer for Maggie's Diet Pepsis. But she *had* suggested it.

"And I'll eat more chocolate. I'll force myself. Now, why don't you bring me some chocolate kisses so I can get through the rest of this paperwork, and I'll finish this one last Diet Pepsi that was in my drawer. I wouldn't want to waste it."

"No, you wouldn't," Claudia said quietly. "I'll get the chocolate."

"Maybe the other professors could use some chocolate, too. The last day of school is always stressful."

Claudia looked back at Maggie as she left the office. "Sometimes I don't know when you're serious and when you're not."

"Don't worry. I'm always serious about chocolate." And Diet Pepsi, Maggie added to herself. She took another swig and glanced at her watch. It was almost time for her meeting with the students and faculty who'd volunteered to help with the antiques show.

Chapter 20

Everlasting Flowers. *Painted for* Vicks Monthly *(an American botanical magazine) and lithographed by Rahn & Karle, Rochester, New York. Bouquet of various wildflowers; colors mainly greens and pinks. 1879. 6 x 9 inches. Price: $45.*

There weren't as many people at the gym for the volunteers' meeting as Maggie had hoped, but the show was being held between semesters. How many students or faculty wanted to return to campus when they didn't have to?

"Hi, Sarah," Maggie said as Sarah Anderson joined them and sat next to Kendall Park and Kayla Martin. Sarah, Kendall, and Kayla had been housemates last semester in Whitcomb House, the dormitory for single parents. Since the death of one of their housemates, some of the parents had gone their separate ways. Maria Ramirez had transferred her credits to the four-year College of New Jersey. Sarah was living with her mother. And Claudia's gossip sources were, as usual, correct: Kendall and Kayla were holding hands. "How're all the kids?"

"Doing fine," answered Kendall. "Josette is running all over the place now, and Katie and Aura are still best friends at day care."

"That's great," said Maggie. "Thank you all for taking the time to help out at the show!"

As she spoke, Claudia joined them, notebook in hand. She was followed by Hal Hanson, the quiet young man living with Carole Drummond's family.

"We figured, you helped us out a few times," answered Kayla. "We owe you more than a couple of hours of work."

Maggie shook her head. "You don't owe me a thing. Now, who else is here?"

Abdullah Jaleel was, as he had promised, and a short blonde girl who introduced herself as "Violet, who loves children." And Paul Turk, a fellow American Studies professor, appeared in the doorway.

"Paul! I didn't know you were joining us."

"Thought you might need some extra muscle," he said, sitting at the far end of the table.

"Then everyone is here," said Maggie, glancing around the room. "Except Eric Sloane. Hal, it's nice to see you."

"Mrs. Drummond said I might be able to help, so I'm here." He slumped down in the chair at the far end of the table, leaned the chair back on two legs, and put his hands in his pockets.

Clearly, Carole had volunteered him. She'd made sure Hal went to every adoptive-parent social event this spring and was hoping to get him to register at the college in the fall. He certainly didn't look thrilled to be at this meeting. He was going through a rough time. Losing both of his parents at the same time, and so suddenly. "We're glad you're here," said Maggie, trying to sound cheerful and welcoming.

Abdullah raised his hand.

"Yes?"

"Professor, maybe you didn't hear. The police found the body of Eric's brother yesterday afternoon. I don't think Eric will be coming this morning."

"They found . . . Jackson's body?" Maggie thought of the news flash on the television last night. "They're sure it's him?"

"It was on the radio this morning." Abdullah looked somber. "They said he was murdered."

There was a rustle around the room as everyone digested the information. It was a small campus. Most of them knew who Jackson was, even if they weren't close friends.

Murdered! Maggie tried to focus. Jackson had been murdered. He hadn't run away from home. Holly and Rob and Eric must be devastated. And all the other children. And Carole. How would this affect the agency? Or publicity for the antiques show?

She felt embarrassed for even thinking about the show.

Maggie tried to shake off a growing sense of dread. She looked at the contingent of volunteers and quickly handed out assignments: Kayla and Kendall preferred to work while the day-care center was open, so they were going to help set up tables and mark booth boundaries Friday morning. Sarah said she'd help out at the café on Saturday and Sunday. Violet wanted to be a porter. And Paul, to Maggie's surprise, volunteered to be a porter both Friday night and Sunday late afternoon. Abdullah also said he'd come Friday morning to help out, porter, and would then be happy to help with any clean-up chores. Even Hal got into the spirit of things and said he'd partner with Abdullah and be available throughout the show. Maggie noticed Abdullah smiling and nodding at Hal. They must know each other from somewhere.

Good. Hal looked as though he could use a friend, and Maggie couldn't remember seeing Abdullah with anyone on campus.

"I'm going to be here the whole time," Claudia assured her. "From Thursday morning until you lock the doors Monday morning. You never know when you might need me!"

Maggie said a mental "Thank you" as well as one out loud. Claudia could be counted on. If someone didn't show up for an assignment, or there was more work in some area than anticipated, Maggie could use another person who was dependable. Knowing Claudia's obsession with organization, and her own lack of concentration just now, Claudia would keep her focused. Even if that focus meant Maggie would have to hear about the evils of artificially sweetened soft drinks throughout the weekend.

And Will would be here. And Gussie and Ben.

Maggie closed her book, her mind already in another place.

Jackson was dead.

Who had murdered Jackson? And why?

And were any of the nightmares the Sloane family was living through connected to those threatening letters? Or to the message on her answering machine?

The antiques show would be filled with people Maggie knew and loved, from antiques dealers to students. She was responsible for them.

Whatever was happening had to be stopped. Now.

Chapter 21

Woman Peeling Apples. A silhouette, one of only seven helio-types done by Winslow Homer. They illustrate James Russell Lowell's limited edition of The Courtin'. *Lowell had trouble selling his long poem to a publisher, so his friend Winslow Homer agreed to illustrate it and drew the silhouettes. They were then heliotyped: reproduced by printing the drawings directly from a gelatin film exposed under a negative and hardened with chrome alum. 1873. Very special examples of Winslow Homer's versatility as an artist. 7.25 x 9.5 inches. Price: $225.*

Maggie's van was steamy from the noon sun as she left the Somerset College campus. She first headed for home, but then changed direction and drove toward the offices of Our World Our Children. Gussie and Ben weren't due to arrive until at least two. She had to know more about Jackson's murder. And Carole Drummond would know more than any other person outside the Sloane family. Or the police department.

Only a few people were at their desks at the agency. "Good afternoon, Maggie," said Priscilla, Carole's secretary. "She should be off the telephone in a minute. Why don't you sit down. I'm afraid we're a bit understaffed just now. Three of the social workers are out making home visits, and everyone else is on their lunch hour."

Lunch. Of course. She'd been so focused on Abdullah's news that she hadn't bothered to think of the time. "I wanted to talk with Carole about the Sloanes." She hesitated. "And the antiques show."

"Such a horrible situation," said Priscilla. "She should be free in just a few moments."

Maggie couldn't relax enough to sit down. She paced the reception area, pausing occasionally to look at the photographs on the wall. Some were of adoptive families; couples and single parents proudly posing with their children. One picture was of the Sloanes, posed in front of their house, perhaps two years ago. Maggie identified a younger-looking Eric. The boy next to him had to be Jackson. He looked like a normal teenage boy, with short hair and glasses. Somehow she hadn't pictured him wearing glasses. As she looked, she suddenly remembered him in another context. He had taken her United States History to the Civil War class during the fall, but hadn't registered for the second semester.

There was also a picture she guessed was Hal Hanson and his parents. She'd met them once, she remembered, at a prospective-parents meeting last December. In the picture Hal was slouching, but smiling, between his mother and father. He looked about ten, and, like most ten-year-old boys, not thrilled at having his picture taken. Now his parents were gone, and he was alone again.

Near Priscilla's desk was a large bulletin board labeled "Waiting Children." Maggie looked carefully at each face. They ranged from infants to young teenagers of various races and backgrounds. Some were in the United States, some in Asia, some in Latin America, and some in Europe. Children who needed families. She looked carefully at the pictures again. Was one of those children her son or daughter? A week ago she would have said "Yes!" eagerly. Today she wasn't as sure.

"Maggie." Carole was standing in the door of her office. "Come on in."

"I just heard," said Maggie. "About Jackson. I'm so sorry. I'm new to the OWOC family, and I was only beginning to know the Sloanes, but I had to tell someone how sorry I was."

"We all are." The left side of Carole's usually sleek hair was standing up at an angle, and makeup wasn't hiding the dark circles under her eyes. "At least Holly was able to go home this morning. But it wasn't exactly a joyous family reunion."

"I heard on the news last night that the police had found a body. I didn't know until this morning that it was Jackson."

"Some children chasing their dog found him in the back of a wooded lot just outside of Somerville."

Maggie shuddered. "And the police are sure he was murdered?"

"Rob called me as soon as he'd identified Jackson. He asked me to call other people at OWOC to let them know. That was late last night. I left you a message this morning."

"I was at the college. I didn't know until one of the students told me during the volunteers meeting. He'd heard it on the radio."

"According to Rob, there'll be an autopsy. But the police said it looked like Jackson had been shot."

The walls of Carole's usually bright office seemed to darken. "They're sure it wasn't suicide?" Anything, Maggie thought. Anything other than murder.

"They didn't find a gun."

They both sat quietly for a moment. Maggie spoke first. "What a horrible reason for Jackson not to come home. And to have people blaming him for Holly's shooting, when he was shot, too!"

"I guess it's still an open question as to whether he shot Holly. But it's obvious that at least one other person was involved. I don't know what the police are considering now. All I know is that two people connected to OWOC were shot. And someone out there still has a gun, unless they've somehow gotten rid of it."

120

Carole leaned against the wall slightly. "I think we need to talk."

Maggie nodded. "That's why I'm here. We'll be starting the setup for the antiques show tomorrow morning." Will and Gussie and Ben would be arriving in a few hours. Everything was happening so fast.

Carole looked defeated. "I'll admit I'm tired. And scared. I don't want anyone else hurt." She hesitated only a moment. "Maggie, I'm seriously thinking we should call off the show."

Maggie sat back in her chair. "I know you want to do the right thing. The safe thing. But stopping the show now would be incredibly complicated. Dealers are already on the road, heading for New Jersey. The contractors would still have to be paid. The agency would end up losing money instead of making it. Besides, if we cancel the show, we're letting some bully win. We're giving in to demands from someone we don't even know."

"I don't want anyone else to be hurt," Carole repeated.

"Have there been any more threatening letters?"

Carole's fingers gripped the yellow pencil she was holding tightly. "Not yet."

Maggie hesitated. "This may not be the right time to tell you, but I got a threatening telephone call Monday. I told the police yesterday."

Carole shook her head and walked across to the window before turning to Maggie. "This can't continue. I can't put anyone else in a dangerous situation. Holly and Jackson have already suffered enough for everyone."

"But if we give in," Maggie pointed out, "we'll be leaving the agency open to more intimidation."

"Then I'm chicken. If it were just you and I in danger, and we decided to risk it, then all right. But we have literally hundreds of people involved in this show now! Even ignoring the major issue of personal safety, what kind of public relations would there be for the agency if we let the show go forward, knowing we've been warned, if there's any kind of trouble! Not to speak of the possibility of a disaster! How would the public feel about

Our World Our Children then? And what about the parents and prospective parents and children we work with every day? We were founded to help children. To help families find each other, and stay together. To continue the show now could be encouraging violence. That's the very opposite of what we stand for."

Maggie was silent. "If we only knew why this person or people are upset about OWOC. Maybe there's a middle road. A way the show can go forward, and we can meet the needs of whoever is causing the problem."

"We're beyond that now, Maggie. I have to believe the two shootings are part of all of this. Jackson Sloane is dead. That shows what these—terrorists—are willing to do. And I don't want to play their games." Carole sat down at her desk and put her head in her hands for a moment. Then she looked up. "You told the police about the call you got?"

Maggie nodded. "They agreed to keep patrols close to the gym, starting when we begin setting up, tomorrow morning. Al Stivali, who used to be a detective and is now head of security at Somerset College, is on board. He's going to do a walk-through tomorrow morning before anyone gets there, and then stay available. He's even going to sleep in the gym Friday and Saturday nights."

"That all sounds good. I'm not questioning that you've done your job, Maggie. I'm questioning whether anyone can stop whatever this group or person has planned. And I'm afraid. No matter what we decide to do, it could be wrong. Very wrong." Carole looked at her with desperation in her eyes.

Maggie nodded. "I know. I'm scared, too."

"We need to share the decision making. I'm going to call an emergency meeting of the board of Our World Our Children tonight. I'll ask someone from the local police force to come. Can you be here? Maybe bring the security guy from Somerset College, too."

"I'll come. And I'll see if Al is free. But we have to find out who is threatening OWOC and stop him or them. Canceling the show won't do that. It will just encourage more demands."

"I'll need time to contact everyone, and some people on the board work in New York, or live in Pennsylvania. So—eight thirty tonight. Here." Carole gestured at the meeting room next to her office.

"At least then everyone involved will be making the decision," agreed Maggie. "And if the decision is to cancel the show, then we'll all have to start making calls."

"Let's just hope nothing worse happens in the meantime," said Carole. "I want to do what's right. For everyone. I just don't know what 'right' is."

Chapter 22

—◦—

The True Old English Pit or Warrior Game. *Drab brown hen and dramatic red and green and black cock, drawn and lithographed by Harrison Weir, 1901, for* The Poultry Book, *1903. 7 x 9.5 inches. Price: $50.*

There were too many things to think about; too many possibilities.

Much as Maggie wanted to see Gussie and Ben and, especially, Will right now, she didn't feel like playing hostess. She headed for home anyway.

Jackson was dead. Carole was seriously thinking of canceling the show.

Maggie changed Winslow's water, gave him a little canned chicken, and cleaned his litter box. Routines on a nonroutine day.

She glanced at her watch. It was almost one thirty. Gussie and Ben could arrive at any moment.

She put clean sheets on all the beds, the only task she hadn't done Sunday night. Doing housework helped her avoid her answering machine. Carole's message about Jackson would be on it, and probably other people asking her to accomplish things. Right now she didn't want to do anything. If she didn't know what she'd been asked to do, she wouldn't feel guilty for not having done it. Shaky logic, but right now it made perfect sense.

She couldn't stop thinking of Jackson, shot and lying in the woods. She wondered how Holly and Rob were coping with the death of one of their children. She didn't want to imagine how they felt.

And people had been blaming Jackson for shooting Holly! His body could have been lying there since last Sunday.

No more excuses. Maggie looked toward her portfolios, but walked to her chair, removed Winslow, who had claimed it, and picked up paper and pencil. She had to face those answering machine messages before Gussie and Ben arrived. She didn't want them hearing the news from a machine. And she needed to call Al to see if he was free for tonight's meeting.

"Maggie? This is Carole. It's Wednesday morning and you should know the police have identified Jackson Sloane's body. It looks as though he was shot. Call me when you can."

Two hang-ups.

Wrong numbers? Something more? But she'd rather have people hang up than leave nasty or threatening messages.

"Professor Summer? Maggie? Eric Sloane. I need to talk with you. Don't call me at home; I'll call you later."

Eric's voice was shaky. He must be taking his brother's death hard. Maybe he had just called to say he was going to miss this morning's meeting. Or . . . did he have something else on his mind? Maggie swallowed and listened to the next message.

"Ms. Summer? I'm Alice Cleary, the head librarian at the Park Glen Library. I've heard you're a real expert on early natural history prints, and wondered if you'd be willing to do a little talk at the library next fall. We're finalizing our speaking schedule, so do try to get back to me as soon as possible."

Maggie shook her head. She'd get back to Alice Cleary another day.

"Professor Summer? This is Jim Hunter. You don't know me, and I know this sounds strange, but I'm worried about one of your students, and he doesn't have any family to talk with. He once mentioned your name, so I thought maybe you'd be able to help. He doesn't know I've called you. Please call me when you get a chance."

One of her students? Maggie frowned. The semester was over; she wouldn't be seeing her students. But she would get back to him. Jim Hunter. She wrote down the name and number. It didn't sound like the kind of emergency she was coping with right now. Mr. Hunter could also wait.

"Maggie, this is Al Stivali, over at security. I heard they found that young man's body. I figured he was the one you were worried about. If I can do anything to help, you be sure to let me know."

Al was a good man, Maggie thought. She had been much less worried about security for the show since she'd talked with him. And now she needed his help with the meeting tonight. At least she wouldn't have to tell him about Jackson; he already knew and no doubt had some thoughts on how the death might influence the show. As soon as she'd heard all the messages, she'd call Al.

"Maggie? Mike Blanchard here. Something's come up, and I won't be able to do your show this weekend. Sorry. Send me the refund when you can."

Maggie underlined Mike's name three times. Another cancellation. Not even an attempt at an excuse. She should have made the deposit nonrefundable, as it was at most shows. Mike Blanchard had a great collection of Belleek and Staffordshire and majolica, all interesting, and very different, types of china. She'd never get anyone else with merchandise that good this close to the show date.

She'd just have to shift the booths, leaving more room for the café. At this point it didn't matter how uneven the rows of booths were, as long as their arrangement looked intentional.

She needed to talk to someone. Someone who would understand her concerns and tell her whether she was being paranoid. Or hysterical. Someone with credibility.

She picked up the phone and dialed the number for Somerset County College. "Security, please."

Al's voice was comfortable and strong. "Security here. Stivali."

"Al, this is Maggie Summer. Sorry to bother you—"

"Maggie! You're not bothering me. I told you to call anytime, didn't I?"

Maggie smiled. Al sounded like a concerned father would. If his daughter had a boyfriend problem, he would probably have stared the young man down and then run him off the premises. Her own father would have told her to call 911 and stop disturbing his nap.

She didn't need a father at her age, but, still, it was nice to have someone reliable to talk with. Someone who cared. "I'm sorry I didn't call you back sooner."

"I've been thinking about you and your antiques show ever since I heard the news about them finding that Sloane boy's body. Horrible situation. And I knew you were connected to the family."

"Indirectly, yes," Maggie admitted. "Through the agency. And Jackson's brother is the one in facilities management group who was going to help us during the show."

"And what about those letters, and that telephone message you got? Any more of that going on?"

"No more messages."

"Good."

"But there's another problem, Al. Our World Our Children is getting really worried about security for the show. They were a little nervous, but now with Jackson's death . . ."

"They're going to cancel it?"

"They may. Carole Drummond, the director, has called an agency board meeting tonight to make the decision as to whether or not the show should go on as planned. I've been asked to go."

"It's a hard call, Maggie," said Al. "Lots of arguments on both sides."

"Exactly. Which is why I'd really appreciate your going with me to the meeting. Carole asked if you would. You have experience, and you'll be at the college this weekend. You could help to pinpoint some of the real issues and eliminate those that aren't so real."

Al hesitated. "The decision is the agency's, Maggie."

"Yes. But I've organized the show, and it's going to be at the college."

Al hesitated. "How are you, Maggie? Really?"

"I'm okay. A little shaky. I wish the show were now, so we could all be doing something concrete instead of just talking about it." In the background Maggie heard a clap of thunder. Just what she needed. A late-day thunderstorm.

Winslow heard the thunder, too. He jumped into Maggie's lap and tucked his head down between Maggie and the arm of the chair. Big brave cat. Maggie absently rubbed his neck harder than usual. He shook his head and jumped down from her lap, dodging under the couch. "And, yes, I'm scared. Especially since I don't know what, or who, to be scared of."

"Where are you?"

"Now? At home. I'm expecting some friends who're coming to help with the show. I guess they've been delayed." Maggie paused. "I'm going a bit nuts."

"Can your friends get into your home if they arrive while you're out?"

"Yes." Where were Gussie and Ben?

"Then why don't you let me buy you dinner. It's a dreary time to be home alone in any case. We can plan what to say at the board meeting. And do some brainstorming about what you should do."

"To protect the antiques show?"

"To protect yourself."

She needed Al's help, and his opinions. "The board meeting is at eight thirty. Would six be too early for dinner?" Gussie would understand.

"Six o'clock, then. At the Somerset Diner? We'll talk. And if you still want me to go to this board meeting with you, then I will."

"See you then. And thank you!" Maggie put down the phone and took a deep breath. Managing this show was getting more complicated every hour.

The telephone's ring interrupted her thoughts.

"Professor Summer? This is Eric Sloane. I really need to see you. Can you meet me at Parkside Library? Over near the reference room. In half an hour."

Chapter 23

—⁓—

Spring Farm Work—Grafting. *Winslow Homer wood engraving done for April 30, 1870,* Harper's Weekly. *Young man standing on ladder, grafting a small branch. Barn, hay pile, and geese in background. WH initials on tree trunk. (Homer did not always sign his work.) 6.75 x 9.25 inches. Price: $150.*

What could Eric want to talk to her about? Maggie called Ian, her next-door neighbor. Ian was a graphic artist who'd added enough skylights and windows to his home so his attic was now a studio. He and Maggie had long ago exchanged keys to their homes, in case of emergency. She explained about Gussie and Ben, and Ian promised to let them into her house in case she hadn't returned by the time they arrived.

Then she drove to the Parkside Library faster than she should have. Parkside was several towns away, but she knew where the library was. It was an old granite building. She'd driven past it often enough, but never been inside.

Eric and his family must be devastated at Jackson's death. They'd already had to deal with their mother being shot in their own front yard. How could this be happening in Somerset County, New Jersey? Somerset County was one of the places people moved to to escape the random violence of New York and Philadelphia. Maggie drove through the quiet suburban streets of Parkside and wondered how many secrets were hidden behind the modern colonial facades and ranch houses. Wide, black-top driveways and pampered lawns shouted their owners' control over their environment. There must be a local ordinance banning dandelions. Much less any other damaging elements.

The main reading room of the library was silent except for the giggles of three middle-school girls crowded together at one of the tables looking at a large book. Anatomy? Maggie remembered when she was thirteen. It seemed a long time ago. An older man sat by the window, immersed in a magazine.

On one wall hung three of John Gould's (1804–93) hummingbirds. Had they been donated to the library individually, or inherited with a collection of books? Automatically, she walked toward them. Nicely matted and framed. Gould birds were large, Victorian-era lithographs; he had overseen more than three thousand prints of birds from around the world. Unframed, most of the lithographs retailed for $800 to $1,600, depending on their condition and the popularity of the bird.

Some "Gould birds" were actually done by Gould; others were done by other carefully selected artists, including his wife, who worked under his direction. The most popular of his prints were his 360 chromolithographs of hummingbirds published between 1849 and 1861. They used special oil colors and varnishes over gold leaf to capture the iridescence of the tiny birds' wings. His formula worked. The wings glimmered. She'd seen those advertised at more than $2,000. Sometimes considerably more than $2,000. The Parkside Library was lucky to have three.

Eric had said he'd meet her "near the reference room."

"Where is Reference, please?" Maggie asked the young woman wearing a yellow, flowered dress who was sorting through magazines at the center desk. The librarian pointed past where the girls were seated, to a hallway.

Eric was hunched over on a window seat near a large section of bookcases. He straightened up and smiled when he saw her.

"Thanks for coming," he said. "You said if I needed to talk with someone, then I could call."

"I did. And I just heard this morning. I'm very sorry about your brother."

"We all are." Eric looked out the window for a few minutes as Maggie pulled over a nearby chair. She didn't want to rush him. Whatever he said had to be on his own time.

"We are—were—almost the same age. Jacks was twenty-two, and I'll be twenty-two next month. But I always thought of him as my younger brother, since I came home before he did. We'd both been in bad family situations and then foster care, and it wasn't easy being moved around a lot. Not being able to count on anyone to be there when you needed them."

Eric's shoulders slumped and he clasped and then unclasped his hands. He looked out the window instead of at Maggie. A small flock of sparrows was chattering and fluttering about one area of the lawn. Someone had probably left part of their lunch sandwich out there.

"Anyway, Mom and Dad wanted us all to be in counseling for a while after we first came home. That was one of the family standards, as Dad says. He believes everyone should have someone to talk with outside the family, and a counselor gave us someone responsible to vent to, or ask advice from, before we were ready to share all that with people inside the family."

"Did it help?"

"It helped me. Yeah. It did. We all had different counselors, because of privacy issues. The guy I talked to was black. He was cool. He understood a lot of the anger I felt about having had such a messed-up life, and being alone so much, and then trying to find my place in this crazy family." Eric looked around at Maggie. "At first, like most of the kids, I put up a big fuss. Didn't want no counseling. Didn't need no help from any shrink. But, yeah, it did help."

This was interesting, but why had Eric wanted to talk with her?

"Jacks wasn't like that. When he said he hated counseling, he really meant it. Once he told me he never talked to his counselor. Never. He went because Dad said that was a rule, but he didn't open his mouth. Just sat there during his sessions." Eric shook his head. "Once in a while I'd try to talk with him. Say, 'Hey, man, how's it going? What're you thinking?' But even though we shared a room and I saw him at school and all, Jacks didn't talk back. Not about anything important. We just talked about school and girls and work and how the little kids were a pain. Everyday stuff.

"I mean, I knew some things. Like, his bio mom was white and his dad was black, and he felt he wasn't black or white. He hung around mostly with the black kids, but he didn't really fit in."

"Aren't several of your brothers and sisters biracial?" asked Maggie.

"Five of them. Since I'm all black, that's one issue I haven't had to cope with. But I know some of the others have had problems. There's always the question of who you hang with. How you fill out forms. What color you feel inside. Everyone treats it differently. For most of the kids it isn't a big deal. It's just part of the package they were handed. Like having white parents now. Weird to some people, but not so unusual for adopted kids. And we know a lot of adopted kids. Those adoptive-parent picnics and Christmas parties and all make sure we do. That's good. People outside the family sometimes have funny reactions to us. Kids see us with our family and ask if we're from the UN or from some exchange program. But we know there are lots of kids in families like ours." Eric seemed comfortable talking about being adopted, maybe because the Sloanes were so open about it. She wondered how it felt to deal with issues of family and race daily.

"But Jacks was mad about the whole deal. Mom thought he was her special boy. He hung around her and talked to her and helped her around the house. More than I did, for sure." Eric looked at Maggie a little guiltily. "But then he'd come upstairs and wonder if his white bio mom was like her. If she was, then why did she dump him and end up in jail? He'd cuss them both out. He used to say if he'd had two parents the same color then he wouldn't be all mixed up the way he was, and living in this crazy family."

"Did he talk to anyone else about how he felt?"

"Not for a long time. Once I told him he should talk to his counselor, but he got angry. Said I could wimp out and talk to some headshrinker, but no way was he going to. That no one knew what was inside his head, and he wanted it to stay that way. After that I left him alone."

"But he did talk to someone?" Maggie persisted, and leaned toward Eric. There was something important in what he was saying. She was sure of it.

"I think so. About six months ago, about the time I started working at the college so I could get some classes paid for, he started hanging around with a couple of new guys. I don't know who they were; he wouldn't tell me. But he said he'd finally found people who understood him, who knew what it was like to feel like a zebra and to hate it."

"Where did Jackson meet these guys? How old were they?"

"He never said. He did say they'd lived more than most of us kids. I figured that meant the guys were older than us. Or at least had a lot more experiences. But I don't think they were a lot older. I mean, I can't see Jacks hanging around with someone in his thirties or something!"

Maggie, aged thirty-eight—almost thirty-nine—tried not to grimace. "He never said who these people were?"

Eric shook his head. "Just that they were like him. I figured maybe they were biracial, since that's what Jacks thought a lot about. Anyway, I didn't want to tell the police, because it sounds stupid that I know there're people out there who might be able to help, but I don't know who they are, or where they are." Eric looked at Maggie and took a deep breath.

"Saturday night Jacks and Mom had a big argument. He wanted to go out and she wanted to know where he was going." Eric shrugged. "They always want to know where we're going. Some of us—oh, hell, we all!—stretch the truth a little when we feel it'll keep the peace. Four of us are over twenty-one! Jacks could have said he was going to a movie with any of the others who were going out, or with someone Mom knew. But he didn't. He made a big scene by telling Mom it wasn't any of her business where he went. She wasn't his real mom, and if his real mom didn't care, then why should she?"

"That was the night before Mother's Day. Maybe Jackson was thinking of his birth mother."

"I guess. Whatever was in his mind, Mom yelled, and he yelled, and then he just took off." Eric hesitated. "The last thing he said was, 'You'll be sorry you ever adopted me!' Then he slammed the door."

"What do you think he meant by that?"

"At the time I didn't think anything of it. We all get aggravated once in a while. It isn't the first time someone's said that to Mom or Dad. But when Mom was shot the next morning, at first I thought maybe Jacks really did it. Although he wasn't ever violent. He just talked a big story. But maybe at least he knew something about Mom's shooting." Eric shook his head. "None of it made sense. I kept waiting for him to come home. To apologize to Mom and put everything back the way it had been." Eric slumped against the window.

Maggie nodded at him. "It must have been very hard."

"*Hard* doesn't begin to say it. Since Saturday night nothing's been the way it was. Even Mom and Dad had a big fight that night, after Jacks left. They never do that. Well, maybe they argue in their room, but never in front of us all. I once heard Dad tell a group of prospective parents that one advantage single parents have"—Eric looked sideways at Maggie— "is their decisions are final. Their kids don't have a 'court of last resort' to go to. Couples won't always agree, but they shouldn't disagree in front of their kids, because then the kids try to divide them. Start taking sides and all." Eric shrugged. "I hadn't thought of that for a long time until this week. It was awful to hear Mom and Dad yelling at each other." He looked at Maggie.

"What were they arguing about Saturday night?"

"Whether Jackson was old enough to do things without telling anyone. Mom said as long as he was living at home, under their roof, they had a right to know what he was doing, and with whom. Dad said no, he needed to have his own friends and make his own decisions to prove he was ready to move into his own place someday." Eric looked up at Maggie. "I forgot to tell you. Jackson was saving up. He wanted to have his own apartment. He even looked at some in Somerville, but they cost too much, with having to put two months' security down and all. He didn't have a regular job, like me. He did stuff like raking leaves in the fall and shoveling snow and mowing grass. A lot of people call our house if they need help. They figure there's always 'one of those poor orphans' who'd like to earn a few bucks. Jackson's been spending a lot of time cleaning people's yards this spring 'cause he was saving for an apartment."

"How much had he saved?"

Eric looked down at the floor with embarrassment. "I knew where he kept it, and I looked after he hadn't come home. I wanted to know if he'd taken the money with him."

"That wasn't bad, Eric. That was smart. To try to figure out what Jackson was planning."

"The money's all still there, Professor Summer. Eight hundred and fifty-three dollars. It's in a peanut butter jar in the back of our closet. If he'd been running away, like some people say, then he would've taken that money." Eric looked back at her. "I told the police that."

"What do you want me to do, Eric?"

"Find whoever Jacks was going to meet that night. Whoever it was might know what happened to him."

Maggie could see fear in Eric's eyes before he moved his head and stared out the window again.

"I can't understand why anyone would've hurt him. He was a little mixed-up, but he was a good kid. A good brother. He was going to be fine. He just needed a little more time to figure his life out. We all need time. Why would anyone kill him?"

Chapter 24

———~~~———

Danger Ahead! *April 1870 Winslow Homer wood engraving printed on the cover of* Appleton's Journal of Literature, Science and Art, *headed by their distinctive logo. Two men lean over the railing of a caboose as they watch the steam engine ahead of them in the night, curving over the bridge they are crossing. Page size: 7.5 x 11 inches. Engraving size: 6.25 x 6.5 inches. Price: $165.*

Maggie drove slowly back through the damp, quiet towns of midcentral New Jersey toward Park Glen, where she lived. The storm was over for the moment, but supermarket parking lots were full of puddles as well as cars. Several young teens on bicycles rode erratically along a slippery road without sidewalks. A jogger crossed in front of her. Three mares and their foals grazed in a field to her right. The hills were covered with blooming dogwoods that looked bedraggled after the downpour.

Not so many years ago this area had all been farmland. Now many of the farms had been turned into executive-home developments, but every mile or so you could still see cows in a pasture, or a stable with a riding ring.

She slowed down in front of Enoch's Antiques. Enoch Spenr went to a lot of auctions in eastern Pennsylvania and often und wonderful folk art there. But a Closed sign was in the window. No bargains today. Maybe he was out scouting for more treasures. And she needed to get home. Gussie and Ben might already be there. Everyone was out in the world, doing what they needed to do. Living their lives.

Except Jackson, whose life had ended. Ended after he had found a home, but, from what Eric had said, before he had totally accepted his new family. His short life had been painful; now his death was painful to those who'd cared about him.

Maggie suddenly thought of her brother, Joe. She hadn't heard from him since a postcard arrived several years ago, postmarked Arizona. If Joe had died, she might not even have heard. He might never have mentioned having a younger sister. As far as she knew, he had no wife, no children. He'd never had anyone, not since he'd left home, when he was eighteen and Maggie was six. Some people seemed suited to live alone. To value solitude over relationships. Did they find peace in solitude? Or were they, as Jackson seemed to be, condemned to live with their own thoughts, to relive the challenges of their lives over and over?

Maggie shivered. It wasn't cold. She was getting too philosophical. Many of her colleagues thought she was a loner; a woman who was too independent; who kept to herself; who didn't need other people. But they were wrong. She couldn't live, at least live comfortably, without people.

She just didn't surround herself with large groups of acquaintances who spent several evenings a month together in various configurations, drinking, socializing, discussing predetermined subjects, or playing golf.

She'd liked being married. Liked having someone to come home to, to share a bottle of wine with and discuss crabgrass or painting the house or who was going to feed the goldfish. Mundane, ordinary, day-to-day sharing.

Maybe she'd been too complacent in her marriage. Maybe she'd ignored behavior she should have challenged. Maybe she'd been more comfortable in the role of wife than in the reality of the relationship. Certainly Michael's philandering proved he hadn't valued the marriage as she had.

She needed to know more about herself before she could open her heart and her life to a child. Ann had said she wanted to adopt so she wouldn't be alone. Maggie suspected that being a parent, especially a single parent, could be very lonely.

There were no guarantees beyond your own commitment to a person. But you couldn't lose yourself in that commitment. The word *mother* encompassed a lifetime of intertwined expectations and roles. Was she ready to play those roles? Or was she just experimenting with the idea of parenthood?

Thank goodness Gussie was coming. Gussie had decided not to have children. But she listened to Maggie, and cared. She would understand some of Maggie's dilemmas. Will had also decided, for different reasons, not to have children. He tried to be supportive, but she knew if she adopted a child, her relationship with Will would not go deeper. It might end.

He, too, would be here tonight.

Did she love him? She loved being with him and missed him when they weren't together. But she hadn't closed her eyes to other men. Her heart, maybe. But a part of her was keeping options open. Life could change in so many ways. By choice, or by chance.

She hated walking into her house and knowing nothing had been moved since she'd left it. Unless, of course, Winslow had decided to play wildcat in the jungle and pounced on a pile of papers left on her desk. Winslow was company. But coming home to him wasn't the same as returning to a husband. Or lover. Or even a friend.

At least tonight she wouldn't be alone.

I could get myself really depressed, thinking this way, Maggie thought. She mentally rapped herself on her head and drove home.

Her house was still empty. She dropped the mail on the

kitchen table and picked Winslow up. He declined the hug, but deigned to accept a few bites of dry food.

Maggie took some filet mignon out of her freezer, covered it with a heavy cat-proof pan, and left it on the counter to defrost. She should have planned for dinner earlier. But steak could be broiled quickly. Even if she was having a fast dinner with Al, she could cook quickly for Gussie and Ben when they got here, and then for Will, later.

She pulled out some mushrooms and onions and started slicing them. There was Italian bread in the freezer, too, and French vanilla ice cream with chocolate sauce for dessert.

Claudia had insisted that chocolate was good, Diet Pepsi was evil. Well, she'd have chocolate later. And maybe she'd even be good and sip something other than Diet Pepsi now.

She poured herself a little Dry Sack, added ice and a twist of lemon, and started cooking the vegetables. The burnished copper pots she'd hung on the wall and the brilliantly colored Cassell rooster lithographs made this room her room. She'd fix the mushrooms and onions, savor her sherry, then sort through the mail.

She flipped through the catalogs and envelopes she'd dropped on the table. An oil company bill. Thank goodness the temperature was warm enough now so her furnace was no longer going full blast.

Telephone company bill. Maggie winced. All those calls to dealers, enticing them to do the OWOC show, and calls to Gussie and Will for encouragement, had inflated the usual monthly total. Maybe the calls about the antiques show could be a charitable tax deduction. She made a note to check with her accountant.

Sears bill. Nothing deductible there. She owed a payment on the small upright freezer she'd bought in March.

A flier for used trucks. A reminder she'd probably have to start looking at used vans soon. Hers was ten years old, and she'd driven it over 150,000 miles. She babied it, made sure she changed the oil without fail every three thousand miles and made any replacements or adjustments her mechanic suggested. But the van wouldn't last forever, and she didn't want it to die while she was somewhere like Maine. Or Buffalo. With a full load of prints.

Three catalogs for summer "togs." I guess I'm not really in a "tog" mood, Maggie thought to herself as she put the catalogs in the recycle pile along with the truck-dealership ad. Who wore "togs" anyway? The word was pretty much obsolete except for catalog appearances.

A plain white envelope, with her name and address hand-printed in red on the front. Postmarked in Somerville. Maggie looked at it for a moment. Sometimes ads and pleas for you to open a new credit card account were sent in plain envelopes, so you didn't know they were junk until you opened them. But even those weren't printed by hand. In red. Just looking at the envelope sent a chill up her back. Carefully she opened it and removed the note, printed in large letters.

STOP THE ANTIQUES SHOW OR YOU WILL BE SORRY. ASK JACKSON.

Maggie dropped the paper onto the table.
Drained her glass of sherry.
And called the police.

Chapter 25

———∽———

"Billy boy blue, come blow me your horn, The sheep's in the meadow, the cow's in the corn: Is that the way you mind your sheep? Under the haycock fast asleep!" Small, lithographed illustration by Kate Greenaway (1846–1901) for Mother Goose *(1881). Daughter of an engraver, Greenaway's depictions of an elegant, graceful, and quaint childhood in which children wore clothing of the late eighteenth century captured the hearts of Victorian England. Reprints of the books she illustrated and reproductions of her drawings are common today. 4 x 6.25 inches. Price: $30.*

"I assume you touched this?" Detective Luciani stood over Maggie as she sat at the kitchen table in the room she had thought so peaceful an hour ago. "You opened it?"

"I didn't think about fingerprints. It all happened so fast. I didn't expect . . ."

"You'll have to come down to the station and be fingerprinted, so we can isolate your prints from any others." He carefully lifted the envelope, with the letter inside, and put it in a plastic bag. "If this is like the ones the agencies got, then there were no prints. Whoever sent it wrote with gloves on. But maybe we'll get lucky." He hesitated. "We'll have handwriting experts compare it to the other notes, but we may not be able to tell for sure if it's from the same person. There could be two people, or more, working together. Or someone who's heard about the letters and sent a copycat one."

"Whoever sent it had my home address," Maggie pointed out. But, today there was the Internet. And she was listed in the faculty directory. All that really proved was that someone wanted to scare her.

"This is the first time someone has threatened you personally. The phone message you got was a threat to the show. At this point I'd advise you to lock your windows and doors. Leave lights on if you're away. The usual. And call us if anything suspicious happens."

Winslow chose that moment to tear through the kitchen, leap onto the top of the refrigerator, and dislodge the electric wok Maggie had stored there, theoretically out of harm's way. The wok crashed onto the floor.

She and Detective Luciani both jumped, as Winslow raced past them into a quieter part of the house. Thank goodness that hadn't happened at three in the morning, Maggie thought. She would have summoned the entire Somerset County police force.

"Is OWOC thinking of canceling the antiques show?" asked the detective.

Maggie hesitated, still feeling silly for the way her heart had raced when the wok fell. "They've called a board meeting for tonight to decide."

"Assuming they go ahead with the show, we've already agreed to drive by every hour or two during the show and check out the gymnasium. Maybe we should also check the inside of the building, before you start setting up, and then again before the show opens."

"That would be reassuring," agreed Maggie. "I alerted the security people at Somerset College. And Al Stivali, the head of security there, is going to sleep at the gym Friday and Saturday nights."

"Stivali's a good guy. I worked with him once when he was ...ill on the Newark force, and a couple of times out at the col-.ege," agreed Detective Luciani. "He doesn't have any official authority now, but he's got good sense and knows when to call for backup. Getting him on board was a good idea."

After the detective left, Maggie covered the sautéed onions and mushrooms and put them in the refrigerator. Where were Gussie and Ben? It was almost five. They were going to hit all the rush-hour traffic coming south on route 287, and then west on 78, just when Gussie would be most tired.

But thank goodness they hadn't been at her house when she'd opened that letter. Or when Detective Luciani was here.

Gussie would have been able to cope. Gussie was a lot tougher than people assumed she was. Having to use an electric wheelchair didn't mean you were weak. In fact, it meant the opposite. It meant you hadn't given up. Gussie wouldn't be thrilled about the letter, of course. But she'd keep calm and discuss options.

And that's exactly what Maggie needed to do. Was Carole right in thinking they should cancel the show? If they did, time was disappearing. They'd need to start making telephone calls now.

If they didn't cancel the show, would it be the rational choice, or just bravado?

No matter what the decision was, Gussie was coming. Will was coming. Ben would be here, too. She wouldn't be alone.

Thank goodness Ben hadn't been here this afternoon. He was twenty-one, but he still lived in a world where right was right, and wrong was wrong. And he'd watched enough TV to have a vivid imagination. She wasn't at all sure she wanted Ben to know about the letter. Or any of the threats.

If only Gussie and Ben would arrive! Maggie glanced at her watch. She'd agreed to meet Al at six. And Gussie had said they'd be arriving between two and four. Something must have happened.

145

Major road construction? Could they have been in an ac
dent?

Maggie realized she was pacing. And then she remembered
she hadn't checked her answering machine. She hadn't been in
her study since she'd talked with Eric.

Eric.

That was a whole separate issue. Who was this older, more
experienced friend of Jackson's? And if the police hadn't been
able to find him, then how could she?

Two messages waited.

"Maggie? This is Gussie. I'm sorry; Ben and I won't be making it to Jersey today. Traffic coming off the Cape was heavy,
and I guess I just don't have as much energy as I'd like to think.
We've stopped at a motel near Hartford. We should be at your
place by noon tomorrow. Just leave the key with your neighbor,
as you'd planned. I know you'll be at the gym setting up. Sorry.
But I'll see you tomorrow!"

Maggie felt her shoulders relax. There hadn't been an accident. Gussie and Ben were all right. Thank goodness. But she'd
miss not seeing Gussie tonight.

She pressed the button for the second message. Will's voice
filled the room.

"Maggie, honey, it's me. I got a late start yesterday, and I'm
still on the road, up around Syracuse. It's about three thirty.
Even with a lot of coffee stops I'm not going to make it to your
place until really late tonight. Or early tomorrow morning. So
don't worry about me. I may even pull over into a rest stop and
take a nap somewhere. I'll be there by morning, though, so
make sure you've got plenty of sausage and eggs for breakfast,
and I'll be ready to go to the gym with you. Wish I were there
now."

Maggie shook her head. Neither Gussie nor Will would be
here tonight after all. And by the time they *did* get to New Jersey, the show might have been canceled.

Thank goodness she'd agreed to have dinner with Al.

Chapter 26

─❦─

"Little Miss Muffet, Sat on a tuffet, Eating some curds and whey; There came a great spider, And sat down beside her, And frightened Miss Muffet away." Kate Greenaway (1846–1901) pastel illustration for 1881 Mother Goose. *Small girl in late-eighteenth-century dress sitting on the grass, wearing a large hat and eating her breakfast. 4 x 6.25 inches. Price: $30.*

Al's suggestion of the Somerset Diner as a place to meet for dinner wasn't Maggie's usual choice of dining locale, but it had two big advantages: it was about halfway between her house and Al's office at Somerset County College, and the parking lot went right up to the door—no allowances for lawns or trees here—so it was only moderately difficult to dodge the raindrops that were falling again.

She stepped inside the restaurant and shook out the rain hat she'd hoped would keep her a little dry. Her long hair was dripping onto the black and white linoleum floor. She glanced into a mirror by the door. It showed all too well the tiny gray hairs that were beginning to be visible on her temple. She brushed them back with her hand. Al waved from a booth down the aisle.

He stood as she took off her slicker and slid across the seat.

"Hope you don't mind a diner," he said when they were both seated again. "Since my wife died, I've found these places provide the closest food to home-cooked, at a pretty reasonable price."

A blonde, heavyset waitress in a white uniform with a pink apron brought a coffeepot over to their table. "Al, you want the usual coffee?"

"You bet, Vera. Maggie, you want some? Great coffee!" The waitress was already pouring Al's.

"No, thanks. But I would like a glass of ice water and a Diet Pepsi with lemon?"

Vera nodded. "Coming right up."

Maggie looked around at the pale yellow walls of the diner and the framed photographs of customers, including former Somerset County residents John DeLorean and Mike Tyson, and Christine Whitman, a former New Jersey governor, who still lived nearby. Jackie Kennedy Onassis had also lived in Somerset County, but perhaps she hadn't patronized the diner.

If this place were spruced up, it could be attractive.

Brighter yellow paint. Narrow curtains at the empty windows. And prints, of course. Late-nineteenth-century lithographs of apples and grapes and raspberries filling the spaces between the windows. They would upgrade the whole look and make the dining room a lot more inviting.

"So you're known here," said Maggie, taking note of the dinnertime patrons on a Wednesday night. Dads with kids; moms with kids. Elderly couples. Two women drinking large frosty ice cream sodas through straws. Was that dinner or dessert? How many years had it been since she'd had a chocolate soda with coffee ice cream? She had a fleeting memory of going to a diner in Bloomfield with her big brother and feeling very grown-up as she ordered one.

"I come here once or twice a week. There's a pretty good coffee shop over in Bridgewater, too. Food's better than those fast-food places, and I can sit and be quiet a little before going home. And"—he grinned at her—"no dishes to wash!"

"You've got a point there," said Maggie, smiling. Some widowers might have found favorite bars to stop at; Al didn't seem to be a drinking man. For an ex-cop, that was unusual, she thought. Unless he was on the wagon for a reason. None of her business in any case. "I've only been here once or twice before, and not recently. It's warm and cozy."

"The food's decent and they're generous with portions." Al's size verified that information. "I usually order one of the daily specials, but everything is pretty good."

Maggie quickly decided on a chicken salad with mandarin oranges and almonds. It had been a while since she'd been at a diner. She'd expected her choice to be between meat loaf and chicken potpie. Al ordered a bowl of chili with garlic toast. Maggie smiled; if this had been a date, that odorous a choice would have been considered selfish. For friends having dinner, it was fine.

"Okay, Al. Now we do have to talk."

"Yes?" He smiled, probably thinking Maggie had a minor complaint to file about his choice of restaurant.

"After we talked this afternoon I got one of those letters. The threatening ones. This time it was addressed to me. Not to the agency."

Al put his cup of coffee down. "Did it go to your office at the college?"

"No. To my home."

He took a breath, staying calm for both of them. His expression wasn't reassuring. "You opened the letter?"

"Yes. Maybe I shouldn't have, but I did."

"And?"

"It read, 'Stop the antiques show or you will be sorry. Ask Jackson.'"

"Jackson's the boy who was killed, right?"

"Right."

Al's voice was careful. "You've turned this letter over to the police?"

"I called them as soon as I'd read it."

"Good. Did they give you any hint about who might have sent it, or whether it was serious?"

"No. They told me to lock my doors and keep my lights on; that they didn't know whether the letter was part of a hoax, or even a copycat."

"But the letter did say 'Jackson.'"

"Yes."

"That's the first direct connection between the shootings of Holly Sloane and her son and the antiques show."

Maggie stopped for a moment. She hadn't thought of that. The other letters hadn't mentioned the shooting. And they had been sent to OWOC. She also realized she hadn't notified the agency of this latest threat. Everything was moving too fast. "I should call Carole Drummond and let her know. I just didn't think of it."

"Don't worry, Maggie. The police have no doubt already told anyone they think needs to know. And we're going to see Carole at the meeting."

They both sat quietly for a few minutes before Maggie spoke. "I know it sounds bad. I know the agency may decide to cancel the show. They're afraid someone might be hurt." Maggie hesitated a moment. "So am I. But I don't want us to give in to threats! You were a detective. You've dealt with this sort of thing before, Al. What's your professional take? Would someone really disrupt the antiques show or hurt me? Or is it all a giant practical joke?" Maggie smiled. "I'll tell you right now, I need some answers before the board meeting tonight."

Al didn't smile back. "It might have seemed like a practical joke before anyone was hurt. But you've got Holly Sloane with a bullet in her hip, and her son dead. That's no joke."

"You're convinced the same person is responsible for both the warnings and the shootings?"

"The cops might not agree, but I'm not on the force anymore, and I'm just giving you my opinion, okay? How many crazies do you think a place like Somerset County has at any one time? Well, we've got our share, of course. Wherever there are people, there is always a certain percentage who're put together a little like Tinkertoys. But most of them have settled in and don't bother no one. But this guy—probably it's a guy, but we don't want to take anything for granted, now—this guy is way out in front of himself. He's warning people about what he might do. I don't get why Mrs. Sloane and her son were shot. But when somebody threatens, you know they're real upset about something. In this case, assuming for argument's sake that it was the same guy, he's upset enough to shoot two people. You got to take that kind of upset seriously."

"Then the show is in danger?" Maggie hesitated. "Then I'm in danger?"

"The good news, Maggie, is that you probably aren't in danger right this minute. But he wants you to be real scared. For some reason he doesn't want that antiques show you're running to happen. He started by warning the agency. Then there were the shootings, which don't fit in directly right now, because we haven't got the whole picture. Then he threatened you. He may figure you'll be afraid, and the agency will listen to you and call off the show."

"If that's what he believes, he's right. I am afraid. Or at least I'm nervous. For myself, and for everyone who may be at that show this weekend."

"And you're not the only one who's not sure how to deal with the situation; that's why they've called the board meeting for tonight."

"But I don't know what to say to the board. Should we cancel the show? Are we putting a lot of people in harm's way by going on with our plans?"

"Did you stop flying in airplanes after 9/11, Maggie?"

"Of course not. That would have been giving in to terrorists." She sat back. "I see what you're getting at. If we cancel the show, that's what we'll be doing. Giving in to someone we don't know for some unknown reason. I've been telling Carole we can't do that. But, Al, I'm beginning to wonder if that's the right course. If anyone were hurt, after I encouraged OWOC to open the show, then I'd blame myself."

"It's not an easy choice, for sure."

"Plus, the agency dropped their other fund-raisers, a cocktail party and a family trip to the United Nations, because they assumed this event could make more money for the time involved. If we cancel the show now, the agency won't make money. They'll lose it." Maggie shook her head.

"Organizing this show's taken a lot of your time, I'll bet," said Al, buttering one of the warm buttermilk biscuits Vera had set in the center of the table.

"More time than I'd anticipated," said Maggie. "I don't know if I'll volunteer to do it again. But it's for a good cause. If it's successful, it will have been well worth the time." She watched a mom at the next table carefully cutting up her toddler's hamburger into bite-size pieces. Would that be her someday?

"How complicated are the logistics? Could you stop the show at this point if the board voted to do that?"

"Sure. But there would be a lot of calls to make and a lot of frustrated and angry people. There's no way to get in touch with all those people now."

Plus, think of all those frozen cookies and cupcakes and muffins in Ann Shepard's freezer. Maggie had a sudden vision of thousands of frozen blueberry and banana and cranberry and cheese muffins neatly arranged in a line across Somerset County. If we canceled the show, she thought, we could still have one hell of a bake sale.

"We're not going to cancel. Period. We just can't lose all the time and money so many people have put into planning this show just because some idiot out there likes to send nasty letters and make phone calls!"

"Okay, okay!" Al said, raising his hand in protest. "I got it. The show goes on. I agree. That's what needs to happen. If, of course, you're able to convince the board."

"The way I see it, I'm not in any danger now. Whoever is threatening me wants the show canceled. I haven't done that yet. But he thinks there's still a chance we'll cancel. Right?"

"Possibly. That may be why he's trying to scare you into making that decision." Al shook his head and downed part of a glass of water. The chili must be hot. "I wish we knew just why this fellow—whoever he is—wants the show canceled. I'm wondering about any connections between the agency and the college. You said Jackson's brother Eric is working for facilities management?"

Maggie nodded. "He'll be helping us out during the show." She took another bite of chicken. Not gourmet. She wasn't sold on the diner food so far, although the Diet Pepsi and the onion rings were just fine. She pushed a still-damp wave of brown hair back from her face. "Eric called me this afternoon. He said Jackson made some new friends a few months ago. He thinks those were the people Jackson was planning to see last Saturday night. Eric thought one of the new friends might be the one who killed Jackson."

"He had no idea who the friends were?"

"He said not. Except he thought maybe the friends might be biracial."

"Biracial what?"

"He didn't say. I don't think he knew." Maggie paused. "Jackson was black/white."

Al shook his head. "That doesn't give us anything. We have no place to start."

"There might be a campus connection, though. Jackson and Eric were both taking courses at Somerset County. Jackson's new friends could be people he met there."

"Sure. But we have over three thousand students, when you count everyone who's there even part-time. Not to mention everyone who works there."

"Maybe someone else on campus saw Jackson with them."

"Maggie, it's semester break. Almost no one's on campus except for some people in admissions and accounting, and groups like facilities management and security. Besides, if the police have been doing their job, they've already covered that territory. As soon as Jackson disappeared, they were investigating where he'd gone that Saturday night."

"But I can't help thinking about possibilities. You rememb̶ Al, when I heard the threat on my answering machine, I thoug̶ it was a voice I recognized. But I couldn't identify it. I keep̶ thinking that if I knew the voice, it must be someone connected to the college."

"Or to the agency. You said you'd gotten to know a lot of people there: staff, adoptive parents, prospective parents."

"That's true. But why would anyone connected with the agency be opposed to a fund-raiser for it?"

"Maggie, we're going around in circles. What you need to do is relax and, just like the cops told you, watch what you do and where you go, and make sure you don't do anything stupid, like leaving your car or house unlocked."

"I won't, Al. I'm going to stay calm. We'll go to the board meeting tonight and help convince them that the show should go on, and then I'll go home and get a good night's sleep. Tomorrow morning I'll be at the gym. The company putting down the protective floor will be there at eight thirty."

"And your friends? When will they be arriving?"

"They were delayed. Tomorrow morning. One very early, and one about noon."

"Good. Then you won't be alone." Al took a last bite of his chili. "I'm going to stay pretty close to my office this week, too, Maggie. And, tomorrow, before anyone else gets there, I'm going to go over the whole gymnasium area myself, to make sure there's no place someone could hide, or leave something we wouldn't see. If I make sure everything is in order before your flooring people arrive, it should be easier to keep an eye on the place and make sure nothing is out of place."

"That would be great. All I want right now is for this show to be over!"

"You mean you wouldn't consider some strawberry pie for dessert?" said Al, grinning.

"Priorities are priorities," Maggie said, smiling back.

Chapter 27

—⁓—

Steeplechase. *Limited-edition etching (black-and-white) by Frederick L. Owens, ca. 1930. Owens was born in Prince Edward Island, Canada, but studied in New York City and was a member of Associated American Artists. His work received special mention in the 1933 edition of* Fifty Best Prints of the Year. *Five jockeys leaning forward, guiding their horses in a jump over a hedge, with water on the far side. Small, semicircular fox mark in lower right corner. 8 x 12.24 inches. Price: $150.*

Al had an errand to do, but agreed to meet Maggie at the board meeting at eight thirty. She stopped at the local police department and was fingerprinted, as Detective Luciani had requested that afternoon.

"Will you keep the prints on file?" asked Maggie as she cleaned the ink off her fingers with the wipes supplied by the young blonde woman who was the clerk on duty.

"They'll be filed electronically," she said, nodding. "So if anyone ever has to identify your body, they'll know who you are."

That was not exactly what Maggie had had in mind. "I meant, if I file a petition to adopt a child from overseas, will I have to have my fingerprints done again?"

The clerk looked blank. "You mean, like if you applied fc gun license?"

Gun licenses and adoption applications, it turned out, wer two of the most common reasons people went to police departments and requested to be fingerprinted. Not counting the fingerprinting now required for some employment applications and usually done at work locations.

And, yes, she'd have to go through the whole procedure again.

So now I'm part of the wonderful world of people who can never get away with doing anything illegal that involves leaving fingerprints, Maggie thought to herself as she drove to the adoption offices. The way this benefit antiques show was going, she was ready to require fingerprints from everyone involved in the entire production. Including the customers.

She was still chuckling at that thought when she reached the Our World Our Children offices.

No one else there was laughing.

Carole was seated, and so was Al. His errand must have taken less time than Maggie's fingerprinting. At the head of the table was a man Maggie had never met, although she'd read his name on the OWOC letterhead: Duncan Thompson, Esq. President of the Board of Directors of OWOC. Mr. Thompson did not look overjoyed.

Nor did the four other board members at the table. Maggie slid into the seat Carole gestured toward and nodded at Al.

"Carole, can we expect anyone else to join us?" Mr. Thompson was looking at his watch. Whatever plans he had made for this evening, they had obviously not included a stop at the agency.

"No," said Carole calmly. "Jim and Hank are out of town on business, and Elizabeth couldn't make it either. I'd like you to meet Maggie Summer, the prospective parent and professor at Somerset County College who organized the show for us."

Maggie nodded at Mr. Thompson.

"Al Stivali, head of security at the college and a former detective with the Newark police force, has also joined us this evening to give us his assessment of the situation." Carole gestured at Al.

"Pleased to be here," he said.

"That's all very well," said Thompson. "But what about the real police? If we're getting involved in a potentially criminal matter, why aren't they here?"

Carole stayed calm. "I've been in touch, as recently as half an hour ago, with Detective Luciani and Detective Newton, who are in charge of investigating this situation. They felt the decision of whether to go ahead with the show this weekend was ours. They're prepared to support whatever we decide to do."

Thompson nodded. "They must not see the threats we've received as dangerous."

"They're urging caution," Carole put in. "As you know, the agency has received three letters that appear to be from the same person. The letter we got last week mentioned the antiques show. Maggie, who's managing the show, received an anonymous call from someone who may be the letter writer. And"—Carole glanced at Maggie—"this afternoon Maggie also received a threatening letter at her home."

Al had been right. The police had notified Carole about the letter.

"Have any connections been made between these anonymous threats and the shooting of Holly or Jackson Sloane?" asked Thompson.

"The police haven't been able to establish a direct connection," said Carole. "Although the letter Maggie got today did mention Jackson by name, his name has been on television and in newspapers. The person, or persons, may just be taking advantage of that unfortunate circumstance to make their threats sound more serious."

"Do we know yet what this person—or people"—Thompson looked directly at Carole—"are upset about? Have they asked for anything?"

"Just that we cancel the show."

They all sat in silence for a few moments.

"Professor Summer and Mr. Stivali, thank you for joining us," said Thompson. "I realize this is a major concern for both of you. Professor Summer, what will actually happen this week end, and who will be involved, and Mr. Stivali, if you could explain what security measures are being taken at the college?"

Al nodded. "Be glad to. Of course, I'm working closely with the local police."

"Professor Summer?"

Maggie had no desire to go through all the gory details. She hoped Thompson wasn't really interested in them. "On-site preparations for the show will begin tomorrow morning. Somerset College personnel, and one or two people I know well, will be in the gym tomorrow and Friday morning, when tables will be brought in, and booths will be laid out. The dealers will set up between four and ten Friday night. The gym will be open to them at eight thirty Saturday morning, and the doors will open for customers at ten. We'll close at five Saturday. Our hours Sunday will be eleven until four."

"And during all that time there will be police patrolling the area?"

Al answered, "Yes. And in addition to the police I'll have Somerset College security people in the parking lots and in the gyms. Both the police and I will go through the gymnasium building tomorrow morning before anyone enters to check that all is in order, confirm that doors that should be locked are, and so forth. And I will personally be spending Friday and Saturday nights in the gym, in addition to hourly police patrols through the campus."

"Stivali, you've been a detective. You know the community, and you know the campus. What risks are we taking?"

"If you cancel the show, there will still be people coming to the campus who'll assume the show is proceeding as it's been advertised. There have been advertisements and signs for a couple of hundred miles around to attract customers. All appropriate precautions are being taken by your agency personnel, by us at the college, and by the local police. If you cancel the show you'll lose money, and, what's more important, lose some credibility in the community."

"I understand losing the money; Carole's briefed me on that," aid Thompson. "But credibility? If we open a show and anyone is hurt, it seems to me we'll be risking our reputation a lot more than if we canceled it."

"There are strong feelings, perhaps particularly here in New Jersey, about giving in to threats. After 9/11 people don't want their actions and decisions dictated by people who don't agree with them. Personally, I think security is well in hand for your show, and it would be a shame to cancel it now."

"There is one other point, too," Carole added. "If anyone should attempt to disrupt the show, we will have Mr. Stivali's staff available, plus the local police, to intercept any actions. If we cancel the show, who knows what this person may want us to do next? We'd be giving in to blackmail. Especially as we don't know why they're upset about support for OWOC."

Thompson nodded. "That makes sense to me. If we knew more, maybe our decision would be different. But these notes and telephone calls may just be from some kid who's just trying to make trouble. They could even," he said, looking at Carole, "be from one of the young people we've placed for adoption. We all know sometimes adolescent adoptees have strong reactions against their adoptive parents and even against the agencies that placed them." He paused. "We'd all feel safer, certainly, if the police had found whoever shot Holly Sloane and murdered her son. But from what's been said here, that very sad and tragic situation may have no relation to the show this weekend." He stood up. "I suggest we go ahead with the show. Does anyone disagree?"

The other board members, none of whom had said a word, shook their heads. Maggie wondered if all OWOC board decisions were made so simply.

"Then it's decided. We will not cancel the benefit antiques show. Professor Summer, I'll see you at the show Saturday." Thompson pushed his chair in and left the room.

The show was on.

Chapter 28

—◦—

The Same Old Christmas Story Over Again. *Wood engraving by Thomas Nast (1840–1902), the nineteenth-century political cartoonist and creator of the image of Santa Claus as we know him today.* Harper's Weekly *centerfold, January 1872. The heads and shoulders of two sleeping children are surrounded by dozens of characters from their dreams: Santa Claus and his reindeer, Little Red Riding Hood, the cow jumping over the moon, a witch on a broomstick, Ali Baba, Robinson Crusoe, Little Boy Blue, and many more. Delicately and memorably drawn. This copy has been hand colored lightly. 16 x 22 inches. Price: $365.*

Wednesday night was "full up with weather," as Maggie remembered a Maine meteorologist saying when she'd been Down East last summer. The wind howled, and the rain poured. At least the thunder and lightning seemed to have stopped.

Per police instructions, and on the possibility that Will would appear, Maggie left all her outside lights on. By ten she'd refrigerated her now defrosted filet and made an executive decision not to pack her van with the portfolios and racks she'd piled near the study doors. She was only sharing a booth at this show,

ɔ she wasn't taking as many prints as usual, and there was no
way she'd take her inventory, even protected by portfolios, out
in bad weather. Maybe Ben or Will could help her pack the van
tomorrow.

Winslow sat on a kitchen windowsill staring out at the sod-
den yard illuminated by the high lights Maggie'd installed late
last fall. Occasionally he reached out a paw in hopes of catching
one of the raindrops dripping down the outside of the glass.

Maggie left him in charge of the kitchen and headed for bed,
but slept little. Wind and rain banged on the roof and window-
panes. Twice she got up to make sure all the windows and doors
were locked. Dreams of bodies and bombs and fires and children kept her alert to the slightest noise in the house. At some
point Winslow joined her. When he jumped off the foot of her
bed at about three thirty, the movement startled her out of her
few moments of deep sleep.

She got up and checked her yard and the street in front of her
house. Will's RV hadn't arrived. He'd probably stopped for
some sleep along the way. It was safer that way.

For him, anyway.

Back under the covers, she listened to the rain. Usually she felt
cozy and safe and peaceful when she was inside on a rainy day.
Now the dank air was suffocating and the heavy rains threatening. Maggie thumped her pillow and turned over. She had a hard
day ahead of her, physically and emotionally. She needed sleep.
She refused to be intimidated.

At six she woke again. The rain had stopped, and May sun
was already drying the puddles and wet trees and lawns left by
last night's storm. Will's silent RV was parked in front of her
house.

Maggie felt herself relaxing. She took a fast shower, put on
enough makeup so she didn't look as though she'd had almost
no sleep, and headed for the kitchen. Winslow endorsed Will's
order of sausage and eggs. He watched as Maggie began heating
the sausages and warming the mushrooms and onions she'd

sautéed last night. They had been planned for the filet, bu
would be just fine added to scrambled eggs this morning.

She set the table and made coffee. After Maggie admitted she
had somehow missed out on Coffeemaking 101, Will had given
her a coffeepot for Valentine's Day. Along with a dozen long-
stemmed red roses. Michael had been a tea drinker and Maggie's
usual breakfast drink was Diet Pepsi with ice. She carefully
measured out the coffee she'd stored in her freezer since Will's
last visit. When he knocked on the door at seven thirty the table
was set, juice poured, and the smells of sausage and coffee filled
the kitchen.

"I'm so glad you're here," Maggie said, once they'd untan-
gled themselves and were just standing holding hands.

"Glad to be of service. As I remember, today is the day we get to
watch other people put the floor down, and then do a lot of bending and measuring and duct-taping to mark out booth locations."

"On target," said Maggie. "You do read my e-mail messages!"

"I treasure every one, my dear. Almost as much as I'll treasure
that breakfast. It smells fantastic in here."

"We have forty-five minutes to enjoy it all before we have to
head for the college." Maggie served the eggs and vegetables
and put a platter of sausages between them on the table.

"Where are Gussie and Ben, by the way? I expected to see
Gussie's van in your driveway."

"They hit bad traffic coming off the Cape yesterday, and
Gussie was too tired to drive the whole way. They stayed in a
motel near Hartford and should be here this morning."

"Sorry we both let you down last night. Shows are getting
harder and harder for Gussie to do, aren't they?"

Maggie nodded as she sat down and picked up her fork. "I'm
afraid so. The growing exhaustion is part of the postpolio syndrome. She's canceled out of a lot of shows, but she wanted to
come for this one."

"Of course. Because you were running it!"

"She's doing the Rensselaer show with us at the end of the month, too. I think after that she'll be home for the summer. Summer visitors to Cape Cod should keep the cash register in her shop ringing."

"I'd guess buying is becoming an issue, too. She won't be able to get to as many other shops and flea markets and auctions and such." Will chewed thoughtfully.

"She still does some, and her sister is doing a little buying for her. She's been in business long enough so sometimes people bring things they're interested in selling to her shop."

"Thank goodness she has Ben."

Maggie nodded. "And Jim. He doesn't know much about antique dolls and toys, but he's stuck with her even when she's had bad days. That must be an enormous emotional help."

"Knowing you're here is an enormous emotional help to me, too," said Will. "But there are moments when being closer would help considerably with the physical aspects of our relationship."

Maggie chewed her sausage and smiled. "At least Gussie and Jim don't have that issue. They live within a few miles of each other."

"So, before we go out into the wilderness of New Jersey, give me an update on terrorism and adoption."

Maggie took a deep breath, prepared to tell all. She was interrupted by the telephone.

"Maggie Summer? This is Jim Hunter. I called you yesterday and left a message, but you didn't return my call."

Maggie sat down, telephone in hand. "I remember. I'm sorry. I've been really busy." Who was this man?

"I thought you might have tried to call when I was out, so I decided to try again."

Maggie didn't say anything. Then she remembered. "You're the one who wanted to know something about one of my students! Has someone applied for a job with you?"

"Ah . . . no. Actually I called to tell *you* something about one of your students."

"Mr. Hunter, we're between semesters just now."

"I know, but he told me he'd be working for you on a special project this week."

Special project? The antiques show. "Who is the student?"

"Abdullah Jaleel."

Maggie relaxed. "He was one of my best students this past semester. And he's volunteered to help out at an antiques show that's being held at the college this weekend."

"He told me he'd be there for several days."

"He was at our meeting for volunteers on Wednesday. As I remember, he volunteered to be a porter Friday night, and then help with any errands or cleanups that were needed during the show, and be a porter again after the show closes Sunday night." Maggie paused. She still didn't know who this man was. "Are you a relative?"

"No, no. I've been working with Abdullah on a committee raising funds to establish a memorial for New Jersey residents killed in the World Trade Center disaster."

"He mentioned he was on that committee." Or, rather, I mentioned I'd seen him on television, Maggie remembered. So many people in New Jersey had lost loved ones and neighbors on 9/11. "I'm sorry, was someone you knew . . . ?"

"My wife. She was on the ninety-seventh floor of the South Tower. She worked with Abdullah's brother."

"I'm so very sorry." Maggie paused. What could she say that meant anything to someone who had lost so much? "I saw a television broadcast about the memorial and mentioned it to Abdullah. He said his brother had been in the Trade Center. That's the first time he'd mentioned it."

"That's what I thought. He's alone now, since his mother died, and his father lives in Saudi Arabia. He doesn't talk to many people. I think he just holds it all in."

"Was his mother in the World Trade Center, too?"

"No. It's complicated, and I don't know all the details. But she killed herself about a year after 9/11. It's been a rough couple of years for Abdullah."

"And you called me because . . . ?"

"He's mentioned you several times, Professor Summer. He respects you. I think he's very lonely and feels isolated. Being Muslim after 9/11 wasn't easy. And at the same time he had to deal with his brother's death, at Muslim hands. I've been worried that he keeps too much to himself; he thinks too much. So when I saw him at the meeting and he mentioned he was going to work on your benefit, I was very pleased. It's the first time he's mentioned doing something other than studying."

"I was pleased, too, Mr. Hunter. Abdullah seems to be a fine young man. I hadn't realized he was coping with so much tragedy in his personal life."

"He doesn't tell people. But now someone at the college will know, so if he should say something a little emotional at some time, you would understand."

Maggie frowned. Why was this man calling her? If Abdullah had wanted her to know about his life, he would have told her himself. "Mr. Hunter, I feel awkward that you've told me all this. How should I react to him?"

"Just as you've always treated him. Like any other student. I didn't mean to confuse any issues. But I did think that if anyone mentioned 9/11, or terrorism, or Muslims, that Abdullah might react in a way you wouldn't understand if you didn't know his background. Maybe I was wrong to call; I know you're just his teacher. But he speaks of so few people. He's a lonely young man, Professor Summer. Although I think he may have made a few friends recently, which is a good sign."

"He's lucky to have you to care about him. Thank you for telling me."

Maggie put down the telephone.

Will had gone into the bathroom while she'd been on the telephone. The house seemed quieter than usual with him gone.

That had been a strange call. She knew a lot about some of

her students because they'd chosen to share their problems or goals or family challenges with her. Most students came to class, handed in papers and tests, and smiled at her in the corridors. She knew little more about them than their names, and sometimes she wasn't as good as she should be at remembering those.

Abdullah was a special young man. She'd seen that from the start.

But to lose a brother and a mother within such a short time. No wonder Mr. Hunter thought he was lonely and isolated. And it couldn't be easy for someone who had ties to the Arab world to live in the United States post-9/11.

Maybe now that she knew about his background, she could get Abdullah to open up, to talk a little and make some more friends.

She was so lucky not to have been directly affected by 9/11. The least she could do was reach out to someone who had been. These were terrible times in the world, and they touched some people closer than others.

Life was not fair. But maybe she could help to even the ground a little for someone for whom life had been rocky.

Will was back. He reached down and kissed the top of her head. "Anything important?"

"Nothing critical," said Maggie. "Just sad. Someone called to tell me one of my students lost his brother in the Trade Center, and then his mother committed suicide, and he's been very lonely."

"And no doubt depressed! What a hell of a past couple of years that kid's had."

"Agreed. And to top it off, he's Muslim, and I suspect may have had to cope with some discrimination issues. In any case, you'll get to meet him. His name is Abdullah, and he's one of the students who volunteered to help with the show."

Will nodded. "Okay. And we need to get over there. I assume you've set up a way Gussie and Ben can get in if we're not here?"

"A neighbor knows about them and will give Ben a key."

"Then why don't you show me this wonderful gymnasium where we'll be spending the next few days?"

Chapter 29

All Aboard! *1894 lithograph by Elizabeth S. Tucker. English. Boy and girl (girl holding doll; boy cracking whip) seated on stool and chair in line, imagining they are in a carriage, and the empty chair in front of them is the trusty steed pulling them. 8 x 10.5 inches. Price: $50.*

They took Maggie's van to the college. On the way, Maggie filled Will in on the challenges of the past couple of days, from the threatening letters and telephone call to Jackson's death to the Our World Our Children board meeting the night before.

With each new revelation Will looked distinctly less happy. "So today we'll be setting up the first antiques show I've ever done that requires police backup and twenty-four/seven security coverage not because there will be valuable antiques there, but because some crazy who doesn't like adoption, or something else he hasn't chosen to share with anyone else, is threatening to make major trouble. And, by the way, two people connected with this adoption agency just happened to have been shot in the past few days, one of them killed."

"Basically, yes," said Maggie. "But I think it's all under control. You'll see."

"If I'd been here yesterday and had a voice at the meeting last night, my vote would have been to get out of town fast. These adoption agency people are crazy for walking into a possibly dangerous situation."

"Remember, Will, I'm one of those crazy people. It's like after 9/11. We couldn't stop living or organizing our lives around fears of 'what might happen' then. We didn't stop visiting New York, or flying anywhere we needed to go, right?"

The more he thought, the more Will's face reddened above his gray beard. He was just managing to control his anger. "But those terrorists had the whole world to choose from. Or at least the entire United States. So the odds were basically in our favor that nothing disastrous would happen in the spot we happened to be on any one particular day. But this idiot who's been making threats has already told you the place and time not to be. And you're making sure that not only will you be there, but hundreds of other people will be, too!"

"Let's just hope you're right, and hundreds of people do come to the show," said Maggie optimistically as she pulled into the parking lot next to the gym. A police car was already parked there.

"Good morning, Maggie," said Al, as they walked into the gym.

"Morning, Al. This is Will Brewer. He's an antiques dealer from Buffalo who'll be helping me out during the next few days."

Al gave them both an appraising glance as he shook Will's hand. "And a close friend I'd wager, too."

"I certainly hope so." Will smiled, trying to follow Maggie's example and be positive. "And you're the college security expert who's moving into these wonderful accommodations for the duration?"

"That's me," agreed Al, appearing remarkably relaxed, while Will looked around as though envisioning a sniper in every corner. "Maggie, I just finished a walk-through. I can guarantee there's nothing, and no one, anywhere in this building that we don't know about. Two local patrolmen were with me for most of the tour, and they're also convinced everything looks fine. Right now they're checking the outside of the building. If all looks okay they'll just be back for the parking-lot drive-throughs today."

"Sounds good to me," said Maggie.

"And I think we finished just in time," Al added as he pointed outside. A large truck marked RENTALS FOR EVERY NEED had pulled up to the loading dock. "Your flooring guys are here."

Within the next half hour they were joined by Claudia ("So *this* is Will! Will and I are going to be great friends") and by Mike Colletto, the tennis coach. ("Well, so far that flooring doesn't seem to have ruined anything.") Eric Sloane was there, too, although he kept pretty much to himself after assuring Maggie he'd help with anything necessary. She introduced him to the crew from the rental company, and he found coffee and doughnuts for them.

"I read something new last night," Claudia added, as Maggie popped the top on her third Diet Pepsi of the morning. "Esophageal cancer. People get it more often if they drink carbonated beverages."

"Not just diet sodas?" asked Maggie, taking another gulp.

"Any soda. Women who drink colas are more apt to have osteoporosis, too, you know. I'm sticking to water and fruit juices from now on."

"That's very virtuous, and I appreciate the information, Claudia, but right now I need all the caffeine I can get. And if I weren't so addicted to the flavor of the diet version, I'd be downing the stuff with sugar, just to keep me going." Maggie smiled.

"You don't have to worry about lunch," Claudia continued. "Yesterday I called Peking Duck and ordered Chinese food for all of us. They're delivering at noon. Here. With green tea. Green tea is excellent. Antioxidants and lots of other good stuff."

"Claudia, you're brilliant."

"I thought you'd like it." Claudia nodded. "And you like green tea."

"Better than black tea, anyway. I will be happy to drink green tea for lunch. Just for you."

"Not for me, for your own sake, Maggie. You have to internalize the need to take care of your own body." Claudia looked grave.

"Whose body is she taking care of?" said Will, coming up to where the women were standing. He'd been helping Eric and Mike move some equipment off the floor and into a closet, and had taken off his shirt. His gray beard was dripping a bit, but he looked good. Damn good.

"Her own body, Will," Claudia enunciated.

Will grinned and his eyes twinkled as they looked up and down at Maggie approvingly. "I approve of that. Maggie, maybe you should go back and see if Gussie and Ben are at your place. It's after ten thirty."

"You're right. Everything here seems under control." Maggie headed for the door. "And, Claudia, I'll be back in plenty of time for the Chinese food!"

Ben was bringing suitcases in when Maggie got home. She hugged Gussie. "I'm so glad you're here. But you look weary," Maggie pronounced.

"I cannot tell a lie. I am tired," said Gussie. "And also glad to be here. I see Will is here, too. You can't miss his enormous RV in the street."

"He got in about five this morning. He's over at the gym now."

"Do you need us there?" asked Gussie.

"Not really. Right now the vendor is just putting down the lining and indoor/outdoor carpeting to protect the gym floor. After they finish, Will and I are going to start measuring out the booths."

"Not something I could help with. I did notice you hadn't had a chance to pack your things for the show." She pointed at the pile of portfolios and racks next to the ramp door in Maggie's study.

"You're right. I got involved in other things. It's complicated, but I'll tell you later. And then yesterday afternoon and evening it poured, and I didn't want to get anything wet."

"We have some space left in my van. Why don't I have Ben pack your stuff in with mine this afternoon? Then we can just unload from one vehicle tomorrow."

"That would be a big help," agreed Maggie. "I hadn't even thought of putting everything in one van. But since we're sharing a booth, it all has to be unloaded to one place anyway."

"That's what I thought. I also guessed you'd want to set up your things before the other dealers get there tomorrow."

"I'd like to do that. Depending on how fast we can get the booths marked out and the electricians can put down the wires. They won't even start until later today. We're hoping the first gym will be ready for measuring and marking this afternoon. The tables will arrive tomorrow morning."

"And chaos will reign from that point on," agreed Gussie. "Why don't Ben and I just stay here for the afternoon. If you decide you need him, or me, just call here. I'll pick up your phone and I can drive over. But don't worry about us."

"Actually, if you don't mind cooking your own lunch or dinner, I defrosted some filets yesterday thinking everyone would be here. Then I ended up going out for dinner. The meat is in the refrigerator and should be eaten. And there's French bread in the freezer."

"Then we'll be more than fine! You go on back to the show, and we'll rest here this afternoon, and Ben will pack your prints and racks. Then tomorrow we'll both be prepared to be at the show all day. Or however long you need us."

Maggie gave Gussie a hug. "I'm so glad you're here! Just make yourself at home. I won't worry at all. Will and I will be back sometime this evening, probably around nine or so, depending on how fast the measuring goes."

"You and Will are a good team. I'm sure it will go well."

All the players scheduled to be present were in Somerset County. Neither Al nor the police had found anything out of place. The sun was shining. Maybe the show would go on as Maggie hoped. Without any problems.

She crossed her fingers and headed back to the gym.

Chapter 30

———⌇———

The Lady in Black. *1860 Winslow Homer (1836–1910) wood engraving of a young woman in heavy mourning, walking with her small daughter. The daughter is carrying a market basket, having left her books on a stoop. Perhaps she is leaving school to help her mother. Illustration for a* Harper's Weekly *story. 3.5 x 4.5 inches. Price: $90.*

The Chinese food (and the green tea) were excellent, and the men from the rental company were experienced in covering floors. Not even Mike had any complaints, although he did check the corners of the flooring a few times. Somehow the need for miles of duct tape had escaped Maggie's mind, so Will borrowed her van and came back with a carton full. The measuring and marking went faster than Maggie had hoped; Claudia and Eric had paired up and seemed to have no problems following Maggie's floor plans. By three o'clock the flooring people had left and the booth dimensions were laid out in one of the two gyms. George Healy's electricians had arrived and were already installing heavy-duty wires and outlets for the booths.

Maggie felt torn. After the electricians arrived, someone

needed to be with them, and that slowed down the measuring that had been going so well in the second gym.

Al stopped in often to bring coffee and moral support. And Diet Pepsi, when Claudia wasn't looking.

"If we can do the second gym as quickly as the first," Will said, standing up and stretching, "then we can begin to think of a dinner a little more formal than the two remaining Dunkin' Donuts Al has dangerously supplied."

"Hmm . . . and maybe even a glass of wine," said Maggie. "After moo shu pork and jelly doughnuts, right now I don't even want to think about food." Her back muscles were tight. Bending and stretching were not movements she did every day.

Things she ought to do this summer:

Buy prints.

Mat prints.

Do shows.

Make money.

Visit Gussie and Will.

Have fun!

Exercise.

Claudia would have added, "Stop drinking Diet Pepsi!" The head of her division at Somerset County College would have added, "Develop new course for American Studies curriculum!" Will would have added . . .

This was her list. No one else's.

"What we need is one more body," said Will. "You or I should be with the electricians to make sure they understand your notes. They're great guys, but I don't think they have the concept of separate booths down quite yet."

"The last time I was in that gym," Maggie agreed, "they'd put all the outlets for three booths in one location. The dealers will be covering all of the outlets with tables and furniture, and most of them won't be bringing cords long enough to get their power from three booths away."

"Not to mention what the dealer who has that booth will

think if people keep coming in to thread cords through his area."

The room was quiet, so when newcomers arrived they were easy to locate. Maggie looked down the gym to where Eric and Claudia were measuring booths. They'd been joined by two more people.

"I think our solution may have just walked through the door," said Maggie. "I'll be right back."

She headed for the four in the corner. "Abdullah," she said, greeting the young men. "And, Hal! You're not due here until tomorrow afternoon."

"I know," Abdullah admitted. "But I had nothing much to do, and I was driving downtown, saw Hal, and stopped to give him a lift. We decided to check and see if we could help with anything today."

"We would love some help!" said Maggie. "Do you both know Claudia Hall and Eric Sloane?"

Abdullah nodded; Hal shook his head. "Hal, this is Eric Sloane and Claudia Hall. And we could definitely use your help."

Carole had said Hal didn't have many friends, and Hunter had said the same about Abdullah. It would be great if they'd found each other. And they had a lot in common: they'd both lost family members recently.

She focused on the tasks at hand.

"We're measuring out the dimensions of the booths. The dealers have paid to rent booths of different sizes, so they can best display their particular antiques. Right now we're marking the corners of the booths. After we finish, the electricians are putting power where it's needed, and tomorrow we'll be moving tables into the booths."

"So what can we do to help?"

"Come with me." Maggie led them toward where Will was standing, several booths away. "Will, this is Abdullah, one of my students, and Hal, who lives with Carole Drummond's family. They've volunteered to help us."

"How do you do?" Abdullah said politely as Will put out his hand.

Hal nodded.

"Will Brewer is an antiques dealer from Buffalo and a friend of mine. Will, since you understand my scribbling, would you mind taking the charts and going to keep an eye on what the electricians are doing in the other gym? I'll explain what we're doing in here and let Abdullah and Hal take over measuring the booths. That will leave me free to keep an eye on the overall setup." And get me up off the floor, Maggie thought to herself. Her knees and back were still cramped. Age!

"We'd be happy to measure the booths," said Abdullah. "Just show us what needs to be done."

"An excellent plan," Will said. "Maggie, would you come with me for a moment to make sure I understand what you want?" He turned back to Abdullah. "I'll have her back in a second."

They walked toward the other gym. "Is that the kid you told me lost someone in the World Trade Center?"

"His brother. Yes. The man who called this morning said he seemed lonely. I was surprised when he came in with Hal. They're both scheduled to help tomorrow."

"And who's Hal?"

"Hal Hanson. He was adopted when he was about ten, and his parents died in a horrible home fire last winter. He's staying with Carole Drummond, the head of OWOC, until he's ready to live on his own."

"Two young men who've had a lot of loss in their lives," said Will. "Well, whoever they are, I'm glad they're on board." Will gave Maggie a quick hug. "You look exhausted, and I drove most of the past forty-eight hours. The more help we get and the sooner we can finish up, the better."

"Especially since we'll have more to do tomorrow," agreed Maggie. "Plus setting up our own booths. At most shows that's exhausting enough." She handed him the clipboard she'd left for the electricians to use as reference. "If you have any questions about my notes, just holler."

Maggie headed back to the gym where Abdullah was already down on his hands and knees while Hal looked carefully at the chart of booth locations Maggie and Will had been using.

"Am I reading this correctly? This booth is ten feet deep, and sixteen feet long. And we're marking the corners of the spaces with duct tape." Hal smiled shyly. It was the first time Maggie had remembered seeing him smile.

"You've got it," said Maggie. The rest of the afternoon was going to go much better than she'd imagined.

The young men spent the next two hours crawling on their hands and knees, stopping to measure, then to cut and tear off lengths of duct tape. Maggie walked in and out of the two gyms, consulting when someone had trouble reading her charts, and improvising when her notes didn't make perfect sense. The time went quickly.

"Everything okay?" called Al from the door to the lobby.

She looked at her watch. It was after five, and Al was still here. "This isn't the night you have to stay, Al!" She walked over to him, shaking her head.

"Oh, I decided I'd just order some pizza and stay tonight, too."

"You think someone might try to break in now?"

"I'm not sure what I'm worried about, Maggie. Everything looks good so far. You're ahead of schedule, aren't you?"

She nodded. "We've almost finished measuring the second gym. Two extra helpers stopped in, and they've been a great help."

"The young Middle Eastern–looking man and the blond?"

"Abdullah and Hal. Bright young men. I just learned this week Abdullah lost a brother in 9/11. He's volunteered to help out with the whole show. And so has Hal. He was adopted through OWOC."

"Was Abdullah adopted, too?"

Maggie looked at him. "I don't know. Why?"

"To volunteer so much of his own time, these young people must really believe in adoption." Al frowned a bit. "I've met Abdullah before, I think. Wasn't he the one who dropped out of school after 9/11, when someone spray painted 'Muslim Killers' on his home? His mother came here to the college to complain. She was sure one of our students was responsible. But she didn't know who. She said the local police weren't doing anything about it."

"How awful! I knew there were incidents against Muslims after 9/11, but I didn't know there were any here."

"They kept it pretty quiet. I asked around, but couldn't come up with anything. I remember the mother though. A pretty blonde lady who was having a rough time. One son murdered by terrorists, and then the other son accused of terrorism."

"I can imagine." Maggie hesitated. "I heard Abdullah's mother killed herself."

"I didn't know that!" Al looked past Maggie into the gym where Abdullah was taping the inside corner of one of the booths. "Poor kid. He has had a rough time. I'm glad he's back in school."

"I'm glad he decided to come and help us; maybe he'll make new friends." Maggie turned toward the other gym, then turned back.

"Al, did you say Abdullah's mother was blonde?"

"Yup. Lots of curls, too."

"Then she wasn't Saudi?"

"No, I don't think so. I asked about her husband, and she sort of fudged around. I don't think she was married. But she did say the father of her sons was Saudi. They'd met in college. She didn't mention working, and she stopped in during the day. I sort of assumed the guy in Saudi Arabia was supporting them."

Maggie nodded. "That's interesting." She checked her watch. "I've got to see how Will is doing. The electricians should be leaving about now."

As if on cue, Will came out into the lobby. "I thought I heard my lady out here. The electricians are cleaning up for the day. That gym is wired, Maggie."

"Great! They'll just have the second gym to do in the morning, and we've almost finished the taping."

"Claudia ordered all that Chinese food for lunch. If you'll let me contribute, why don't I order pizza for all of us for dinner," said Al. "You two, and me, and Claudia and the three young men. We're all tired and I suspect the young people could use some sustenance."

Will and Maggie looked at each other. Earlier they'd thought of something a bit more special. But now they were both exhausted. And Gussie and Ben had the steak to eat at home.

Maggie voiced Will's thoughts, too. "Maybe pizza would be good for all of us. That's kind of you, Al."

"I'm not that altruistic," said Al. "I'm starving, too. I'll go ahead and order several pizzas with different toppings. The pizzeria should be able to deliver within half an hour or so."

"Why don't you walk through the gym I've been working in to make sure everything is the way you want it, Maggie," Will said. "I'll go and deliver the good news that pizza is on its way and see how the rest of the crew is doing."

Maggie walked through the first gym quickly. All was in order: booth boundaries marked on the floor, and electrical power outlets in the booths that had paid extra for it. So far, so good; they'd finish marking off the booths in the second gym, and then everyone could go home and get a good night's rest.

Except for Al, who was sleeping here.

Right now it looked as though all the planning was paying off.

The setup was on target. Nothing unexpected had happened. The police were no doubt right: threats were nothing unless actions followed them.

By the time she got back to the lobby she felt much more relaxed. It seemed everyone else did, too. The pizza was on its way, and Eric and Will were sitting on the floor and chatting quietly, while Claudia was walking through the gym, picking up pieces of tape and paper that had fallen on the floor. Abdullah just stood, stretching a bit, watching the others. Hal was checking his watch. Maybe he had to be back at Carole's at a certain time.

"Your help has made the work go so much faster this afternoon," said Maggie. "Hal, I saw you looking at your watch. If you need to go somewhere, please, go ahead. Although we'd love for you to stay and have pizza. And help us finish this room!" She touched Hal's arm lightly.

"I'm happy to help out. I don't have any other plans for right now."

Maggie nodded. "Great! And, Abdullah, I've been meaning to ask you . . . I'm grateful, but why did you volunteer to help with this antiques show? Most students don't want to spend their vacation time on campus!"

"Adoption is a good thing," Abdullah said.

"A lot of people think so," Maggie said carefully, thinking of the threatening letters and telephone call. "Especially when they're involved with adoption in some way. Like Eric, over there with Will. He's adopted, you know. And Hal, you were adopted."

"Yes."

"And I'm thinking about adopting a child."

Abdullah looked at her. "I wondered if you were. Why else would someone do so much work for an adoption organization?"

"Maybe because, even if I decide not to adopt, I'm impressed by everything OWOC does. They help children all over the world come home to families who want them. That's a wonderful purpose for an organization."

"Children who don't have families can be in difficult situations. Or they can be well cared for by institutions," said Abdullah.

"Organizations and institutions may be well meaning, but

they can't always give the individual attention and love that children need and deserve."

"But to do that families must understand the individual needs of the children," added Hal.

"Exactly!" Maggie nodded. "If you don't mind my asking— were you adopted, Abdullah?"

"No!" His voice was louder than necessary. "Do I look as though I were adopted?"

"You can't tell someone is adopted by looking at them," said Maggie. "I just wondered whether you had ties to adoption, since you were taking so much time to help us." Abdullah looked uncomfortable, and Maggie felt bad for pressing the issue just to satisfy her own curiosity.

"Pizza's here!" called Al from the door of the gym.

They sat on the lobby floor and focused on who wanted plain slices, and who wanted mushrooms and onions. Important issues. Issues that could be resolved.

Al's phone rang once.

He walked away as he answered it.

When he got back, he said quietly to Maggie, who had just finished her second slice of fully loaded vegetarian pizza, "That was the police. They wondered how long everyone would be here tonight. They're keeping track of cars in the parking lot."

Maggie hesitated. "Have they seen anything suspicious?"

"No, not at all," Al said. "They'd just thought we'd all be home by now. I told them I was staying the night, and which car was mine. The rest of you were finishing up and I thought you'd be gone by seven thirty or so."

Maggie nodded. "I hope so. Everything's gone better than I thought it might today. And we all need some rest before tomorrow. The gymnasium should be quiet for the night."

"I'm hoping so." Al smiled. "Now I've had dinner, and there's candy in a machine for dessert, and no competition for the showers. I even brought in a portable TV. So I'll be set. I figure every couple of hours I'll do a walk-through, unless I hear something in the meantime. The police know I'll be here, so they won't worry about a light or two. And they'll drive around the parking lot a few times during the night. None of us expect any problems. Tomorrow is the real test."

"I don't even want to think about it," said Maggie. "This has been such a lovely, peaceful, productive day."

At that moment the gym shook. A loud explosion erupted close by. Claudia screamed; Maggie froze. Al dialed his cell phone as he ran to the window overlooking the parking lot.

"We need fire and police help outside the Whitcomb Gymnasium at Somerset College. Stat. A car in the parking lot's just exploded, and it's burning." He hesitated. "No, thank goodness. No injuries."

Chapter 31

—⁓—

Godey's Fashions for December 1872. *A double-fold, hand-colored engraving from* Godey's Magazine, *illustrating the latest fashions from Paris for American women. (It also often included patterns for trimmings and embroideries.) This unusual print features a bride, in the center of the page, being handed a black mantilla by a sad-looking woman in an elegantly embroidered dress. A woman and a young boy wearing purple, the light color of mourning, are to the side. Has the bride just learned of the death of someone close to her? The question is raised, but left unanswered. 8.75 x 11 inches. Price: $65.*

Al immediately turned to the six people who were still eating pizza in the lobby of the gym. They could all see what had happened through the large glass window overlooking the parking lot.

"No!" Maggie whispered, her hand over her mouth. Will put his arm around her and tried to turn her away from the view, but she refused to move. Abdullah sank down to his knees, covering his head.

How awful. He must be reliving the explosions at the World Trade Center. Eric, who had also lost a brother, knelt down and put his arm on Abdullah's shoulder. Hal just stared, in shock or fascination.

"What the hell happened?" asked Claudia, running toward the glass window. "Maggie's van just blew up!"

"That's exactly what happened," said Al. "I've called 911. Everyone, get back as far as you can from the window. If there are any other explosions the glass could shatter."

They all moved back, but everyone kept watching in fascination. Parts of Maggie's blue van were all over the parking lot. What was left of it was burning in a blaze of fiery gasoline as high as the gym. The van was gone.

The next question was, would it take anything else with it?

Thank goodness the gym is made of steel and concrete, Maggie thought. Her van was in the center of the parking lot, about fifteen spaces from the building. Three other cars were in the lot. They must be Al's, Claudia's, and either Abdullah's or Eric's.

The one closest to the fire was a small red sedan.

"How the hell could this have happened?" said Claudia. "And how fast will that fire department get here?" Her usually animated face was pale, her wavy hair flying in all directions. She pointed toward the parking lot. "The red car near Maggie's. That's mine."

Its body was already scarred by flying fragments.

"Was there anything in your van that would fuel the fire, Maggie?" asked Al.

"Nothing except the gas in the gas tank," she said. "I hadn't packed my van for the antiques show yet."

Will's arm tightened around her shoulders. She had lost her van. It had been part of her life for ten years, and she would miss it. And not relish having to buy another. Tears of grief and anger filled her eyes. But at least she hadn't also lost thousands of dollars worth of prints. And she was still alive. Maggie started to shake when she realized that in another forty-five minutes or so she and Will would have been in the van.

As they watched the pyre, two fire engines and three police cars converged on the parking lot.

"Maggie," said Al. "Can I see you for a moment?"

Chapter 32

—◦—

Untitled. Three women crudely whittled out of wooden pegs; each has a painted face and black hair and a colored peg "body." Each ends in a rough squared-off peg apparently for display in some sort of stand. From Czechoslovakian Folk Toys *by Roberta Samsour, folio printed in Prague, 1941. 8 x 10.5 inches. Price: $40.*

Will followed Maggie into the small room Maggie had used for her meeting with the facilities management staff only three days before. Al closed the door.

"I assume your friend knows what's happening?" Al said to Maggie.

She nodded. "Will knows what I know. I'm not sure that covers what's happening now."

"I don't want to alarm any of the younger people."

Maggie felt old. Claudia was thirty-two, but, indeed, under these conditions, in Al's mind she was as much a "young person" as Abdullah or Eric or Hal.

"I know you haven't been home all day, but you said you had a friend there."

Maggie nodded.

"If any threats or messages had been called to your home, then you would have heard about them."

"Gussie said she'd answer my phone. She didn't have a telephone number for the gym, but if something were critical, she would have driven here." And thank goodness she hadn't, Maggie thought.

"And I'm assuming if the agency had heard anything, they would have found you."

"Everyone on the OWOC staff knew I'd be here at the gym today."

"So let's assume there were no additional warnings. No additional threats."

Will put his hand over Maggie's. "You're ruling out the possibility this was some sort of automotive malfunction. You're assuming someone blew the van up intentionally."

Al nodded. "Absolutely. You can be thankful it wasn't set to explode when you turned the ignition on." He glanced at his watch. "It blew at about six o'clock. The van's been parked here all day, right? You got here about eight thirty."

"Yes. But I left from about ten thirty until eleven thirty."

"And I used the van about one o'clock to go and buy some duct tape," added Will. "So the van has only been parked there since about one thirty."

"Then whoever put something in it or on it or under it did it after one thirty." Al nodded. "Okay. I just wanted to make sure we all agreed on a time line before the police started asking questions."

There was a knock on the door. It was Abdullah. "Excuse me, but there's a cop out here who wants to see you, Professor Summer."

They all went out into the lobby. In the short time they'd been away from the window, the fire department had covered Maggie's van with foam. The fire was under control. At least Claudia's car hadn't been demolished, too, thought Maggie, trying to take solace in something.

"Hi, Al," said Detective Luciani. "And Professor Summer. And . . ."

"This is my friend Will Brewer, Detective. From Buffalo, New York. He's here for the antiques show."

"Will, do you think you could get the others away from the windows and see if you could all finish up taping the floor for the show?"

Will hesitated.

"Please? They don't need to hear and see everything now. The excitement is over. And it would really help if you could finish the floor." Maggie looked at him meaningfully. "I'm all right. Really."

"I'm not sure doing more to get this place ready for an antiques show is a good idea," said Will. "But all right. For now." He went over to where the others were silently standing, staring out at the parking lot, and headed them back into the gym. None of them wanted to go back to the work they'd been doing all afternoon.

"Remember when I told you chances were that threat you received was just talk?" said Detective Luciani.

Maggie nodded. "Right."

"Well, now we're beyond talk. Have you heard or seen any new threats today?"

Al and Maggie shook their heads. "So far as we know, there's been nothing," said Maggie. "Unless something was received at the agency."

"We've already been in touch with Mrs. Drummond. She hasn't heard anything new. And it was your van that was blown up, Maggie. That had to be intentional."

"Was it a bomb?" asked Al.

"Some sort of detonating device, I'd guess. We'll get the experts in to decide officially," said the detective. "Did either of you see anyone in the parking lot this afternoon?"

"The car was parked in that spot about one thirty," said Maggie. "Will did an errand and left it there."

"How long have you known Mr. Brewer?" asked Detective Luciani.

"About a year," said Maggie indignantly, "and there's no way he blew up my van! He's a close personal friend."

"He just got here today from Buffalo?"

"Early this morning. His RV is parked in front of my house right now. He's a dealer doing the show this weekend. He came early to help set up."

"And he was the last one you know was in your van."

"Yes." Maggie's voice was wavering. "But that doesn't mean he blew it up!"

"I didn't say he did. But we have to know who's been here."

"I haven't been watching the parking lot all afternoon, but I did look out whenever I walked around. I've been keeping an eye on doors and windows and such," said Al. "I didn't see anyone in the parking lot who isn't here now."

"Who, other than Mr. Brewer, are these people?"

"My secretary, Claudia Hall. She works here at the college in the American Studies department," said Maggie. "And Eric Sloane."

Luciani nodded. "I recognized him. He's the brother of the boy who was killed earlier this week. I'd think he'd be with his family now."

"It was his choice to volunteer to help out here. He also works here at the college. The antiques show is supporting the agency which placed him, and most of his brothers and sisters, in their family. He could have stayed home. I certainly would have understood. Maybe he wanted to get away from home for a few hours."

"And the other two men?"

"Abdullah Jaleel. He's a student here. He also volunteered to help out with the show. And Hal Hanson. He was adopted by a couple here in town ten years ago, but they were killed in a fire last winter. He's staying with Carole Drummond and her husband. All four of them have spent the whole afternoon in the gym, measuring out booths. They weren't wandering around the parking lot!"

"And whose cars are out there? Besides yours, Professor Summer."

"Mine is the blue Plymouth over in the far corner," said Al. "The red sedan belongs to Claudia."

"Glad we got here fast enough so that one didn't blow, too," said Luciani. "And how did the other three volunteers get here? There's only one other car out there. A gray Honda."

"Eric was here all morning. Someone must have driven him. Abdullah and Hal came together this afternoon."

"What time was that?"

"I don't remember exactly. After lunch," said Maggie. "They weren't scheduled to work until tomorrow, but came by in case we could use their help. And they've been indispensable. We wouldn't have gotten this far without them."

"I'll need to talk to all of them. Maybe they saw something neither of you noticed." Detective Luciani paused. "And the show is going to continue? Even after this?"

"The show will open Saturday morning," said Maggie grimly. "Somehow."

Chapter 33

—⁓—

The Bullhead (Ameiurus nebulosus). *Chromolithograph, 1901, by Sherman Foote Denton, American naturalist and illustrator, of a variety of catfish that lives in muddy ponds and streams, feeding on bottom plants and animals. Common in waters of Central and Eastern states. 8 x 11 inches. Price: $55.*

Eric Sloane's father had dropped him off at the gym in the morning. Abdullah offered him a ride home, and Eric gratefully accepted. They'd finished outlining the rest of the booths in record time, and everyone could hardly wait to get out of the gym.

The police still had to pin down the cause of the explosion in Maggie's van. It was staying at the gym, as was Al, who gamely declared, "All the excitement seems to have happened already, so I'll probably have a boring night."

Claudia offered to drop Maggie and Will off. When they got to the parking lot, she first walked around her car, touching it lightly where the finish had been dented or marred. "It was such a pretty red color," she said quietly.

"I'm so sorry, Claudia," said Maggie. She took a last look at what was left of her van. Yes, the van had been old. But she hadn't planned to replace it this year. Now she was going to have to buy another van. Soon. She'd need it for the show in New York State over Memorial Day.

But thank goodness she hadn't lost her inventory. Or her life.

They were all silent on their way to Maggie's house.

"Maggie, that Abdullah is really nice. But he doesn't seem like the other students," said Claudia, finding a topic of conversation that did not involve burning vans.

"No?"

"He told me he lives alone."

"His brother died in the World Trade Center, and I heard his mother killed herself after that."

"How horrible for him! Is his father dead, too?"

Maggie thought a moment. "I don't know. Someone said his father was in Saudi Arabia."

"Oh. Abdullah doesn't look like a terrorist."

Maggie grimaced. She was tired. "There are lots of Saudis who aren't terrorists. I'm sure neither Abdullah nor his father are. After all, his brother was killed on 9/11."

"That's right."

"And it can't be easy for Abdullah, with all the controversy over terrorism and Muslims and Saudis."

"No. But it's funny he lives alone and he's going to Somerset College."

"Claudia, I don't follow you."

"Well, didn't the families of the survivors get insurance money? And you said yourself, Maggie, that he was really bright. So why doesn't he go to a four-year college instead of a community one?"

"That's a good question, Claudia. Why don't you ask him yourself? Except I don't think you'd better mention anything about insurance money."

"Of course not, Maggie. I was just curious."

They were all silent for a few more minutes.

"Will there still be an antiques show this weekend?"

"Yes. If I have anything to say about it."

Claudia pulled up across the street from Maggie's house, and Will's RV. "Well, I guess I'll see you back at the gym tomorrow."

"If you don't feel comfortable coming back, that's fine. You need to get your car fixed."

"Maggie, if you're going to be there, I'm going to be there."

"See you tomorrow then!"

Gussie and Ben were waiting for them; Ben had turned on a small TV in the kitchen and was watching a baseball game. Gussie was sipping white wine.

"So, how was the day?" asked Gussie as Will poured wine for Maggie and himself. "You're here earlier than you thought, and I didn't even hear your van."

Maggie was exhausted, but the story had to be told.

"So someone blew up your van with a bomb, like in the movies?" asked Ben, who had decided Maggie's story was even more exciting than the Red Sox game.

"Just about like that," agreed Maggie.

"With lots of smoke and fire? And firemen?"

"Smoke and fire and, thank goodness, lots of firemen."

"I wish I could have seen it! It must have been cool! I've never seen anything blow up!"

"It wasn't really cool," said Maggie. "But I'd never seen anything like it before either."

"How are you going to go places now?"

"Tomorrow," Gussie said, "we are all going to go to the gym and set up the show. We'll take our van, and Will will drive his RV, since that's where all his antiques are. I'm sure between us we can fit Maggie in somewhere."

"It will be tight in our van," said Ben. "Especially since I put all of Maggie's prints and racks and bags of stuff in it this afternoon." He paused for a moment. "Do you think they'll blow up our van, too?"

"No!" said Maggie. "Nothing else will be blown up." Under the table, her fingers not intertwined with Will's were crossed.

"Thank goodness you hadn't loaded your van," said Gussie.

"I keep thinking that," agreed Maggie. "It's always been one of my nightmares that I'd be in an accident on the way to a show and not only total my van but lose my inventory."

"That's every antiques dealer's nightmare," agreed Gussie.

"But more important, you're all right," said Will, who had been holding Maggie's hand tightly since they'd left the campus.

"We're both all right," agreed Maggie. "And, like Scarlett O'Hara said, tomorrow is another day."

After Ben had gone to bed, and Will had gone to his RV to get a suitcase, Gussie asked the hardest question.

"Maggie, do you feel you can go ahead with this show? Whoever this person is, they may have shot two people, killed one of them, and now they've blown up your van. On the phone and in e-mail you made it sound as though someone was making idle threats. Right now none of the threats sound like idle ones."

"No. They don't," Maggie agreed. "I am getting scared, Gussie. When we heard that explosion, and I looked out the window and parts of my van were up in the air, my first reaction after 'Oh, shit!' was anger. Now I just feel tired and frustrated."

"And still angry."

"And still angry. I'm angry that I have to find the money and time to buy a van when I'm already behind on getting prints ready for the next show. I'm angry that we have a dear man you'll meet tomorrow sleeping in the gym for three nights just in case someone tries anything else crazy. I'm angry that I'm now on a first-name basis with most of the detectives in Somerset County. And I'm scared, because tomorrow dealers we've worked with for years and some of the new friends I've made at the adoption agency will all be there together. In the same place some idiot decided to blow up my van!"

"At least it was just a van."

"But, Gussie, what if there is a next time? And what if the next time it isn't just a van?"

Gussie was silent.

"I don't know what to do. I thought I was doing the right

thing by standing up to the threats. But if anyone else is hurt, then it will be my fault."

"You're not the only one in this, Maggie. The police know, and the school knows, and the agency knows. If anything happens, it won't be your fault."

"Yes, it will, Gussie. I've been the calm one, the one telling everyone there would be no problems. And now . . ." Maggie suddenly couldn't stop the tears. "They blew my van up! My own van, that I'd driven to all those shows, and classes, and . . . it was *my van*! They had no right to do that! I just want everything back the way it was a week ago. Before all of this started."

She put her head down on the table and sobbed.

Chapter 34

Independence Hall. Hand-colored steel engraving, ca. 1850, of the room in Independence Hall, Philadelphia, where the Declaration of Independence was signed. One man is telling visitors about the room, as elegantly dressed tourists admire the portraits on the walls and the tall windows draped in red velvet. 9 x 11.5 inches. Price: $65.

Friday morning wasn't bright, but at least it wasn't raining. Somehow a bright sunny day would have been too much like a joke, Maggie thought, as she broke eggs and shredded cheddar for a breakfast omelet and poured orange juice. She'd braided her hair, pinned it up, and put on jeans and a red Somerset County College T-shirt, prepared for a hard working day. Then added a blue cardigan to her outfit, in case they turned the air-conditioning on in the gym. All I need is a white scarf to be patriotic, she thought. Although somehow today she wasn't quite in the mood to wave flags.

Winslow said good morning, then retreated to his windowsill. An electric wheelchair and three extra people in his house were a bit disconcerting.

After a quiet breakfast they all headed for the Somerset College gym. Maggie rode with Gussie and Ben in Gussie's van, and Will followed them in his RV.

Kayla and Kendall were already there, ready to help with booth layouts and tables, and Eric had already cleaned up the first cup of coffee spilled on the rented carpet. Hal and Abdullah had teamed up again and were checking the duct tape they'd put down all too quickly the night before, reattaching the pieces that were coming away from the carpet.

Gussie volunteered to station herself in the main lobby with a list of everyone they expected, so she could direct traffic. And, as she quietly pointed out, monitor who was in the building and who wasn't. She could also see the parking lot from where she was sitting, in back of the large window.

When the rental truck arrived with the tables, the first two were put in an L-shape around her so Gussie would have plenty of space to spread out the cartons of papers Maggie had luckily left in her house yesterday, not in her van.

Will made sure the right number of tables was delivered and started Kendall and Kayla and Eric and Ben moving the correct configuration of six- and eight-foot tables to each booth without disturbing the electricians, who were back at work, this time wiring the second gym.

Claudia arrived at Maggie's side with a peace offering. "Last night I couldn't sleep. I was upset about my car, but I was really scared about your van blowing up. Then I realized this was a sign. It was a message telling us that maybe we just need to enjoy life when we can. You know? Maybe I've been too serious. So I brought you this. It's an early birthday present."

She handed Maggie a large carton, wrapped in pink and blue flowered paper and crowned by an enormous bow.

"It's not my birthday!" Maggie smiled self-consciously as people passed her and eyed the gift.

"I know. But it will be soon enough," said Claudia complacently. "So open it!"

Maggie put the carton on one of Gussie's tables, broke the

bbon, and pulled back the paper. It was a twenty-four-pack of Diet Pepsi cans. She burst into laughter.

"I didn't guess!" Maggie gave Claudia a big hug. "Does this mean it's okay for me to drink Diet Pepsi?"

"It means maybe there are things more important than doing everything just right. At least today," Claudia added, glancing at the spot in the parking lot where Maggie's van had been before it was towed early that morning.

"Does this mean if I get brain cancer or something else horrible, I can blame it on you?"

"As long as you know in your heart that you're the one responsible for your own life."

Maggie put her hand up. "Okay, Claudia! Peace. And thank you for the Diet Pepsi. That's definitely the best thing that has happened so far today." Maggie left the cans in Gussie's care, so they wouldn't disappear.

Claudia huddled with Gussie, going over all of Maggie's notes for the day. This was by far the busiest day of their schedule. Tables delivered. Check. Tables set up. In progress. Electricity installed. In progress. Claudia had made a pile of signs for the dealers' booths on her computer, and she assigned herself the job of checking each booth after the tables and electricity had been put there, making sure the right number and size of tables were in the right places, then leaving the booth sign, so each arriving dealer could easily identify his or her own space this afternoon.

Gussie alphabetized the pile of dealer name-tags that Claudia had also printed out, then sorted through the booth rental statements and put them with the tags. Dealers checking in could pick up their tag and pay their remaining balance before setting up.

"During the setups, all the doors to the gym have to be open," Maggie was explaining to Al.

He shook his head. "That concerns me, Maggie. The more doors we have open, the less we're able to keep an eye on who is coming in or out."

Detective Luciani interrupted them. "Everything okay here this morning?"

"Fine, Detective," Maggie answered. "I see you had my van towed. Do you know yet exactly what happened to it?"

"We've pulled in an expert to confirm our suspicions, but right now it looks pretty simple. Appears an alarm-clock explosive device was put under your gas tank. When it went off at six last night, it ignited the fuel in the van."

"I had less than half a tank of gas," said Maggie. "So if I'd filled the van before driving to the gym yesterday . . ."

"Then there would have been a bigger fire; probably that second car would have gone up as well."

Maggie said a silent "Thank you" to herself for rejecting the high gasoline prices at a station near the Parkside Library and deciding to look for gas at a local station later. And then forgetting to fill the tank.

"Detective, is there any progress on figuring out who set the explosives? Or who killed Jackson Sloane?"

He shook his head. "The device that set off the bomb was very simple. A teenager could have found instructions on the Internet. It didn't involve any complicated ingredients we could check out. And as for Jackson Sloane . . . frankly, we haven't got a lot to go on. His father's gun is still missing. We were able to confirm that the gun that shot Holly Sloane was the same one that killed Jackson."

"Did you find whoever Jackson was with after he left his home Saturday night?"

"Jackson walked out of his house and disappeared until those kids found his body. No one saw him. He didn't take any of the family cars or bicycles, so we're assuming either he walked or someone picked him up. It was after dark, and the houses where the Sloanes live aren't too close together. Someone would have to have looked out a window at just the right moment or been out themselves. We've talked with neighbors, but no one's come up with leads that go anyplace."

Al shook his head. "If you knew who'd done the shooting, I think you'd also find the person who set off that bomb yesterday."

"You may be right. But we can't assume that either. The only connection is the Our World Our Children agency, and they don't know anything. If someone were angry at the agency, you'd think they'd threaten it directly, not threaten families connected with it, or fund-raisers."

"Carole Drummond said she'd asked for more surveillance of the agency offices," said Maggie.

"And we're checking their offices regularly. But all the action seems to be away from the agency itself. Like here."

"That could change," said Al. "Someone could be trying to draw your efforts away from the agency."

"That's why we have extra guys keeping alert for the next couple of days. Especially Saturday and Sunday, when most of the agency people will be here. OWOC has hired private security people for the weekend, too."

Earlier that week Carole had said the offices held irreplaceable papers critical to bringing children to this country or to finalize adoptions. Carole hadn't even been near the gym yesterday, so far as Maggie knew. It sounded as though she'd been busy protecting her own turf.

Detective Luciani took out his notebook. "I've been checking the records of everyone who was here in the gym yesterday. Everyone who had an opportunity to place that bomb. All they had to do was tell someone they were going to a restroom. It wouldn't have taken long."

"But just a few of us were here, and I can't imagine any of us doing it! Someone else could have driven or walked into the parking lot during the afternoon. We weren't watching it every minute while we were working in the gyms."

"I understand, Professor Summer. But we had to start the investigation somewhere. As you say, though, we didn't find much." Luciani looked down at his notebook. "You had two parking tickets about four years ago. That's the only record we had for you. And you left your fingerprints with us earlier this week, so we'll be able to check those out."

"You think I bombed my own van? You must think I'm totally insane!"

"Al, your record is clean. Eric Sloane had several juvenile arrests, but they must not have been serious; they've been sealed. He's had nothing since he was seventeen. Abdullah Jaleel has had three speeding tickets within the past five years. We also found records that one of his neighbors, and several anonymous callers, reported after 9/11 that he might be a terrorist." Luciani raised his hand to shush Maggie's aggravated expression. "Nothing was found; nothing was done. They were just hate calls so far as I could tell. There was also some racist spray painting at his home, and his mother reported she'd overheard people making anti-Arab remarks. The usual 'Camel jockey, when're you going on your suicide mission?' sort of talk."

"The 'usual talk'?" said Maggie incredulously. "What's 'usual' about discriminating against someone who lost his brother *in* a terrorist attack?"

"People listen to the news, and they worry. They go on the offensive," said the detective, adding, "And I guess you know his mother killed herself."

"I'd heard."

"Abdullah was the one who called 911 when it happened. She hung herself. Left a note about being tired and not able to cope anymore. It wasn't pretty."

"She killed herself because of the prejudice?"

"It looked as though that pushed her over the edge, after her older son was killed."

Al asked, "There was no question it was suicide?"

"No question. From the investigator or from her son. She did it."

"This is awful," said Maggie. "I can't believe you're rehashing all the terrible things that happened to these good people in the past, when I'm sure someone else set that bomb!"

Detective Luciani continued, unfazed. "Will Brewer has no record of any sort we could find, although we have faxed the police in Buffalo to verify that."

Maggie almost stamped her foot in rage. Was all this necessary? There was a killer out there! And these idiots were investigating victims, like Abdullah, and innocent bystanders, like Will.

"The only one here who had any sort of significant record was Claudia Hall."

"Claudia?" Maggie stood absolutely still.

"Yup. She has a sheet."

Maggie felt a bit faint.

"Shoplifting, a couple of times, about ten years ago. Drug possession, once."

"Drugs?" croaked Maggie. The woman who was condemning her for drinking diet cola?

"Marijuana. She was in a car accident; police found it in her pocketbook. And there was a protective order taken out against her, four years ago."

"A protective order?" Al frowned. "She was abusing someone?"

"Harassing. Former boyfriend. He said she was following him and sending him threatening letters. She was pissed because he had a new girlfriend. A couple of new girlfriends, actually." Detective Luciani shook his head. "Anyway, it didn't come to anything. She stopped bothering him, I guess."

"But she did send threatening letters." Al was looking back toward the gym, where Claudia was working.

"She did. And," Detective Luciani looked at Maggie, "she does have a gun."

"I know that. It's licensed." Last fall Maggie had had a serious talk with Claudia about why one shouldn't carry a gun to work in one's pocketbook. Even if it was licensed.

"And, luckily for her, it's not the same type used to shoot Mrs. Sloane or her son. But we're going to watch her, I have to

tell you. If you see anything suspicious, with her or anyone els
let me know as soon as possible." Luciani paused. "Maybe i
would be a good idea if she didn't work so closely with you on
this show."

"No!" said Maggie. "I'm sure there's a reasonable explana-
tion for everything. And let's assume for a minute that she is
responsible for all this chaos. Which I don't for one minute
believe. Wouldn't it be better if she were right here with us, so
we could keep an eye on her?"

"I suppose that's right, Professor Summer. But be careful. She
might be a dangerous person." Luciani looked down at his
notes. "And then there's Hal Hanson."

Maggie felt her level of frustration rising. "I suppose he's a
dangerous criminal, too?"

"Possibly, yes."

Maggie took a deep breath. "What did you find out about
Hal?"

"He was adopted about ten years ago, by Sheryl and Len
Hanson, who lived in Somerville. Didn't make a good adjust-
ment; had been abused by his parents and as a kid in foster care,
and was seriously hyperactive. So hyperactive the local school
system said they couldn't handle him; he was hitting other kids
and throwing things out windows during classes. His parents
had him in counseling, tried different medications and different
schools. None of them worked out."

Maggie listened carefully. Life had been difficult for Hal. And
his adoptive parents.

"After he set a few small fires at home, he ended up at an adolescent psychiatric facility in Pennsylvania."

Fires.

"He was released from that hospital late last fall and moved
home, on medication."

"And in January his parents' home burned down, killing
them both," said Maggie quietly.

"That's why we have a whole file on him. But I want to

emphasize—there was no proof the fire was set, or that he had anything to do with it. It appeared to be electrical. Hal was in a first-floor bedroom; the fire started in the middle of the night. He called 911. His parents were in bed and trapped on the second floor. There was nothing he, or anyone else, could do."

"You investigated and found nothing."

The detective shook his head. "We had some questions, but nothing conclusive. Then the Drummonds took him in. They knew his history, and they believed he was innocent."

Carole and her husband wouldn't have offered Hal a home if they'd felt there was danger to their other children. Maggie was sure about that.

"So . . . ?"

"No proof. No reason to investigate further. But Hal has a history of emotional disturbance and a connection with fires."

Maggie thought a moment. "Has he had any connection with guns? Or bombs?"

"None that we know of."

She nodded. "So it may all be a coincidence that he was here."

"It may be," agreed the detective. "And it may be a coincidence that all three of the young men here yesterday afternoon have lost family members to violence. But we in law enforcement don't like it when there are too many coincidences connected with one event."

"Incidents of violence and death of family members is much more common among adopted children and adults than it is among the population in general," Maggie put in. "Two of those young men were adopted. And Abdullah lost his brother in the World Trade Center. You can't put that loss in the same category as the others!"

"That's very different, of course," said Detective Luciani. "But it is interesting that the three of them were together."

"All helping to support adoption," Maggie reminded him. "*Support* adoption. Not threaten it."

"We're exploring all possibilities. Let me know if you hear or see anything that might be helpful to the investigation."

"Of course," said Maggie.

"Or if you see or hear anything that could potentially lead to another incident."

"You mean another threat?"

"Another threat. Or worse."

Chapter 35

—⁓—

Crossing a Deep Ravine Dangerous to Pafs *(sic)*. *One of six hand-colored etchings in the "Steeple Chase" series by Henry Thomas Alken (1785–1853), perhaps Britain's most famous painter of sporting subjects. His satirical view of sports was popular in England in the 1820s and 1830s. This etching, published by S&J Fuller, shows four horses and riders in a race. One horse and rider have fallen into a deep ditch, while the other three proceed to the next hazard: bushes in front of a fence. Matted, in modern antiqued gold frame. Frame: 12.5 x 15.5 inches. Price: $250.*

By one in the afternoon it was beginning to feel as though there might really be an antiques show.

Signs appeared all over town announcing the show and directing potential customers toward the college. And with the help of some ladders Eric had located, Skip Hendricks and his committee put a big vinyl banner on the gym declaring OWOC ANTIQUES SHOW—MAY 14 & 15 in red letters on a white background. Maggie had seen signs for professionally run shows that weren't as clear.

Volunteers who believed in their cause were invaluable. Maggie realized it was a slight miracle that everyone who'd been working in the gym yesterday when her van blew up was back again today.

She looked around. Additional handicapped parking spaces had been reserved.

The electricians had finished putting the cables and outlets down, tables were in the booth spaces, and dealer signs were in each space.

Maggie hated to do it, but, without giving a reason to anyone, even Will, she'd asked Will and Claudia to work together to check the booth contracts Gussie had organized, and to verify that each dealer had the electricity and the number and size of tables he or she wanted. Just in case one of the students had made an error or left anything in one of the booths. Or that Claudia had uncharacteristically left something undone.

I'm getting really paranoid, thought Maggie to herself. But she double-checked everything.

They'd shortened one line of booths to make up for a cancellation, and Gussie had the brilliant idea to use one of the canceled booths as a lounge, leaving a dozen extra chairs there for people who wanted to sit for a while, to wait for a spouse who was still shopping, or to make a decision about a major purchase.

The tables and chairs for the café looked fine. Ann would check that setup after the bank closed at three.

Eric had listened to Maggie's concerns. Twice he'd assured her there was plenty of toilet paper in the bathrooms, including the bathrooms in the locker rooms. Maggie made a note to make sure the locker rooms were locked before the end of the day.

"Okay, Ben," she said. "I think it's time for you to be a porter and bring in Gussie's and my stuff from the van so we can get our booth set up before the other dealers arrive. Will, if you want to start setting up, too, I don't see any reason why you shouldn't. I might need your help with something else after the other dealers arrive."

The people who'd volunteered to be porters weren't coming until four, but Kayla and Kendall volunteered to help Will unload now, and Eric and Abdullah went to help Ben.

With that many porters, loading in was going to be easy, Maggie thought. At too many shows she'd had to heft and carry all her inventory and racks and table covers and tools herself. It often took over an hour just to get everything from her van to her booth.

Her van. She tried not to think about the logistical issues of not having any transportation, as she kept an eye on the door while Gussie supervised the unloading.

She'd mentioned the lockers to Al, and he was off making sure everything there was secure. If he needed a shower tonight, he assured her, he'd briefly unlock just one area.

So far, so good, Maggie said over and over to herself. No more threats. No more shootings. No more explosions.

Maybe whoever had done all this was satisfied he or she had already gotten enough people upset and wouldn't try anything else.

Maggie's fingers were crossed, and she looked around quickly for some wood to knock on.

"Your table covers or mine?" asked Gussie. "I think the guys have unloaded everything. Ben and I can set up our part of the booth, but you'll have to put up your Peg-Boards and racks."

Just like a regular antiques show, thought Maggie. She followed Gussie into the gym. She'd put Will's booth across from theirs, and his porters had been working just as quickly. It looked as though almost everything he'd planned to display was piled on the floor between his tables.

They chose Gussie's table covers, which were navy blue. Maggie's were black, and today, they both decided, something a little brighter would be good. Ben set Gussie's folding bookcases on the back of her tables, forming a wall of sorts to fill with dolls and toys, while Maggie attached Peg-Boards to the tables on the other side of the booth, so she could hang prints on them.

Setup would be much faster than usual, since she hadn't brought many prints. She put a high rack in the corner to hold Victorian lithographs of children and used lower racks on the tables for the children's illustrators she was going to feature.

She put Winslow Homer wood engravings on one end of the front table. No matter what show she did, she always took her Homers. Some Thomas Nasts were right for this show, too, since he had lived in New Jersey and his Christmas engravings featured Santa Claus and children. Even in May there were customers looking for Christmas gifts and collectors looking for Santa Clauses.

Several groups of hand-colored and lithographed flowers fit well in one corner of the booth, with a rack holding astronomy and astrology behind them.

There was less room for anatomy prints than she'd planned, so Maggie left prints of animal anatomy in her portfolio. She pulled out the 1912 foldouts of the digestive system of man, and of the stages of human pregnancy, and a wonderful Victorian lithograph illustrating where to provide pressure should the pictured mustached gentleman have the unfortunate luck to be bitten by a mad dog. Parts of the ear. Parts of the eye. Skeletal structure. Muscular structure. All wonderful prints for doctors, nurses, physical therapists, surgeons, and others professionally involved with the human body. At her last show she'd sold several skulls to a father who planned to give them as graduation gifts to his daughter, who was studying to be a psychiatrist. Skulls were always dramatic to put in front.

There. She pulled out one of a skull, front and back and top views, and one of a series of skulls showing anatomical differences in anthropological divisions of *Homo sapiens*. Interesting. She checked the date. Was this still as true as had been believed in 1888? Or was it politically incorrect now? She looked at it again. And then a third time. The skulls were labeled as different races, but many of them were what we would now call different cultures. Maggie put it in back of the other prints and stood back.

Not bad. Her part of the booth had come together better than she'd hoped, considering the short time she'd taken to go through her portfolios and then to plan what she would bring, and how she would display everything.

And, as often happened, going through her prints had calmed her. Had let her see life in a little different light.

Ben was arranging a group of cast-iron banks in the shapes of horses, elephants, and bank buildings on one of Gussie's bookcases, while Gussie set up a lovely pink, flowered Victorian dolls' tea set. "Make sure that's not too close to the edge of the table," Maggie advised. "There will be more children than usual at this show."

"You're right," agreed Gussie. "In fact, I thought of that when I was packing." She pointed at her front table. It contained more twentieth-century toys than Gussie usually brought, but they were certainly all collectible, from early Tonka trucks to elaborate pink and blue plastic 1950s dollhouse furniture. And Gussie had added a sign: EVERYTHING ON THIS TABLE $15 OR LESS.

Maggie gave her a "thumbs-up." "Good marketing! And once you get the children occupied . . ."

"Then we entrance the parents with your prints and my nineteenth century French fashion dolls. The ones arranged far from the edge of the table."

Chapter 36

—⁓—

Gathering Corn. *Wood engraving from 1865 by Edward Forbes. Black man dumps basket of corn into a wagon pulled by a pair of oxen, one black and one white, who are nibbling on cornstalks. One white man shucks corn, while another removes cornstalks. 11 x 15 inches. Price: $60.*

By three thirty Maggie was glad she'd finished setting up her booth early. Dealers and their vans and trucks lined the parking lot. She walked through the lot, checking to make sure she knew everyone there, and handing out name tags.

If people inside the building were not wearing name tags, they'd be stopped by Al or one of his assistants so their identity could be verified. If they didn't have a good reason for being there or were just trying to get an early look at the merchandise, their names would be recorded—as they were accompanied to the door.

Luckily this was not far from standard procedure at many antiques shows. None of the dealers would suspect there were any more reasons to be concerned than the need to protect their antiques. But there are no secrets at antiques shows; within an hour of their arrivals, Maggie knew all the dealers would have heard about her van being blown up.

Violet, one of the students who'd volunteered to be a porter, arrived. Kayla and Kendall left to pick their children up at day care. George Healy stopped in to check on Eric and make sure everything in the gym was all right.

Ann arrived with two friends, demanding that porters unload the small refrigerators she'd brought, along with cartons of napkins, cups, sodas, hot dog rolls, and what looked like four cartons of electric deep fryers ("So we can cook hot dogs!") and frying pans ("For the onions and sauerkraut!").

Maggie sent Abdullah and Violet off to find Eric and see if there were any additional dollies they could borrow for Ann. Gussie was still setting up her booth, but Josie Thomas had stopped in to see where the admissions table would be on Saturday, and Maggie recruited her.

Would she stay and check the dealers in, see that they paid the rest of their booth rent before they set up, give out the name tags everyone should be wearing by now, and keep a current list of dealers who'd requested porters? In the order they'd requested them, please.

Josie nodded and went to work.

Volunteers were wonderful.

Paul Turk arrived, as good as his word, to be a porter, and so did Oliver Whitcomb. Maggie put aside any hesitations about ordering a philanthropist to get his hands dirty. She asked Oliver to find George Healy and check that there was enough power for all the electrical appliances Ann and her café staff were unloading.

Another note for future shows, Maggie thought: ask café people how much power they'll need.

And if there wasn't enough power, Oliver would be the best person to tell Ann.

Was Ann really going to sue OWOC?

If she was going to do that, then why go to all this trouble for the show?

Maggie had a sudden horribly funny vision of Ann as the

wicked witch in *Snow White,* handing out poisoned apple muffins to everyone at the agency.

It was not the moment to share that thought with anyone.

Abdullah was helping Will set up his booth. Where were all the other people who'd promised to be porters?

She breathed a sigh of relief when an OWOC parent waved to her from an SUV and unloaded six teenagers, four girls and two boys.

"When should I come back for them?" called the mom.

"Seven o'clock," Maggie called back. All the dealers should have their inventories in their booths by then. They might still be setting up, but they wouldn't need porters at that point. The busiest time was the next hour, with tired dealers anxious to unload and start arranging their booths. Many had left home early this morning to get here by setup time.

At quarter to four Maggie let the dealers come in, see how the gyms were arranged, find their booths, and identify the door closest to their booth to use for unloading. Several grumbled. Others quickly moved their vans to more strategic parking locations around the gymnasium.

All part of a usual setup, especially for the first show in this location. If the show was held again next year, all would know their booth locations and the best parking spaces.

Maggie said a mental prayer that if there *were* a show here next year, she would *not* be the one managing it. Once was enough. Maybe once was too much.

Josie figured out the logistics like a veteran. Mothers seemed to have a lot of logistical skills, Maggie noted.

She made new name tags for each of the volunteer porters, most of whom she recognized from OWOC adoptive-parent parties and picnics. She spoke sharply to one dealer she overheard trying to bribe a girl to unload his van before helping someone ahead of him on the porter list.

Finally, at four, porters assigned, Maggie gave the word. Dealers could unload.

Dealers and porters streamed through every door into both gyms. Many of the dealers had already piled cartons outside their vans or even carried their inventory to right outside the doors of the gym. Others had loaded their own dollies while they were waiting.

Maggie walked through, nodding and waving and answering important questions. ("Are there special restrooms for dealers?" No.) ("Is there free coffee for dealers?" Soon.) Many dealers were already frazzled after long days. Tonight most would unload and set up as well as they could. They'd come back tomorrow morning at eight to rearrange and perhaps bring in some particularly special items they hadn't wanted to leave in the gym overnight. And check other dealers' booths for any bargains before the show opened at ten.

She looked over at the café. Oliver and George had determined what was needed, and Ann had two tables of electrical appliances already set up. Coffee was perking. Maggie poured herself a paper cup of one of the no-name sodas the agency was providing for the dealers and porters during setup. Even no-name diet cola was better than no diet cola. She made a mental note to take her gift carton of Diet Pepsi home.

Everything was working. Maggie kept walking down the aisles, keeping an eye on the dealers and porters and the few other people approved to be here now.

Aisles and booths were jammed with boxes and furniture. Most of the tables were now covered to the floor with black or blue or white or red flameproof fabric table covers. Walls surrounded three sides of some booths. Oriental carpets were on the floors of others.

Maggie reminded one dealer that not even masking tape could go on the gym walls; another, that he could only attach spotlights or lamps to the outlets he had requested and paid for. The ones already in his booth.

The merchandise was as varied as Maggie had hoped. One dealer specialized in metal lunch boxes and pottery cookie jars.

Another in oyster plates and sterling silver. Pine colonial furniture was arranged in one booth; a careful selection of grandfather and grandmother clocks in another. One dealer displayed nothing but barometers, antique microscopes, and early surgical equipment.

"Did you find anything for me at the estate library?" Maggie asked Joe Cousins, as he unloaded a dolly full of boxes of books.

"That sale was a bust," Joe said sadly. "The idiot running it didn't know the difference between a first edition and a book-club edition."

Maggie shrugged, smiled, and waved as she walked on.

Maybe everything was going to work out. Maybe there would be no problems.

She kept an eye on Claudia, who was portering for a woman who'd brought several dozen cartons of printed tablecloths and aprons and dish towels dating from the 1920s to the 1950s. Linens were popular at many shows, but a dealer would have to sell a lot of dish towels to equal one grandfather clock. In fact, the clock dealer would probably consider this show a major success if he ended up selling one clock. A strong show for him would be making contacts with one or two people to repair clocks they already owned.

Eric had to be exhausted. He'd been running since before Maggie had arrived. And how could he have slept much with all that was happening at his house? But he must have kept George happy, since George appeared to have left. Hal was helping Abdullah bring in a large Pennsylvania Dutch pie safe.

At least after tonight the only lifting and carrying would be if any customer bought a large item that had to be taken to a van or car or truck. Often purchases like that were picked up on Sunday, after the show was over. A dealer was lucky if he had to worry about the number of red and black sold stickers he had in inventory. (One show Maggie did supplied sold signs for the dealers to use that said, "Sold! Watch this space for another wonderful item to appear!") Optimistically, most dealers carried one or two extra pieces of furniture or special framed items in their vans or trucks in case a major sale emptied their booth.

Maggie crossed her fingers that this would be that kind of a show. Although the first show in any location could not expect spectacular sales. It sometimes took years for dealers and collectors and decorators and other regular customers to learn that a particular show was worth attending. That's why dealers were cautious about committing their time and money to a new show. Many of these dealers had agreed to come because they knew Maggie, or because they lived close by and it would be an easy show to do. Or because they strongly supported adoption. It was amazing how many people Maggie called who had some connection with adoption. Dealers shared that they had been adopted, or a brother or sister or cousin had been. Or their best friend had relinquished a child for adoption. Or their son had adopted three children.

Will's booth looked good, Maggie noted. He'd brought the iron devil andirons he'd told her about months before. When there was a fire, red and yellow flames would shine through the devils' grins. Very nice. Gussie and Ben had finished their side of the booth and placed a Booth Closed sign on the chairs they'd used to block the entrance.

Where had they gone?

Maggie found them quickly. Ben was helping Violet bring in cartons of crystal.

Maggie said a small prayer they didn't drop anything.

And Gussie had replaced Josie at the front desk, where the action had slowed down considerably.

"I told the nice pregnant woman who was here—Josie?"

Maggie nodded. "Josie Thomas. She and her husband adopted two really cute eight-year-olds last year. Twins."

"Well, the way she looks, she could be having another set pretty soon. Anyway, I told her she could go on home. She did fine, and all but eight of the dealers are here now." Gussie glanced at her list. "Two are still waiting for porters, but I expect they'll have most of their things unpacked before any of the porters are available."

Maggie nodded. "No show ever has enough porters."

"That's one of the things we dealers always say. 'If *we* ran the show, there'd be a lot more porters.'"

"Right. Well, now I know why that's hard to do. All the dealers need porters at the same time. The porters work like crazy for an hour or two. And then it's over. No one needs them until pack-out on Sunday."

Gussie handed Maggie the list of dealers who hadn't arrived. "Will anyone on this list want porters? I hate to tell the kids to stick around if no one needs them."

Maggie looked. "Two or three of these dealers are local; they may be planning to set up tomorrow morning. One is the guy with the estate jewelry. I know he won't leave anything here overnight. He'll arrive at eight tomorrow morning, cover his tables, bring in his display cases, attach a few Tensor lamps to his tables, and be in business in an hour. The porters can leave when they're finished helping the dealers they're with now."

She realized it was dinnertime. "Want me to get you some pizza? I saw them unpacking boxes in the café a few minutes ago."

"Yes, please. Two pieces of pepperoni," said Gussie.

In the café dealers and porters were taking full advantage of the stacks of boxed pizzas that had just been delivered. Another five minutes and the pizza would be gone. Maggie filled one plate for herself and one for Gussie and returned to the lobby.

"I'll admit I'm wearing down," said Gussie. "If all stays quiet, I think I'll finish my pizza and head for home. Ben can come with me or go home with you and Will later. I know you have to stay until the bitter end."

"Either the bitter end or ten o'clock. Whichever comes first," agreed Maggie. "But there's no reason you have to stay. You've been an enormous help today. I really appreciate your being here."

"Glad to be of service. And glad I didn't get to see the kind of fireworks you saw last night."

Maggie grimaced. "The show opens tomorrow morning. Let's just hope no more fireworks. Not even a sparkler."

But that reminded her. She needed to talk with Al.

He was eating his pizza in a quiet corner of the conference room. "I just needed a bit of peace," he admitted, when Maggie found him. "What's up?"

"After yesterday, nothing, I hope," said Maggie. "But have you seen what a mess the gyms are now? That's just part of setting a show up, I know. But do you know the guys on the county police force well enough for them to do you a favor?"

"That depends, Maggie. I'd say right now they have so much on their plates they couldn't do something extra even if they wanted to."

"But what if it might keep people from being in danger?"

"That's different. What do you have in mind?"

"Does Somerset County have any bomb-sniffing dogs?"

Chapter 37

My Little White Kittens Playing Dominoes. *One of the "My Little White Kittens" series lithographed by Currier & Ives. The kittens are famously demonic-appearing, with pointed ears and eyes. In this lithograph two kittens are knocking over a carefully aligned wall of dominoes. In period frame. Print has several small holes in margins, and one tiny one in a kitten's paw. Margins intact, except for holes. Small folio: 11 x 14 inches. $170.*

Maggie and Will got to the gym before eight Saturday morning, leaving Ben and Gussie at home to get a little more rest. The sun was already hot, and the dampness of the past couple of days promised humidity would be rising with the sun. Several dealers were already parked outside, waiting for the doors to be unlocked so they could finish setting up their booths.

Usually Maggie wore a long skirt to antiques shows, but today, not knowing what she might have to do, she'd put on a pair of navy linen slacks and a dressy overblouse and added one of her brass *M* pins for luck. At least pants meant she could avoid stockings. She wiggled her toes in her comfortable open, navy blue sandals. Will was wearing pressed jeans, with a blue

ess shirt, open at the chest. That color blue always reflected the color of his eyes. A devastating combination.

They'd brought Al some doughnuts and coffee, assuming, correctly, that Ann's café staff wouldn't be there at eight on the dot.

"How're you coping with sleeping here?" Maggie asked.

"I must admit, I'll be glad to get back to my own bed and off that cot," said Al. "I must have heard a dozen noises last night that weren't there. Everything went so well yesterday I kept waiting for a disaster to strike."

Hal, Eric, and Abdullah came in together. "Good morning, guys!" said Maggie. "You didn't all need to be here this early."

"But Eric did, so I thought I'd offer him a ride," said Abdullah. "And Hal figured he'd come, too. Their families are pretty busy now."

Hal's family was dead; Abdullah must have meant Carole's family. Strange—with all the excitement, Maggie hadn't even realized that Carole had never stopped in to see how the setup was going. And, of course, Eric's family was still dealing with Jackson's death.

"Are you okay with spending this much time here?" Maggie asked Eric. "Things must be pretty intense at home. Has a date been set for Jackson's funeral? And how is your mother doing?"

"The funeral will be Monday. Mom's still in a lot of pain, and she can't climb stairs, so Dad's set up a bed for her in the living room. She's using a rented wheelchair. With all the confusion and telephone calls and people dropping in to say they're sorry, or just to check up and see how we're all doing, I'd just as soon be here. I'm doing something productive, and I don't have to think as much."

"I understand. And you've been a big help. I'm going to write to George and point that out after this show is over."

Eric looked down, but his eyes shone. "That would be great."

As if to answer the other question on Maggie's mind, Carole Drummond was the next to appear.

"Good morning! Everyone set for the show? Hal, there yo͏ͦ
are! I saw your note that you had a ride this morning. Could yoᴜ
unload the cartons I have for the display and handouts in the
agency booth?"

"I'll help, too," said Eric, and Abdullah nodded and followed
him. Maggie wondered what she would have done during the
past couple of days without the three of them. They'd been
essential parts of the team. And they seemed to be getting along
well.

She suspected they each could use a new friend. Maybe they'd
found one. Or two.

"Hal's been a great help, Carole," said Maggie. "Thanks for
suggesting he volunteer."

"I'm glad. And I'm so sorry about your van. Let's hope that
was the last unfortunate event. After all, three is a charm!"
Carole peeked inside the gyms. "The sign outside looks terrific,
and everything looks amazingly organized." Several dealers
were still bringing in merchandise; others were arranging items
already in their booths. "I just have to make two more calls, and
then I'll set up the agency booth." Carole headed for the
OWOC booth, cell phone in hand.

Coffee was beginning to perk; Ann must be here. Coolers full
of baked goodies were beginning to appear in back of the café
service tables.

"Carole, here's your name tag!" called Maggie, fishing it out
of the box of unclaimed name tags on the front table and following Carole into the gym. "All the dealers are accounted for,
and everything is set up except for the café, which Ann and her
committee are working on, and your booth."

As Carole pinned on her name tag Hal passed them, carrying
some large blowups of OWOC families.

"Those are for the walls of the booth," explained Carole.
"We'll put handouts and pictures of waiting children on the
table in front of the booth."

"Josie and her husband are taking turns at the admissions

table," Maggie continued. "They're putting the raffle items for the table over there." She pointed at a spot just inside the door of the gym.

"What's the other table for?" asked Carole, indicating a second one nearby.

"Handouts. Many dealers bring postcards and other promotional information for the next shows they'll be doing, and a couple of regional antiques newspapers have donated copies to be given away, in hopes of getting new subscribers. Plus some sponsors, like motels and restaurants, and local antiques shops and malls, have given us maps or copies of menus that customers can pick up and take with them."

Carole nodded. "You've done a great job, Maggie."

"With a lot of help," Maggie acknowledged.

Carole moved a little closer and spoke softly. "No more phone calls or letters?"

"Not to me. Has the agency gotten any?"

"No, thank goodness."

Two uniformed policemen nodded as they walked by.

"I see we have some local support."

"Yes. They were here early, before the dealers arrived. Patrols are watching the parking lot a little closer than they'd planned after the problems Thursday, and Al has four of his security people specifically watching the doors. Right now they're all open, because dealers are still unloading. But fifteen minutes before the show opens, we'll lock all the outside doors except the main one near the admissions desk. After that the security guys will just walk around, keeping an eye on everything."

"Are they wearing uniforms?"

"Al told them they'd have to. We're trying to intimidate anyone who might try to make trouble. And the police are also in uniform, except for the detectives. I don't know if they'll be here or not. They have a lot to work on now."

"Yes." Carole watched Eric walk past her with another load of cartons from her car. "Yesterday one of those detectives called again. This time they were asking about Hal." She looked at Maggie. "Have there been any problems with him?"

"Not one. He's been an enormous help. The police were just checking on everyone who was in the gym when my van burst into flames."

"Did they find anything?"

"They did say Hal had some history with fires." Maggie said it quietly.

Carole nodded. "True. But that's history. He wouldn't have done this, Maggie. He's had a hard life, and he's pulling it together. He's taking his meds, and he's doing fine."

"I understand. But they were asking about everyone. Even me, and it was my van that was murdered."

Carole smiled at Maggie's choice of words. "Then I won't worry. And I guess I'd better get to work in my booth. I wouldn't want the agency booth to be the only one unfinished when you open the doors at ten."

"I'll be close to the front lobby until Josie comes. If you need anything, look for me. Or Eric Sloane. He knows this building better than anyone."

"Thank you, Maggie. For everything. We were right to decide to go ahead with the show. I just know it's going to be a fantastic success!" Carole turned and started making her second cell-phone call.

Maggie hoped Carole would have time to set up her booth. After all, promoting Our World Our Children was one of the reasons for the show.

The only hassle in the next hour was Ann's realizing that despite the extra tables and outlets she'd gotten last night, she needed one more table for bake-sale items. Eric moved a table from the conference room into the gym. Maggie made a note to make sure they counted the tables when the rental company came Monday. She didn't want them to accidentally take any tables owned by the college.

Josie and Sam Thomas appeared promptly at nine fifteen

with the raffle items and their twins. At almost the same time Ben and Gussie arrived. Ben went to see if Eric needed any help, while Gussie went to their booth to get out her cash box and separate Maggie's sales books from hers.

At nine twenty Maggie went around to all the dealers announcing that *now* was the time that all dealers' vehicles should be moved to another lot, if any were still parked by the gym. Spaces close to the gym were for customers. Dealers' vans and trucks should be in the lot next to the dormitories.

At nine thirty she asked Al to have one of his security staff walk through the parking lot to make sure the vehicles had been moved. "The white van with the wheelchair lift and the Massachusetts plates can stay in handicapped parking," she reminded Al. "No other vehicles with dealers' cards should be in the lot. If there are any, have your guys make a note of the license plate numbers, and I'll find the owners."

Only one van had to be moved, someone who'd arrived late and was frantically trying to unpack and bring order out of chaos.

"I'm sorry," Maggie told him. "You'll have to move your vehicle to the dormitory lot. Now."

He stomped across to the door with his car keys, muttering.

She wasn't sympathetic. With that much inventory he should have gotten here last night, like most of the dealers. Every dealer had been sent vehicle identification cards and instructions on where to park in the information packages she'd sent out two weeks ago. Asking dealers to move their vehicles away from the site of a show was not an unusual request. Parking spots had to be left for customers. At some shows dealers had to park miles away and be taxied back to the show site.

Customers were starting to line up outside the doors. Maggie crossed her fingers. A good crowd waiting to get in was a positive sign. The publicity had worked. People had heard about the show.

Maggie let them stay outside until nine fifty, when the doors were unlocked and customers could come in, pay their admittance fee, and wait in the lobby until the doors to the gyms opened at ten.

It was almost showtime, Maggie thought. "Magic time" they called it in the theater. She could feel her adrenaline on "high," and she'd only had one Diet Pepsi this morning. It was all going to work.

Chapter 38

⎯⎯⎯◡∽⎯⎯⎯

The World. *Steel engraving of "The Western Hemisphere, or New World" and "The Eastern Hemisphere, or Old World." Published by Lincoln and Edmunds, Boston, 1827, from Adam's School Atlas. Continents outlined lightly in different-colored watercolors. The "Old World" is fairly accurate, despite Siam's covering most of Southeast Asia and what is now Australia labeled "New Holland." Outlines of North and South America are less accurate, but approximate. Light line down the center, where the pages were folded into the atlas. 16 x 12 inches with mat; modern wood frame. $150.*

By eleven o'clock the show was in full swing; customers were wandering through the aisles, browsing in the booths, and washing down their maple blueberry muffins with coffee in the café. Josie and Sam reported the gate was over two hundred. For a small, brand-new show in western New Jersey, that was an excellent beginning.

Maggie hoped they would all buy. One thing each, she wished silently.

If only.

As she walked by the booths, she saw fellow professor Paul

Turk in what appeared to be an intense discussion of nineteenth-century inkwells with a dealer who specialized in desk items and antique pens. Will was wrapping up an iron match safe for a young woman carrying one baby and wheeling another. Maggie tried to peek, but couldn't tell if they "matched" their mother or might be adopted.

Gussie had planned well with her "bargain table"; every time Maggie passed, adults were looking at toys they'd grown up with, or their parents had told them about.

The booth with the elegant grandfather clocks was empty of customers, but the dealer seemed to have settled himself with a paperback of Jonathan Kellerman's *Bad Love*. Antiques shows were, unfortunately, sometimes quiet places to catch up on reading. The dealer might not be expecting to be overwhelmed by business, but he was still hoping. Otherwise he wouldn't be here.

As the sun on the roof increased in intensity, and the number of people in the gyms rose, the building began to get stuffy.

Maggie found Al talking to one of his men by the side door to the second gym. "Should I see you, or Eric? I think it's time to turn on the air-conditioning. Not high, but enough so there's some air circulating in here."

"Good idea. Eric's the one to ask. I heard him going over instructions for the air-conditioning system with George yesterday."

"No problem," said Maggie. "Any security issues I should be aware of?"

"It's all amazingly quiet," said the guard. "Here we were expecting some excitement. Now, I'm not looking for any disasters, but so far we're pretty bored. I'm supposed to keep an eye on this door. Which is locked. Unless there's a major problem, it will stay locked. I haven't even seen anyone trying to slip a piece of sterling silver into a pocketbook."

"And let's hope you won't," said Maggie. "But I'm still glad you're here. After all, it was only two days ago that my van went up in smoke."

"I heard."

"And the show's barely begun. There are plenty of hours left. Right now I'm going to find Eric and get some air on in this place."

She walked up the far aisle, checking out the OWOC booth as she went. Carole and two other OWOC staff members were busy charming show visitors. One couple took a brochure about the agency. Another woman was looking through the binders filled with pictures of waiting children.

Skip and Jennifer Hendricks were attracting attention to the OWOC booth just by proudly carrying Christina. Nothing like a visual aid to prove that adoption works, Maggie thought. Christina was adorable.

She squelched the impulse to go over and look through a binder of "waiting children" pictures herself. When she was ready, her child would be there. Something inside of her said so. Right now she wasn't ready. She wasn't ready for anything but getting this show finished, making money for the agency, and then sleeping for two days straight.

Where was Eric? She checked the café, and walked quickly through both gyms. Probably he was also walking around. She stopped in the lobby and waited until Josie made change for an elderly gentleman paying admission for himself and three other people. "Josie, if you see Eric Sloane, would you tell him I'm looking for him?"

"Will do. Last time I saw him he was heading for the men's room with a mop and pail."

Not a good sign, Maggie thought. But cleanup was definitely Eric's department. He'd volunteered to be here, but she was going to check with George to make sure he got a bonus for the weekend. Even if she had to pay it herself. He and Abdullah and Hal had outdone themselves in helping with this show. And Claudia . . . where was Claudia today?

Maggie walked back into the gym and there she was, working in the café. Sarah was there, too, making a poster listing the varieties of available muffins. She waved. Ann must have needed extra help, and Claudia had moved in to supply it. Thank goodness for reliable people, Maggie thought. Imagine Detective Luciani suspecting Claudia of being trouble. What would she do without Claudia?

"Maggie, the show is wonderful," Ann said, coming up behind Maggie with a carton of napkins and spoons. "And thank you for listening to me vent at dinner the other night."

"It was fine, Ann. It made me think harder about some parts of this whole decision process."

"It isn't easy, is it?" Ann said, shifting the box in her arms. "It's so easy to say you want to love a child and give them a good home. And then all the doubts and complications creep in. I hope my misgivings won't discourage you from adopting."

"No," said Maggie. "You voiced some thoughts I've had. And you reminded me I need to make sure that when—if—I decide to adopt, it will be for the right reasons. For me and my child."

"Then I hope we can still be friends," said Ann. "I probably overreacted by talking to a lawyer. I'm just very nervous right now. Here I've been dreaming of being a mother for years, and I'm getting cold feet when OWOC says it really can happen."

Maggie smiled. "In the meantime we can help other people who've already made that decision. Your café looks wonderful, Ann."

"Now I just need to make sure we don't have customers waiting in line for too long!"

Maggie paid for a large chocolate cookie. Perhaps not a nutritious lunch, but one she could eat on the go. "Ann, as soon as the rush here ends, would you have one of your younger helpers fill a serving cart with sandwiches and cookies and drinks and take it down the aisles to the dealers? Some who're running their booths alone may not be able to come and get their own lunches."

"Will do," said Ann. "You know, I was wondering if we'd

brought too much food, but even people who aren't eating lunch here have bought bake-sale items to take home." She leaned over and whispered, "Some of them say they want to buy something to support OWOC and couldn't find anything they wanted, or could afford, in the booths."

Maggie nodded. "It's good they're buying the food. But I hope some of them also find some antiques to buy." No matter how many customers came, if they didn't buy, then the dealers wouldn't come back next year. *If* there was a show next year, Maggie cautioned herself quickly. Next year seemed a long time from now.

She stationed herself in the vicinity of the men's room, feeling self-conscious hanging out at that end of the corridor, and was rewarded by Eric's appearing within a few minutes, complete with pail, mop, and toilet plunger. "Problem?"

"Not anymore," said Eric with a bit of pride. "When you live in a family of sixteen, clogged toilets are not major problems."

"Thank goodness," Maggie said under her breath. "Eric, after you put that stuff away, could you turn on the air-conditioning? It's getting stuffy in the gyms, and we need some air flow."

"No problem. The control panel is just down the hall. The air should be on in five minutes."

Just then Ben came up. "Aunt Gussie wants to talk to you," he said. "I think it's about a price on a print."

Maggie followed Ben back to the booth and was quietly delighted when the question involved how much of a discount she would take if someone bought six Arthur Rackham prints marked $65 each.

"The regular price would be $390," she said. "A ten percent discount, which is what I usually give, would bring that down to about $350. What if I make it $330? That would almost be getting one of the prints free."

The customer agreed. Gussie, with receipt book in hand, said, "Now, there'll be tax on that, too, of course," and Maggie walked on. She wondered if that was her first sale of the day. It was

strange to have someone else making her sales, even if the someone was Gussie. She suspected Gussie's own inventory was selling
well. Based on the number of toys on the front table, Aunt
Augusta's Attic had been selling in quantity, if not in quality.

"You gotta have a gimmick," Maggie said to herself, remembering the song from *Gypsy*. Whatever got those customers into
the booth and pulling out their wallets.

The grandfather clock dealer was now having a serious conversation with two people. Were they one of those two-income
couples who furnished their executive home before they had
children? Carole would be happy to help them fill up any empty
rooms they might have. After they'd bought a $12,000 clock.

She heard the quiet roar of the air-conditioning coming on.
Eric, as usual, was true to his word. The air should make it more
comfortable in the gyms within a few minutes.

Maybe she should get Gussie or Will something to eat or
drink. Ann's young helpers couldn't have had time to get to all
of the dealers yet.

Everything was on schedule; everyone was smiling, except
maybe the bored security guard, and the day was beautiful.

Then the lights went out.

Chapter 39

⸻〰️⸻

Fire-Works on the Night of the Fourth of July. *1868 wood engraving in* Harper's Weekly *by Winslow Homer. Wonderful close-up of faces turned to the sky looking up at the fireworks. One distinguished gentleman is being hit on his head by a stray rocket. Homer signed W. H. in the lower right-hand corner. 11 x 15 inches. Price: $225.*

As George had predicted at the meeting Monday, even after the power had blown, the gyms were not totally black. The emergency generator kicked in after five seconds, providing low lights by the exits, and a few dim lights on the ceiling. But the sun outside didn't reach into the gyms.

The booth walls blocked any light from the exit signs, and of course, all the lamps carefully placed in booths to show off the merchandise had also gone out.

Making her way through the aisles of confused dealers and customers, Maggie headed to the front of the building. Maybe turning the air-conditioning on blew the electrical power for some reason. If Eric turned the air-conditioning off, maybe the lights would come back on. She hoped.

In the meantime, she also hoped no one would stumble on the

electrical cords duct-taped on top of the carpet, or knock against tables covered with crystal, or take the opportunity to relieve a booth of a piece of jewelry or silver.

The good news was that no one was panicking. Some people were even laughing. Dealers and customers were in the aisles. Everyone thought it was a glitch, a momentary outage. The lights would come back on any moment. Maggie hoped they were right.

She kept her eyes open, looking for Eric.

He'd said the electrical panel was in a closet down the hall and pointed to an area near the entrances to the locker rooms. There were no generator-created lights along that hall. Maggie touched the masonry wall gently as she felt her way down the corridor.

Suddenly she heard someone in back of her. "Eric?" she called out, turning around.

A piece of duct tape was swiftly pulled across her mouth and twisted behind her head. As she reached to pull it off, someone yanked her arms down and behind her back before she could react. Her wrists were held firmly, despite her struggles. She felt duct tape bandaging them together. She smelled spicy sweet after-shave.

She wriggled and kicked, but that didn't seem to bother whoever was holding her. Why hadn't she worn high heels that would hurt someone, instead of comfortable sandals that could do no damage? She twisted, trying to see who was holding her, but he held tight and pushed her against a doorway. One of the doors into the locker room.

The locker room was unlocked. Inside, he pushed her down on the concrete floor, hard, on her stomach and lay on top of her. Her struggling didn't seem to make a difference. He was a lot bigger and stronger than she was. He duct-taped her ankles.

Then he released her. She lay on the floor, fighting the duct tape for a few minutes. When she stopped, she heard the sound of a key in a lock. She was being locked in. Her nose picked up the flowery scent of powder. Deodorant. Hand lotion. The girls' locker room. Her eyes began to adjust to the dim emergency light from the exit signs on the doors. Then she saw Eric, similarly bound, perhaps ten feet away. They were both lying in one aisle of gym lockers.

No one would be turning the electricity back on.

She twisted her body and looked up. Hal stood over them, on the other side of a low bench. A gun and a cell phone lay on the bench between him and his prisoners. He put a key ring down next to them. His tools.

"I warned you. I said to cancel the antiques show. But you went ahead and did just what you wanted. You ignored me, no matter what I did. People have always made that mistake. They never take me seriously."

Maggie squirmed, trying to loosen the duct tape. But Hal had twisted it. The tape that covered her mouth and was fastened at the back of her head was pulling her hair. It hurt even more when she moved her head. Eric was watching her; she saw his eyes in the almost darkness. He was scared. Hell, she was scared.

"I like you both. I do. So I'm going to give everyone at this show one last chance. You're not the people who need to suffer."

Hal picked up the cell phone. Where had it come from? She hadn't seen him with one before.

He dialed.

"Hello, Carole?"

Carole always had her cell phone. Thank God she'd picked it up now.

His voice was calm and slow. "No, it's Hal. I'm calling from Al Stivali's cell phone."

Carole must have caller ID and thought Al was trying to reach her. Where had Hal gotten Al's phone? She hoped Al was all right.

"No, he didn't give it to me." Hal grinned.

He was enjoying this! Maggie tried to kick with both of her

feet and managed to hit the bench in front of the lockers. The noise was minimal. And her naked toes hurt like hell.

"Stop talking and listen to me. I sent those letters. You know what letters. And the telephone message. I thought I was being clear. I want this show to stop."

He paused. Maggie wondered what Carole was saying. She hoped Carole was walking quickly toward wherever Al was. Or one of the other security men. Someone else must have a phone. Someone that could call for help. Police should be patrolling the parking lots about now.

"Two reasons. One, you're messing with people's lives. Your agency gave me to two people who didn't listen. They said they loved me, but they didn't care enough to even keep me around. They sent me to live with a lot of crazy people. Do you have any idea what it's like to spend years living with psychos? They drug you to control you, and then they lock you up in rooms with bars and glass that won't break. They laugh at you and talk about you behind your back. And then they spew you out and send you back to live with the people who sent you there in the first place. And those people act so sweet and nice, but then you find out they're adopting other kids behind your back. Other kids they can put in places like that." Hal paused. "I couldn't let that happen, you understand?

"And the second reason isn't for me. It's for Jackson, and all the kids like him you placed with parents of different colors. You mess with ethnic purity. You condemn the future of America by creating families of mixed races. Those families can't protect their kids from hatred. Those kids won't fit in. And they'll be blamed for everything done by anyone who looks like them. They'll have no place to go."

Maggie looked over at Eric. He was listening carefully, and his eyes were no longer full of fear. They were angry.

Hal paused for a moment. "Good. You're hearing me. Adoption between the races is wrong. People can only become who they're meant to be when they're raised by people like them."

He paused again. He was close enough so Maggie could see the muscles in his face tense. "*Listen!* This is not a discussion! Listen carefully!" Hal looked down at his watch. "It is now approximately twelve forty. Two bombs are set to go off at one. One in each of the gyms. They're the same kind that blew up Maggie Summer's van. But no one paid attention to that bomb. No one took me seriously. Nobody stopped this show. I couldn't let it earn more money so you could make victims of more innocent children like me!"

He was quiet for a moment. What was Carole doing? What was she saying? What was happening in the rest of the building? Maggie looked for something that would cut the tape that was binding her.

"I am in the building. I have Maggie Summer and Eric with me. Even if you evacuate the building, you won't find us. The three of us will blow up with the show."

Carole was trying to find out something.

"I've said all you need to know! Stop interrupting me! You have to close the show down! And stop placing children with parents who don't understand them! If you promise to do that, then call me back. If you call me in time, I can locate the bombs and disengage them. If you don't call, Whitcomb Gymnasium is going up, with everything and everyone in it. You now have"— Hal looked at his watch again—"sixteen minutes until one o'clock. But I'll need time to disconnect the bombs. So you have ten minutes." He put the cell phone down on the bench and walked over to where Eric lay.

"I'm sorry about Jackson. I thought I was doing him a favor. After we met at one of those rah-rah-adoption picnics at your house, he told me what it felt like to be biracial. He hated it. He said he hated his mother; she was white, like his birth mother, and she thought she could take the place of a real mother. But a real mother would have cared enough about him to have made sure he had a father of the same heritage."

Hal looked over at Maggie. "Abdullah met Jackson here on

campus. He told Jackson and me about that melting pot you talk about in your classes. He tried to tell us we were all Americans. Abdullah is mixed race, too. But Jackson and I knew better. You can't mix rice and noodles and potatoes and couscous in a bowl and expect to end up with anything you can eat. It just doesn't work. Jackson and I talked about it. He told me how when adoption agencies can't find families with the same race as a child, they put them with anyone who'll say yes. Jackson hated that. He told me he couldn't stand his mother; he wished she were dead.

"He told me his father had a gun, and he could get it. So I told him to do that; we'd find a way to make things better for him." Hal looked down at Eric. "Only when I shot his mother—your mother—I messed up. She didn't die. And then Jackson got all turned around. He said he didn't mean to have her hurt. That he loved her! After all he'd said about her. When she was white! "He said he'd turn me in. He'd tell everyone. I couldn't let him do that. He let me down. I was his friend, and doing him a favor, and he was letting me down. He'd promised to help me stop the show."

Hal's voice was almost pleading.

"You understand, I couldn't let the show go on. I couldn't let more kids be put in wrong families. I couldn't let it happen again in my family. I couldn't let it happen in anyone's."

He looked at his watch. "They're probably trying to get everyone out of the gyms. The walls are too thick to hear anything in here. Maybe I'll be nice and take the duct tape off your mouths. Just your mouths. Then in case they call and want you to prove you're here with me, you'll be able to talk.

"But don't count on saying much. If they don't call in another few minutes, I won't have time to disconnect those bombs."

Hal reached into his pocket and pulled out a small pocketknife. Maggie saw the handle as it went by her face. Boy Scouts of America. Always prepared. She winced as Hal sliced the duct tape and then pulled. Skin and hair came away with the tape. He then went to Eric. "I like you, man. Even though you didn't see things as clearly as your brother did."

Before he had a chance to cut Eric's duct tape, the phone rang.

"Right on time," Hal said. "Very good. Very organized." He picked up the phone and sat on the bench between Maggie and Eric, his feet between their bodies.

"Yes?"

Maggie reached out with both her arms and legs, angling so they hit the top of the bench. Eric watched and immediately did the same. Hal, concentrating on the phone, slipped backward off onto the floor as the bench tumbled, putting it between him and Maggie and Eric. "The girls' locker room!" Maggie screamed, hoping whoever was on the other end of the phone would hear. "We're in the girls' locker room!"

Hal threw the phone across the room. "You think that's going to help? They were going to let me out. And both of you. I'm going to die anyway. I killed that idiot brother of yours who didn't know what he wanted. But you might have survived. Before you started doing crazy things. Before you started thinking you were in control.

"You both saw the van, right? Blew pretty high. And I put more stuff in these bombs. I'm not as dumb as everybody thought. I know about fires and bombs. I can put things together. I read all about how to do it on the Internet. That idiot Carole and her husband never paid attention to what I was doing. They were just happy I was being quiet and not bothering their kids. But now you two aren't going to get to see all the excitement. Because you're going to die before the fireworks."

When the bench had overturned, the gun had slipped onto the floor near where Hal had fallen. Just the bench was between Hal and his prey. As he reached for the weapon, Maggie kicked the bench again, pushing it and the gun farther away. Hal slipped as he reached again, and this time Eric and Maggie kicked the bench together and the bench moved on top of the gun. Pain streaked through Maggie's bare toes.

As Hal reached to move the bench, the locker door opened.

The light of a torch blinded all of them. A policewoman was there, with two other cops in back of her. She held her gun on Hal as one of the other officers pulled him up and handcuffed him. Then she reached down and pulled the gun from under the bench.

"You think after that sort of treatment I'm going to tell you where the bombs are?" said Hal. "You think I'm not brave enough to die?"

"I don't know how brave you are. But you're plenty crazy. And we've already found the bombs."

"I don't believe you!"

"We figured if anyone was going to set off another bomb, they'd set it up yesterday. Maggie said anything could be brought in and hidden under table covers while the dealers were bringing in boxes and packages. So late last night, after everyone but Al had left, we brought in a bomb-sniffing dog. You were pretty smart. The bombs were on twenty-four-hour clocks. Not bad. But not good enough."

The cop pushed Hal through the door. Another policeman knelt and cut the duct tape holding Maggie and Eric. "Eric, can you get these lights back on?"

"Yes, sir," said Eric, stumbling a bit as he regained his balance. "The master key is somewhere on the floor. George left it with me, in case of emergency. Hal followed me when I was turning on the air-conditioning and took it. That's how he turned off the lights and got into the locker room." One flashlight survey of the floor and the keys were in Eric's hands.

"Sorry, Maggie. I didn't think it was anything important when he followed me to turn on the air-conditioning. He was being really friendly. I . . . I liked him."

A few minutes later the lights and the air-conditioning came on. Maggie limped out into the hallway. Will was standing there. She hobbled into his arms. "Thank God you're all right," he said, holding her tightly.

Then he let her go and looked down at her. Her face was bleeding in patches from the duct tape. And she had left a trail of blood from the locker room. "I think I may have broken a toe. Or two," she said. "Is the show still open?"

"It will be as soon as we know all the lights are on and no one's in danger," said the officer.

"That's good," said Maggie, leaning on Will's arm and limping toward the lobby. "The show must go on."

Chapter 40

———~~———

Gloucester Harbor. *Winslow Homer wood engraving, 1873. One of Homer's well-known "Gloucester Series," among the finest of his wood engravings from* Harper's Weekly. *Seven children lounging in two dories in the harbor, looking out at vessels in full sail. H.W. signature in water, lower left. 11 x 15 inches. Price: $360.*

The rest of Maggie's Saturday went by in a haze. The show stayed open. Claudia and Carole and Al answered questions; Josie and Sam kept track of admissions; Ann supplied food to everyone, whose appetites increased as soon as they knew any danger was past. Al called George, who came in and took over the maintenance job.

Gussie insisted that with Ben's help she could watch Will's booth as well as the one she was sharing with Maggie, so Will went to the emergency room with Maggie and Eric. Rob Sloane met them there, looking pale, but grateful when his son was pronounced fine except for some bruises and scraped skin. Rob had already lost one son that week.

Maggie had fared worse. Besides the bleeding scrapes on her face (and the pain from the hair that had been pulled out), she had, indeed, broken three of her toes. She left the emergency room with a green cast on her right foot.

As soon as Will had driven her home, Maggie called Al to check on how the show had gone and invite him for a Chinese dinner, delivered. She told him to bring Claudia. Al readily agreed. "But I won't stay long. I'm already looking forward to sleeping in my own bed tonight."

Will contributed the bottles of wine Maggie had requested he stop for in New York State, although he made sure Maggie stuck with Diet Pepsi. Wine and painkillers were not a good combination.

By the time Gussie and Ben had gotten home and reported that even in their absence Will and Maggie had each totaled several hundred dollars in sales, the Chinese food was on plates, the wine and Pepsi cooled, and Maggie was happy to stretch out on the lounge chair in her study with her foot up, per doctor's orders.

"Maggie, did you know it was Hal?" asked Gussie. "He seemed so polite, and enthusiastic, and helpful. Just a nice young man."

"I wasn't sure," admitted Maggie. "But I kept eliminating other possibilities. At one point I was even suspecting Ann, because she has a major problem with Our World Our Children. But I didn't think she'd set a bomb. I knew Abdullah was sad, and troubled. And I knew he questioned the 'America as melting pot' myth; he wrote a paper on it this spring. So for a while I thought he was the one responsible. Especially after what you told me about his mother, Al."

Al nodded. "I remember. I told you I'd met Abdullah's mother, and she was blonde."

"I realized that, like Jackson, Abdullah had parents who represented two different cultures. Not races, but cultures. And Eric had said Jackson's new friend was 'like him.' It all came together when I was setting up the booth yesterday and noticed an engraving of skulls that were supposed to represent different racial groups. They included a Caucasian skull, a Negroid, a Turkish, a Chinese, and so forth . . . and I realized that, of course, the word *race* means different things to different people. Do you know," Maggie continued, putting on her professor's hat, "in New York City at the beginning of the twentieth century some Protestant families refused to adopt children of Irish parents? They said they were of another, lower race." She shook her head. "Perspectives change."

"But it wasn't Abdullah who was responsible. It was Hal!" said Gussie.

"That was the hard part," Maggie agreed. "Eric said he thought his brother Jackson had found a couple of new friends. Friends who understood him. Hal had moved home about six months ago and would have met all of the Sloanes at adoptive-parent activities. When Abdullah brought Hal to the show a couple of days ago, I realized they knew each other. Then I found out Hal had a history of mental illness and violence."

"Then was Abdullah involved at all?"

"I don't think he had anything to do with it. From what Hal said in the locker room, Abdullah might even have argued with Jackson and Hal about their anger at their parents and the agency. I don't think he knew anything about Hal's shooting Holly, or killing Jackson, and he certainly didn't know about the bombs. He was really scared when my van blew up. After all, his brother died as the result of a terrorist attack." Maggie took another sip of Pepsi. "Basically, it was a process of elimination. I wasn't absolutely sure, but Hal was the most likely suspect."

Al nodded. "But the best thing you did, Maggie, was to suggest getting the dog in before the show started. After your van had been blown up, bombs were on all of our minds, and the bomb squad agreed checking would be a good idea. Everyone knew I was planning to spend the night in the gym, so there would be lights on. The dog found the bombs right away. They were in cartons dealers had unpacked and left empty under their booths to use when they pack up tomorrow afternoon. The explosives weren't very sophisticated." He paused. "But they could have done a lot of damage."

"So at least I knew something Hal didn't: I knew the bombs he'd left yesterday were gone. But I didn't know whether he might have other explosives. And he had that gun." Maggie winced slightly. Her foot hurt. "I never asked you, Al. What booths were the bombs in?"

"Yours and Gussie's," he answered with a grimace. "And that crystal dealer's in the other gym."

Maggie shivered. "Can you imagine the damage crystal would have done if it had blown up?"

"I know I shouldn't," said Gussie, "but I keep thinking about all the young men involved. Hal had a traumatic childhood and even a caring family couldn't help him. Jackson never felt accepted, even when he was. Abdullah lost his brother and his mother. All of them were trying to make sense of life in their own ways. I hope at least Eric and Abdullah are able to get through all of this and have good lives. They deserve them."

Al shook his head. "It is sad. Jackson Sloane didn't get a chance. He may have just been starting to figure out who he was when he made the fatal mistake of choosing the wrong friend."

They were all silent for a few minutes.

"What are you going to do, Maggie? You can't drive anymore." Ben pointed at her cast. "And your van blew up."

Maggie burst into laughter. "You're right, Ben," she agreed. "Those are real, immediate issues."

Then she burst into almost hysterical giggling. Maybe it was the pain pills. Maybe it was the relief of not having to worry about threatening letters and telephone calls. Maybe it was just that the semester was over and the antiques show was going on. Will reached out to touch her shoulder.

Then she pointed to a corner of the room. Winslow had somehow dragged a small insulated bag of Chinese barbecued pork there and was carefully and neatly devouring it.

"That is going to be one sick cat," Will predicted, risking

being scratched as he retrieved the pork from an indignant Winslow. "And, Ben, you don't have to worry about Maggie. I've decided to stick around here for a couple of weeks, while she's still limping. Most of my inventory is in the RV, so I can manage the next show without going back to Buffalo. Somehow we'll get her prints into my RV for the Rensselaer County show, and while she's healing, we'll investigate used vans."

"So you're not going to change your plans for the summer, Maggie? You're still planning to come to the Cape?" asked Gussie.

"Absolutely. I'll let you know as soon as I'm mobile again. I plan on spending the summer buying and selling prints, eating well, and"—Maggie smiled at Claudia—"drinking red wine. I don't want to think about school, or antiques shows, or even about adoption, for at least the summer."

"And Aunt Nettie is looking forward to seeing you in Maine, Maggie," Will reminded her. "You have friends Down East."

"Not as many as I have right here," Maggie said, looking around the room. "And I'm so glad you're all here. Because the show isn't over. And I'm going to need all the help I can get to make sure it runs smoothly tomorrow."

"I suspect you'll have a few extra customers," Al added. "News of everything that happened today will hit the newspapers, and there will be people coming just to sightsee."

"As long as they pay admission and we make money for OWOC that will be just fine," said Maggie. "But if they want another antiques show next spring—they'd better look for someone else to run it!"

About the Author

Lea Wait comes from a long line of antiques dealers, including her mother, her grandmother, and her great-grandfather. She has owned her antique-print business for more than twenty-five years. She now lives in Edgecomb, Maine, where she runs the business and writes historical novels for young readers as well as the Maggie Summer series.

1

244